Hybridity as a Rhetorical Strategy
in Doris Lessing's Narration

多丽丝·莱辛
叙事中的杂糅修辞策略研究

黄春燕 _ 著

外语教学与研究出版社
FOREIGN LANGUAGE TEACHING AND RESEARCH PRESS
北京 BEIJING

图书在版编目 (CIP) 数据

多丽丝·莱辛叙事中的杂糅修辞策略研究：英、汉／黄春燕著. —— 北京：
外语教学与研究出版社，2017.9
ISBN 978-7-5135-9483-7

Ⅰ. ①多… Ⅱ. ①黄… Ⅲ. ①莱辛 (Doris Lessing, 1919–2013) – 小说研究 –
英、汉 Ⅳ. ①I561.074

中国版本图书馆 CIP 数据核字 (2017) 第 239618 号

出 版 人 蔡剑峰
责任编辑 孔乃卓
封面设计 蒋宏工作室
版式设计 付玉梅
出版发行 外语教学与研究出版社
社 址 北京市西三环北路 19 号（100089）
网 址 http://www.fltrp.com
印 刷 北京九州迅驰传媒文化有限公司
开 本 650×980 1/16
印 张 13.75
版 次 2017 年 9 月第 1 版 2017 年 9 月第 1 次印刷
书 号 ISBN 978-7-5135-9483-7
定 价 49.90 元

购书咨询：（010）88819926 电子邮箱：club@fltrp.com
外研书店：https://waiyants.tmall.com
凡印刷、装订质量问题，请联系我社印制部
联系电话：（010）61207896 电子邮箱：zhijian@fltrp.com
凡侵权、盗版书籍线索，请联系我社法律事务部
举报电话：（010）88817519 电子邮箱：banquan@fltrp.com
法律顾问：立方律师事务所 刘旭东律师
中咨律师事务所 殷 斌律师
物料号：294830001

序

祝贺黄春燕博士的新作《多丽丝·莱辛叙事中的杂糅修辞策略研究》问世！春燕是北京物资学院副教授，多年来潜心研究莱辛，发表的成果得到同行的赞许。这部新作是春燕博士多年研究成果的集中展示，特表祝贺！

多丽丝·莱辛是英国当代女作家，2007年诺贝尔文学奖得主，诺奖官方主页宣布获奖消息时，称其为"以女性体验创作史诗的作家"，赞其特有的"怀疑、激情和远见"，对"一个分裂的文明进行了审视"。莱辛是小说家，她审视西方世界的工具便是其独特的叙事手法。春燕多年前就开始研究莱辛的一个重要的叙事特征——杂糅性，而这个修辞手法似乎尚未引起足够的重视。这部新著便结合米哈伊尔·巴赫金和霍米·巴巴的杂糅理论，集中探讨了莱辛在小说叙事中如何匠心独具地运用杂糅策略。

作者首先证明，杂糅性是莱辛小说创作的一个主要修辞策略。她在文本中呈现多种声音间的平等对话；在叙事中构建出作者、文本以及读者三者之间的互动关系；她与其他作家和理论家有多种呼应与对话；哪怕对自己的创作理念及手法她也不断修正，体现出自身的矛盾性，这些都可以看作是莱辛在文本内外唤起不同的声音、创立对话机制的结果。正是这种对话机制，使文本由单一话语变为混合了多种社会语言的载体，而莱辛是促成这种转换的好手。

这种转换看似魔术师的一个戏法，但不要小看了这种"戏法"，因为它产生的效果是革命性的。巴巴把这种由"混杂"而产生的杂糅称之为"一种颠覆性策略"，无中生有地产生出一个"第三空间"，使貌似的统一与和谐发生质变，产生出作家所期待的变化。"第三空间"貌似多余之地，可有可无，实际上却是一块是非之地，为各种新生力量、复调话语或"异质"文化提供了栖身之地，使它们从压抑中得到释放，在排斥中得到展现，无论这样的"释放"与"展现"是多么的微不足道。无论是出于创新或突破意识，还是纯粹的无心所致，莱辛借助在小说叙事的不同层面安插"异质",为自己的小说开拓出一个个"第三空间",其中的对话与互动呈现出一种与众不同的丰富性、包容性以及审美性。

春燕认为,莱辛的杂糅不仅体现在具体的叙事技巧和写作手法上,她在自传、访谈以及文学评论中,就文学创作做过长达几十年的探究与阐述,在创作思想上也体现出混杂性与发展性。她对莱辛杂糅性的论证从其文本中的杂糅策略逐步推进,一直延伸到作家精神上的丰富性。

莱辛是"混杂"叙事要素的高手,这种"混杂"看上去十分自然,说明莱辛做得得心应手,对"混杂"有极好的驾驭能力。借助于多重叙述声音、多样化的叙事者以及混杂的视角,莱辛创造出一个个双声或多声的场景。无论是回顾型和体验型视角的并存、黑白视角有意无意的混杂、还是女性作家投射出外在或内化的父权视角,都是莱辛在叙事层面摆脱"单一话语"的体现。此外,她在虚构作品中呈现出繁杂与多变,这与她在各种访谈和文学评论文章中的阐释和自我辩护并非总是互为观照,而是在写作理念与实践之间常常存在错位。她在叙事技巧上变化频繁,不仅增加了文本意义的含混,也给读者造成了一定的阅读障碍。不过,如此不确定恰好导致作者—文本—读者之间的互动增加,用伊瑟尔的话说,增强了作品的审美性,也为巴赫金所谓的"无限的"意义阐释提供了基础,莱辛倚靠这种后现代手法,使自己小说的含义变得更为开放,呼唤着巴巴所预期的那种对意义的不断"再阐释"。

莱辛还极善于融会贯通批评流派和写作手法,创新与发展不同体裁,混杂使用不同主题。即使采用某种特定的风格写作,她也并非墨守成规,而是不断尝试融入新的风格元素。她在处理虚构和非虚构作品时刻意模糊虚与实的界限,把现实主义手法融入科幻小说。她热衷于科幻小说,不是为了逃避现实,而是期望藉此为自己的表现手法发掘更多的灵活性,从而能更真实地反映现实。她创作的半传记式小说,她就真实性与虚构性所做的连篇累牍的陈述,都表明她对体裁与风格问题的关注。批评家们常说,早期的莱辛倾向现实主义,之后转向现代主义和后现代主义,最终又回归了现实主义,但这里的"倾向"、"转向"和"回归"都只是批评家的整体把握,其实莱辛的"主义"间不乏混杂,你中有我,我中有你,很难找到符合某种定义的写法。莱辛作品的主题也极其丰富,涵盖她对多种文化、思想、族裔、人群以及社会热点的关注。

莱辛对杂糅策略情有独钟,其根源可以归结到莱辛本人博大的人文主义关怀。她旗帜鲜明地反对同时期英国文学中的狭隘思维，指出这种思维"受限于英国人自身最直接的经验和评判标准"，因此常常流露出"欧洲中心"视角。她提倡开放的姿态，鼓励跨界意识，也因为如此，她反对别人将自己简单地归类为某种形式的现实主义、现代派或女权主义作家。尽管她的作品对性别问题尤其关注，《金色笔记》等一批作品也确实在第二次女性主义浪潮中颇具影响力，但莱辛始终否认自己是"女权主义"作家，而宁愿做一名被"三重"流放的边缘作家。

即使对自己提出的创作理念，莱辛也一再修正，甚至体现出思想上的不确定性和矛盾性。例如关于作者功能，她从深信其肩负说教和改造的职责，到逐渐对作者的职责失去信心，甚至一度将其等同于普通读者，经历了一个由信心满满到怀疑甚至否定的过程。同样，她对文本是否应该反映道德也由立场坚定过渡到模棱两可，导致她的作者可以是凌驾于读者之上的全知全能式的人物，也可以是冷静抽离的旁观者，摇摆于两者之间，更增加了叙事的复杂性。

作者春燕试图告诉我们，由于以上的"杂糅"因素，莱辛一方面有意寻求边缘化及个性化，试图与主流话语保持距离；但同时她又常常不自觉地表现出与主流话语的认同，尽管这种认同最终仍然会表现出某种摇摆性。换句话说，莱辛消除界限的方式是首先突出对立，再模糊差异，最终谋求共存，但这样的共存仍然具有"和而不同"的性质。

莱辛在文本构建与精神本质上体现出的杂糅性，不仅使她的左翼知识分子形象更为突出，文本更加丰富多元，也为她的作品打上了鲜明的个人烙印。这是春燕对莱辛的解读，这样的解读也许存在一定的"误读"，但无疑为我们理解莱辛提供了新的视角。

是为序。

朱刚

2017 年 8 月 31 日于仙林侨裕楼

Contents

Introduction

Doris Lessing (1919–2013) is a widely studied writer for her contribution to British literature. She began writing in the 1940s and has produced more than fifty books in almost every genre, including more than thirty novels, several collections of short stories, one play, a good number of critical essays, several autobiographies, and some other writing. In recent years, scholars have paid more attention to Lessing's narration. Yet up to now few critics have approached Lessing from the perspective of hybridity, which turns out to be a distinctive narrative feature of her writing. Therefore, this book focuses on the hybridized narration in Lessing in light of Mikhail Bakhtin and Homi Bhabha's concept of hybridity. It tries to argue that Lessing makes hybridity one of her rhetorical strategies by establishing a dialogic mechanism in her writing, a fact that can be demonstrated in the multi-voiced dialogue within the text, the interaction among the author, text and reader, her response to or inheritance of other writers and theorists, as well as the adjustments and occasional self-contradiction apparent in her writing philosophy. Thanks to this dialogism set up both inside and outside, her text, to quote Bakhtin, becomes "a mixture of two social languages within the limits of a single utterance" (Bakhtin 358), an effective strategy to replace the single-voice authority in the traditional fiction. In this sense, hybridity is reconstructive as well as subversive.

Bhabha regards hybridity as "a strategic reversal" (Bhabha *Location* 112) and highlights its significance in the Third Space enunciations. The Third Place is productive in that it embraces new power. This hybrid strategy opens up "a space of negotiation" which calls for neither "assimilation" nor "collaboration" (Bhabha "Culture's In-Between" 58), but a space open for reconstruction. Lessing is perseverant in making something anew to fight against the dominant discourse through a multi-dimensional dialogue in which different voices integrate into each other without losing their own distinctive features.

This kind of hybridity in Lessing not only manifests itself in her specific narrative skills, but also in her writing philosophy which turns out to be the outcome of her decades-long contemplation on novel writing in her auto-biographies, interviews and literary essays. This book, then, delves into the following three aspects of her work: (1) the diversified voices, narrators, perspectives and the dynamic author-text-reader relationship; (2) the juxtaposition of styles, genres, and subject matters as well as the "dialogue" or "negotiation" between Lessing and other writers and theorists; and (3) the sources of her re-constructiveness and de-constructiveness as reflected in her protesting, adaptive and experimental spirit as well as her ever-evolving writing philosophy.

Firstly, by resorting to diversified voices, narrators and perspectives, Lessing manages to produce in her writing either a double- or multi-voiced dialogue. The co-existence of retrospective and experiencing perspectives, the white-and-black viewpoint and the internalized patriarchal perspective combined help to break the limits of the authoritative discourse, or of "a single utterance" (Bakhtin 358). A new space is thus created, characterized by "difference and sameness in an apparently impossible simultaneity" (Young *Colonial Desire* 25). This polyphonic narrative grows out of both her "unconscious, organic" hybridization and her "intentional" efforts (Bakhtin 358). Besides, the diversity as manifested in her fictional writing does not always keep in line with her views on literary production she presents in the non-fiction. This occasional incompatibility between her writing philosophy and writing gives rise to misreadings on the part of the reader and encounters unexpected reader responses. What's more, the hybrid use of narrative skills not only brings more ambiguities to the text, but also makes the reading process a difficult one. Nevertheless, this unstable author-text-reader relationship best proves the nature of hybridity as explained by Bakhtin, namely, the "limitless" production of meaning, or the possibility of the "reinterpretation" of meaning.

Secondly, Lessing's experiment with different styles, genres, and subject matters contributes to the hybridity in her writing. Rather than adhering to set principles, she constantly brings new elements into her texts even when she writes in conventional styles. When dealing with fiction and non-fiction, for example, she purposely blurs the demarcation between the real and the imaginative and thus injects freshness into the two genres. In addition, her space fiction is not a break with realism but rather a kind of inheritance and development from it. Far from a gesture of escapism, her fondness for space fiction indicates an effort of getting rid of the provincialism of British literature by telling a more universal truth. The semi-fictional writing growing out of her own experience and that of her parents, and the lengthy statements she has made on the topic of fiction and non-fiction all show her concern for the issues of genre and style. Lessing in her earliest years of writing tends to be more realistic, then she turns to modernistic and post-modernistic ways of writing, and finally she seems to return to realism, although these "turns" and "returns" never indicate a complete break. In spite of all these turnings, namely, it is hard to put her into any one of these "-isms", for she seldom sticks to any single way of writing. Apart from styles and genres, the hybridity of Lessing's works also reveals itself in her choice of subject matters which cover a wide range of cultures, ideas, races and social issues. As she experiments with different styles, genres and subject matters, the hybrid construction in her work becomes more congenial to her social criticism than any conventional narrative she could ever attempt. It can be proved that she benefits as well as makes breakthroughs from the politics and poetics of the day. Apart from the dialogue with herself, Lessing, by "negotiating" with others, makes her contribution towards the construction of a heteroglossia in literature.

Thirdly, apart from the textual construction, the cutting edge of Lessing's hybridity comes from her awareness of cultural legacies. Her educational, literary, and ideological background contributes as much to her hybridized way of writing. Lessing protests against the provincialism in British literature and the practice of labelling. Besides, her preference for an open stance and the practice of border-crossing is also held accountable for her strategic use of hybridity. Lessing blames contemporary British writers for their narrowness, declaring that their "horizons are bounded by their immediate experience of British life and standard" (Lessing *ASPV* 14), hence a Euro-centered perspective, a major concern of post-colonial theorists like Bhabha and Said.

Besides, Lessing is unhappy about the fact that she is often regarded as a realist or modernist, or in particular, a feminist writer. Although she cares much about gender issues, for some of her works such as *The Golden Notebook* do have some influence on the second-wave feminist movement, she always stands clear of the feminist group. Being one of the practitioners of border-crossing and the self-styled "thrice-exiled", Lessing protests against the practice of categorization and turns out to be highly hybridized both in writing and in mind. The frequent revision of her writing philosophy not only shows her fluidity and paradoxy, but also has a direct bearing on her choice of narrative skills. As for the author's function, she begins with a firm belief in the author's preaching and transforming power and ends as a disillusioned writer who does not see any superiority in the writer. Similarly, she gradually becomes doubtful about the necessity of integrating the moral issue into writing which she at the very beginning has strong faith in. Due to these changes in attitude, Lessing frequently modifies her role as an author, from an omniscient authority towards a cool-headed and more detached observer in the later years of her writing. No wonder there have been some backtracks and self-contradictions between her writing principles and practice, which all add up to the hybridized nature of her narration.

Bakhtin applies the theory of hybridity to the examination of language and pays more attention to the dismantlement of the single-voice utterance. Bhabha, by focusing on the cultural and post-colonial context, goes on to highlight the active role that hybridity plays in the construction of the Third Space. If the development of language tends to prioritize the independence and individuality of each utterance, the interpretation or translation of cultures calls for more attention towards common ground with differences. bakhtin points out that the tension caused by the contradiction or conflict between two discourses within one single utterance provides the text with productive power. Bhabha regards hybridity as an effective strategy in bringing forth negotiation and dialogue between different voices, a co-existence of difference and sameness on the margin or in a space "in-between" (Bhabha *Location* 38). Both of these ideas find resonance in Lessing, that is, the pursuit of differentiation and individualization as well as the construction of a polyphonic narrative which is open to multi-voiced negotiations. This doubleness, however, gives rise to an inner contradiction which Lessing is not totally unaware of, namely, on the one hand she tries to speak out from the margin, in an effort to subvert the dominating discourse; on the other hand, she identifies herself, however reluctantly, with the voice from the center. She disagrees with the binary opposition while at the same time tends to turn it into a means of deconstructing the binary opposition. In other words, to blur the difference, she often foregrounds the disparities at first in a way to bring forth the ultimate reconciliation between different parties.

As it has been briefly introduced above, Lessing's hybridity contains deconstructive and re-constructive elements constantly supplementing each other, so that the text becomes highly polyphonic. To approach Lessing's narration from the perspective of hybridity helps to highlight her distinctive narrative features as well as best demonstrate her spirit of resistance and the will to experimentation.

Although acknowledged nowadays as one of the most significant British writers of the time, Lessing has nevertheless had controversial evaluations on her literary achievements especially during the earlier stage of Lessing criticism. In 1965, the first Lessing biography-writer Dorothy Brewster regarded her as "one of the most gifted of the younger group of English novelists" (Brewster 3). In 1978, Michael Thorpe praised her as "the most widely recognized and most seriously considered woman novelist writing in English since Virginia Woolf died in 1941" (Thorpe *Africa* 3). One year later, Roberta Rubenstein, a distinguished Lessing scholar and author of *The Novelistic Vision of Doris Lessing, Breaking the Forms of Consciousness* (1979), speculated that Lessing "will be remembered for the sheer scope, breadth, vividness, and depth of her endeavor as a chronicler of major strands of contemporary experience" (Rubenstein *Novelistic Vision* 26).

Despite these positive views, Lessing has been frequently criticized for her dry voice, the didactic tone of a moralist, aesthetic slackness, clumsy language and structure, one-sided politics, and limited conceptions. Some critics hold an ambivalent attitude. They, on the one hand, praise Lessing for her distinctive features and, on the other hand, regard them as her shortcomings. Harold Bloom (2007), for one, expresses his dissent against Lessing's winning of Nobel Prize by declaring her works after 1990s quite unreadable and her science fiction fourth-rate[1]. Bloom also regards Lessing's style and language as "a kind of drab shrug" (Bloom 6). Though critical of Lessing's weakness, Bloom nevertheless recognizes her strengths, claiming that she is the perfect spokeswoman of the time, for she "has the spirit, if not the style, of the age" (Bloom 7).

　　Unlike Bloom, James Gindin criticizes Lessing's intensity and steadfast conviction and commitment because he believes that "intense commitment can cut off a whole dimension of human experience" (Gindin 85). Similarly, Water Allen regards *The Golden Notebook* as a sociological work which is too honest to be attractive from an artistic perspective: "As a work of art, *The Golden Notebook* seems to fail. The structure is clumsy, complicated rather than complex" (Allen 276). However, he also admits that "it must also be said that it is essential reading for anyone interested in our times" (Allen 277) for its honesty and uniqueness. Nevertheless, due to the increasing influence of Lessing's writing, especially after she was awarded the Nobel Prize for Literature in 2007[2], her work has drawn more attention worldwide and there have been more and more positive responses to her works. Scholars have conducted research on her from multiple perspectives such as, among the most popular, the feminist, psychoanalytical, realist, deconstructive, formalist, and ecological. Critical studies of her work have mainly focused on her African settings, social-political issues, feminist concerns, Marxist and humanistic elements, treatments of time and space, and philosophical, religious, and mystical elements in her later works. It is not until recently that the narrative part of Lessing has aroused attention among Lessing critics.

1　For more details about Bloom's criticism on Lessing upon the awarding of the Nobel Prize to her, see Sarah Crown's essay "Doris Lessing wins Nobel Prize". *The Guardian.* Oct. 11, 2007. Apr. 15, 2013. Retrieved from http://www.guardian.co.uk/books/2007/oct/11/nobelprize.awardsandprizes.

2　In 2007, 87-year-old Lessing was awarded the Nobel Prize for Literature, which makes her the oldest woman to receive this award.

Lessing study in the West emerged in the 1960s, when responses to her work were not as positive as they would become in the following decades. Initially, Lessing scholars conducted textual analyses of several of her representative works, especially the earlier ones such as *The Grass Is Singing* (1950), *The Golden Notebook* (1962), and the five-volume *The Children of Violence* series, which extend from 1952 to 1969[1]. These early works of Lessing criticism, introductory in nature, mainly focused on her life as a feminist and on African matters. In 1965, the first Lessing biography, written by Dorothy Brewster, was published, which, besides offering a biographical sketch of Lessing, elaborated on the theme and techniques of her early fiction and short stories.

In the 1970s, due to the influence of *The Golden Notebook*, there were more controversial responses to her work. In *A Literature of Their Own, British Women Novelists from Brontë to Lessing* (1977), a landmark monograph based on feminist literary criticism, Elaine Showalter praises *GN* as "such a monumental achievement that it is tempting to see it as Lessing's ultimate statement about 20th-century women and the female tradition" (Showalter 308). Showalter is among the first to deal with feminine writing and sexual politics in this novel.

Along with feminism, early criticism also focused attention on African matters in Lessing, the most brilliant among these being Michael Thorpe's *Doris Lessing's Africa* (1978), a collection of essays addressing African materials in her early novels and short stories. More importantly, Thorpe is one of the earliest critics to notice Lessing's shifting points of views although at that time it "may be simply a shifting of her Zambesian eye to new subjects" (Thorpe x).

---

1 In recent years, some of Lessing's later works have added to the topics of discussion, in particular the *Canopus in Argos: Archives* series, her four-volume science fiction published continuously from 1979 to 1982, and *The Good Terrorist* (1985). In order to trace the trajectory of her writing, this book will integrate several significant yet less discussed works, including *The Summer Before the Dark* (1973), *The Memoirs of a Survivor* (1975), *Love, again* (1996), *The Diaries of Jane Somers* (1983), and *Alfred and Emily* (2008).

Ruberta Rubenstein pays attention to the presentations of consciousness in *The Novelistic Vision of Doris Lessing: Breaking the Forms of Consciousness* (1979). According to Rubenstein, "the common denominator in Lessing's fictional world is the mind: the mind discovering, interpreting, and ultimately shaping its own reality" (Rubenstein *Novelistic Vision* 7). Rubenstein's viewpoint was quite insightful for later Lessing critics, for Lessing has been known to be involved in consciousness and dreams in her later writings due to the influence of Jungian psychoanalysis and oriental mysticism, such as Sufism[1].

As critics became more concerned with Lessing and her writings, *Contemporary Literature*, an academic quarterly in the United States, published a special issue on her in 1973[2], followed by another special issue published by *Modern Fiction Studies* in 1980[3]. The decade also witnessed the appearance of several significant Lessing monographs that proved to be milestones in Lessing scholarship. For instance, *Notebooks, Memoirs, Archives: Reading and Rereading Doris Lessing* (1982) edited by Jenny Taylor, "is representative

---

1   Lessing has been heavily influenced by this Islamic mysticism in her later years. A more detailed analysis can be found in Muge Galin's *Between East and West: Sufism in the Novels of Doris Lessing* (1997).

2   In this special issue on Lessing, 11 critical essays plus 1 introductory article and 1 interview were collected, covering a wide range of topics, perspectives, and approaches for a study of Lessing's earlier works. This edition also offers a checklist of Lessing criticism with almost 80 critical essays starting from the 1960s. This collection of essays makes a good beginning in the study of Doris Lessing and calls for more diversified critical views in Lessing study. It not only touches upon the structural features of Lessing's work, but also discusses from such perspective as socialism, feminism and archetypal analysis, so as to further the understanding of Lessing's experimentalist way of writing and "encyclopedic range and complexity" (Pratt 416–417). In a sense, this special issue on Lessing is a critical initial step in Lessing studies.

3   The special issue on Lessing published by *Modern Fiction Studies* is composed of 13 critical essays plus 1 book review and a checklist, adding up to 176 pages. The checklist "is essentially an updated supplement to Selma Burkom's 1973 checklist" (King 167), consisting of criticism, interviews, biographical commentary, and bibliography.

in many respects of the sins and virtues of Lessing scholarship" (Knapp 182). A remarkable monograph in the early period of Lessing studies, this book, however, is criticized for its over-emphasis on the feminist elements in Lessing's novels, a perspective which Lessing constantly complains about as a "sin" and which has been blamed for an "overly personal and emotional standpoint which interferes with the reader/text relationship" (Knapp 183). This so-called "sin" may result from the fact that all eight contributors to this book are female. Similarly, most Lessing criticism in this period puts emphasis on her early works in the 1950s and 1960s to the exclusion of her works of 1970s, such as *Briefing for a Descent into Hell* (1971) and *The Summer Before the Dark* (1973).

In 1985, Eve Bertelsen published *Doris Lessing*, a selection of press reviews of Lessing from 1950 to 1982. Katherine Fishburn also published *The Unexpected Universe of Doris Lessing: A Study in Narrative Technique*, in which she addresses narrative technique in Lessing's seven science fiction works. One year later, *Modern Critical Views: Doris Lessing* (1986), edited by Harold Bloom, was published and a second edition came out in 2003 enriched by new perspectives and viewpoints[1].

One of the most important monographs for Lessing studies is Claire Sprague's 1987 *Rereading Doris Lessing, Narrative Patterns of Doubling and Repetition*, which provided an examination of the narrative patterns—in particular, the patterns of repetition—in Lessing's work. Probing into Lessing's separate and merging selves, as well as her dialectical use of name patterns and repetitive motifs, and tracing them back to her narrative adventures as a whole, Sprague concludes that it is with the help of the narrative patterns of doubling and repetition that Lessing is capable of presenting her major themes and concerns. Before Sprague, few Lessing scholars or critics had approached Lessing from the perspective of narrative patterns.

---

1   In 2003, Bloom published a new edition entitled *Bloom's Modern Critical Views: Doris Lessing*, replacing the 9 essays with 8 new ones, with the intention to bring together what he judged to be "the most useful criticism yet published on the fiction of Doris Lessing" (Bloom 1986 vii).

From the 1990s to the 21st century, Lessing criticism boasts two distinctive features. Namely, it has shifted attention to the inter-relations between Lessing and the broad socio-cultural, post-colonial context in which she wrote and provided various comparative studies between Lessing and other novelists. The year of 1994 witnessed three important books on Doris Lessing dealing with the psychological aspects and spiritual evolution in Lessing. Based on an overview of Lessing's work, Margaret Moan Rowe in *Doris Lessing* "traces how Lessing resolves—or refuses to resolve—tensions between the paternal and maternal perspectives" (Draine 194). In *Doris Lessing: The Poetics of Change*, Observing from a different perspective, Gayle Greene "also notes the continual struggle in Lessing's narratives between the force of visionary imagination and the drag of quotidian reality" (Draine 195). Unlike the first two scholars, Shadia S. Fahim and Palgrave Macmillan in *Doris Lessing and Sufi Equilibrium* explore the influence of Sufism on Lessing's later works, which has become one of the hottest issues in Lessing criticism.

In the first years of the 21st century, more and more critics have become concerned about the spiritual growth in Lessing. *Doris Lessing, Border Crossings* (2009), co-edited by Alice Ridout and Susan Watkins, *The Adventures of the Spirit* (2010) by Phyllis Sternberg Perrakis, and *Doris Lessing Interrogating the Times* (2010), edited by Debrah Raschke and two other scholars, go deep into the mentality of Doris Lessing to explore the formation and evolution of her spirit of resistance and border-crossing. Therefore, they serve well for discussing the spiritual, psychological, and socio-cultural resources of Lessing's hybridized narration. In 2011, Susan Watkins published another collection of criticism on Lessing entitled *Doris Lessing (Contemporary World Writers)*, in which Watkins conducts a postcolonial critique and examines Lessing's consistent concerns about nation, empire, gender, race, and self-collective interrelations. The post-colonial approach, by integrating Lessing research into social-political and cultural contexts and identity issues, enriches Lessing studies both in breadth and depth. Besides, its emphasis on and concern for post-colonial issues such as resistance, border-crossing, and politics of discourse is enlightening in the study of Lessing's hybridized narration by resorting to her spiritual, psychological, and socio-cultural resources.

Another important characteristic of current Lessing criticism is that scholars tend to conduct more comparative studies between Lessing and other writers. The most frequently chosen writer to compare with Lessing is Virginia Woolf. *Woolf and Lessing: Breaking the Mold* (1994), co-edited by Ruth Saxton and Jean Tobin, may be the first book that ushers in more similar criticism conducted between these two female writers. For example, the Chinese scholar Ching-Feng Tseng published *The Imperial Garden: Englishness and Domestic Space in Virginia Woolf, Doris Lessing, and Tayeb Salih* in 2003, a book growing out of her doctoral dissertation. In recent years, scholars have published a great number of essays in this regard which, to some extent, are supporting evidences of Lessing's correspondence with other writers.

Outside the rising enthusiasm in Lessing studies, there is a strange neglect, or under-statement, of Lessing. Her name is sometimes excluded from authoritative books. For instance, in *The Cambridge Companion to Modernism* (1999), Lessing is not on the list of the modernists, although she is elsewhere noted as one of the most frequently discussed modernistic writers. She is also "forgotten" by *Lives of the Novelists: A History of Fiction in 294 Lives* (2012), written by John Sutherland and published by Yale University Press, a book meant to acclaim the finest writers of English and American fiction. According to one book review made by Robert Gottlieb (2012), the author of this enormous book of more than 800 pages totally forgets about two Africa-born women Nobel Prize winners: Doris Lessing and Nadine Gordimer[1].

Lessing study in China has made remarkable headway in recent years. Although Lessing was introduced into China as early as in 1956 with the publication of the Chinese version of *The Grass Is Singing* translated by Wang Lei (Jiang Hua 58), it is not until the 1980s that the study on Lessing found

---

1 For more details about John Sutherland's ignorance of Lessing and several other significant writers, see "A Very Lush Garland of Writers". *The New York Review of Books*. Aug. 16, 2012. Nov. 20, 2013. Retrieved from http://www.nybooks.com/articles/archives/2012/aug/16/very-lush-garland-writers/.

its voice. Unlike the Lessing criticism of the early years mainly consisting of translations and brief introductions, Sun Zongbai is "the first domestic scholar who introduces Lessing into China" (Lu Jing 76). Huang Mei is one of the earliest to focus on *GN*, while Li Fuxiang draws attention to the consciousness in and general characteristics of Lessing's writing. Apart from the above mentioned three, Feng Yidai, Hou Zongrui, Zhang Zhongzai and several other Chinese scholars have approached Lessing study from various perspectives in the 1980s and 1990s.

Lessing study after the new millennium became more systematic, covering a wider range of topics and perspectives coupled with diversified approaches and perspectives. As is observed by Lu Jing in her essay "Doris Lessing Studies in China Since the 1980s" (2008), Lessing study in China has become more concentrated in "thematic criticism, feminism criticism, religious-philosophical criticism and form criticism" (Lu Jing 75). Scholars have begun to focus on the religious and philosophical elements in Lessing's works from the perspective of spatial theory, identifying her as a modernist or post-modernist writer rather than a traditional realist, or making a comparative study between Lessing and Chinese writers such as Zhang Ailing, Wang Anyi and Tie Ning. Towards the end of the 20th century, the space issue in her writing became one of the most frequently discussed topics. Meanwhile, Chinese scholars keep a watch on Lessing's reception in China. Deng Zhong liang for instance tries to "trac[e] the process of the translation and research" of Lessing (Deng Zhongliang 270) in China to her latest work published in 2008[1].

The first domestic master's dissertation on Lessing appeared in 2001—"The Breathless Spiritual Wasteland—*The Grass Is Singing*", authored by Fu Li from Sichuan Normal University. Since then, there have been more than three hundred masters' theses on Lessing, covering a wide range of perspectives and approaches. The year of 2009 witnessed a sharp increase in the number of masters' dissertations which shows a growing interest in Lessing and in 2012 alone, about 60 dissertations got publicized.

---

1 Deng's essay is one of the seven collected in a special edition of *English and American Literary Studies* (2008) in honor of Doris Lessing.

Compared with the number of masters' dissertations, domestic doctoral dissertations in the past decade add up to about a dozen. Among them, the latest include Yan Wenjie's "A Semiotic Interpretation of *The Golden Notebook*" (2014) and Zhang Qi's "On Cultural Identity in Doris Lessing's Space Fictions" (2014). While Yan from Nanjing Normal University tries to prove the effectiveness of form from the perspective of "Susanne K. Langer's statement that 'art is the reflection of emotional symbols'" (Yan Wenjie iii), Zhang Qi from Xiangtan University adopts a postcolonial perspective. Zhang's dissertation deals with the cultural identity of the marginal Other in space and the power discourse and social reality by focusing on *Canopus in Argos: Archives* (1979–1983) series, Lessing's representative space fiction. Jiang Renfeng from Shanghai International Studies University in "Space and Self in Doris Lessing's Major Fiction" (2013) discusses self by resorting to spatial theories. Deng Linna in her dissertation "Life Experience and Self Transcendence—Sufi Thoughts in Doris Lessing's Fiction" (2012) chooses to relate the discussion to Lessing's Sufi thoughts and reaches the conclusion that "the pursuit of life experience and self-transcendence in Sufism has positive influence on Lessing's fiction" (Deng Linna 131). Like self, identity and space, trauma is one of the focuses in recent Lessing study. Zhou Guijun from North-East Normal University, in his dissertation entitled "Trauma Writing of the Cross-Cultural Writers in the Context of Modernity" (2010), conducts a research on Doris Lessing, Patrick White, J. M. Coetzee and V. S. Naipaul. Zhou concludes that their writing "begins with an analysis of trauma and ends with healing the wound" (Zhou Guijun 141), each in their own way.

Apart from these latest doctoral dissertations, Lu Jing from Nanjing Normal University explores into the strategic use of textual structure, time, space and body images in *GN*. She argues, in her book *The Artistic Forms of The Golden Notebook and Lessing's Life Experience* (2008), that "various artistic skills, delicate frame settings, together with the clever arrangements of the layout" (Lu Jing 2) serve well the author's self-expression and the representation of the ideological content of the work. *A Study of Doris*

Lessing's Art and Philosophy (2007) written by Wang Lili provides a succinct overview of Lessing criticism. She focuses on the structures in Lessing's novels, the underlying relations between the form and psychological and philosophical ideas, with a focus on the philosophical and psychological meanings of some of the concepts in Lessing's writing, such as "whirlpool" and "fountain". Another monograph on Lessing in the same year is *Doris Lessing's Colonial Ambiguities: A Study of Colonial Tropes in Her Works* (2007), written by Chen Jingxia where she discusses how Lessing makes use of colonial tropes in order to show her "ambiguous attitude towards colonialism" (Chen Jingxia 24).

In 2008, Xiao Qinghua published *Urban Space and Literary Space—A Study of on Doris Lessing's Fiction* (2008), a book on the inter-relations between urban space, experience and civilization in Lessing's works. Similarly, Jiang Hua, the author of *The Repressed Self and Alienated Life: A Study of Doris Lessing's African Fiction* (2009), probes into the urban issues by making "a relatively comprehensive and profound analysis of Lessing's African fiction revolving around the individual and the collective relationship" (Jiang Hua 225).

Despite the efforts made by scholars and researchers, Lessing's own elaborations in various forms at different times turn out to be insufficiently explored for scholarly discussions. The "talkative" Lessing published, altogether, four collections of critical essays and public speeches, covering a wide range of issues concerning literature, politics and social affairs, which are quite expansive and inclusive in terms of time and subject matter. The four collections were published in different periods of her writing career, and hence offer a dynamic self-confession of her writing philosophy: *A Small Personal Voice* (1974), *Prisons We Choose to Live Inside* (1987), *The Wind Blows away Our Words* (1987), and *Time Bites* (2004).

Among these four book*s, A Small Personal V*oice is a collection of Lessing's essays, reminiscences, reviews and interviews ranging from 1956 to 1973. It contains her reflection on some literary issues, in particular, the writer's function. In this small personal voice, Lessing talks about her insights into and attitudes towards literature, the relations between life and work, her admiration for her fellow writers, her African experiences, the political issues and the family relations as well. The most valuable part of this book is her illustration on the responsibility of the writer and the dynamic relations between writer, reader and the text. Lessing's views on these aspects have contributed to her choice of narrative strategy, hence, her hybridized narration. If *A Small Personal Voice* can be regarded as the declaration of a young and radical Lessing, then *Time Bites* is the one that presents a much more experienced and mature Lessing. Published in her 80s, *Time Bites* contains the wisdom and calm reflections of a writer who keeps learning and growing from her writing. Although she never changes in terms of spirit— "tough, uncompromising, direct and courageous" as the comment made by Elaine Showalter on the cover of the book, Lessing is willing to admit that being an old female writer now, she reads the world differently. In addition, what inspire the present book are her comments on and evaluations of such writers as Virginia Woolf, D. H. Lawrence, Tolstoy, Goethe and Stendhal, her reflections on the differences between fiction and autobiography, her analysis on the storyteller's voice in her works, and the personalities of the roles and authors respectively. The traces of all these can be found in the above mentioned four collections.

Lessing also wrote several autobiographies and memoirs published in a time span of about 40 years, a group of writings keeping a record of her life at different stages and shedding light on both her personal life and thought: *Going Home: Autobiography Essay* (1957), *African Laughter: Four Visits to Zimbabwe* (1992), *Under My Skin: Volume One of My Autobiography, to 1949* (1994), and *Walking in the Shade: Volume Two of My Autobiography, 1949 to 1962* (1997). What is particularly inspiring for this study is a collection of 24 Lessing interviews entitled *Putting the Questions Differently, Interviews with Doris Lessing, 1964–1994* (1996). These interviews offer a reflection on the following aspects of her writing philosophy: the role of the writer, the relations between the writer and reader, the position of the literary critic, the specific technique she uses in her novels, and the broader literary trends in British literature. To some extent, this collection of interviews helps to reveal a dynamic overview of her writing, from idiosyncratic skills to her sense of the overall function of a writer in society. The evolution of her writing philosophy helps in deciphering her strategies at different periods, as well as the twists and turns in styles in her individual works. In addition, some of her novels— such as *The Golden Notebook*, *Martha Quest* and *The Four-Gated City*—also address issues relating to literary criticism, so that an integration of Lessing's own critical essays, autobiographies, interviews, and fictional works enable the critic to track the evolving trajectory of her thoughts and writing which help to demonstrated her strategy of hybridity.

The development of Lessing's writing indicates that she has experienced ups and downs. Whenever she takes some turns in her writings, negative voices would emerge. Most of the time, the responses to her works are controversial. It is true that after the publication of *GN* and her winning of the Nobel Prize, she is accepted more positively. But still, the reception of her works sees periods of reticence and blank fields. For instance, the issue of hybridity in Lessing's writing has not been sufficiently discussed.

As one of the core concepts in post-colonial studies, hybridity has undergone changes and become a complex term in itself. Mikhail Bakhtin is the first to adopt this concept in the cultural study, praising hybridity for its power of subversion and construction. Homi Bhabha applies this notion to his study of postcolonial novels and regards it as a strategy of resistance claimed by the colonized. Before the detailed discussion on Bakhtin and Bhabha's interpretation of hybridity, it is necessary to first of all have an overview of the concept of hybridity. Robert Young, the British postcolonial theorist and cultural critic, drawing an overall picture of hybridity, conducts a comprehensive study of some of the most significant "hybrid" theorists. By tracing the evolution of hybrid discourse and its interpretations in different contexts, Young helps to broaden the scope of application of hybridity.

In *The Colonial Desire: Hybridity in Theory, Culture, and Race* (1995), Robert Young presents a detailed genealogy of hybridity, originally a biological and botanical term referring to "mixed species" and now used in many fields of study, including linguistics, racial theory, cultural studies, literary theory, and so on:

The word 'hybrid' has developed from biological and botanical origins: in Latin it meant the offspring of a tame sow and a wild boar, and hence, as *OED* puts it, 'of human parents of different races, half-breed'. The *OED* continues: 'A few examples of this word occur early in the seventeenth century; but it was scarcely in use until the nineteenth'. 'Hybrid' is the nineteenth century's word. But it has become our own again. In the nineteenth century it was used to refer to a physiological phenomenon; in the 20th century it has been reactivated to describe a cultural one (Young *Colonial Desire* 6).

Young briefs the reader on the history of "hybrid", a word deriving from its biological and botanical origin that was later defined as a physiological phenomenon (in the 19th century) and revitalized again (in the 20th century) to carry with it a cultural connotation[1]. Young further examines different positions people take in their discussions of hybridity in different periods, such as biological, ethnological, or evolutionary. According to his observation, the study of hybridity in the 19th century was closely connected with races, species, and fertility as a result of which the discussion in that century was mainly focused on cross-bred species: whether the products of mixed races or species were less fertile than those of the same species, or whether this kind of hybridism would lead to diminished fertility and even extinction.

Among the 19th century debates on this term, Darwin's view, as presented in *The Origin of Species* (1859) which explores the relation between "hybridism" and fertility from the perspective of races and species, became one of the most influential. Based on his years-long observations, Darwin claims that "the question of sterility has little to do with absolute distinctions

---

1 Young also points out that the first use of the term "hybrid" appeared as early as in 1813 by ethnologist J. C. Prichard in his study of human races, though the OED (Oxford English Dictionary) locates its earliest recorded use in 1861. The *OED* confirms the link between hybridity in language and race in an 1890 passage: "Aryan languages present such indications of hybridity as would correspond with... racial intermixture" (cited in Young *Colonial Desire* 6).

between species and varieties: the facts, rather, 'clearly indicate that the sterility both of first crosses and of hybrids is simply incidental or dependent on unknown differences, chiefly in the reproductive systems, of the species which are crossed'" (qtd. in Young *Colonial Desire* 12). Darwin declares that there is no clear evidence to prove the connection between "hybridism" and fertility; in other words, neither the purebred nor hybridized can be held more accountable for sterility than the reproductive systems of the species themselves.

Compared with Darwin's neutral stand perceiving from a biological perspective, quite a few writers have expressed their opposition to hybridization in their literary works. For instance, Rudyard Kipling protests against the "monstrous hybridism of East and West" (Kipling 288) in his masterpiece *Kim* (1901). E. M. Forster regards it a disaster if the English people mix together with Indians in *A Passage to India* (1924). Unlike Kipling and Forster, Daniel Defoe speaks highly of the significance of hybridity in the development of England: "'It is multiplicity and plurality that make England a more glorious, resplendent country,' Defoe proudly says, meaning that the combination resulting from hybridity 'is productive of strength, creativity and courage in the English. It is as if he was suggesting what post-colonial theory refers to as *in-betweenness*...'" (Guignery *et al.* 14). Being an 18th century writer, Defoe is prophetic in the sense that he notices the core elements of hybridity such as multiplicity, plurality, and creativity and claims that the strength and glory of England partly comes from it since it is capable of generating more power and creating a space of an "in-betweenness" which says no to any single authority.

Although the productive power of the hybrid was not acknowledged by biologists and anthropologists at the very beginning, more and more people tended to believe that "gene mixing is invigorating and that combining diverse strains creates '*hybrid vigour*'" (Pieterse 226). From the turn of the 20th century onward, the recognition and affirmation of "hybrid vigour" was not limited to the discussion on biology. It began to be applied to the study of many other fields, including cultural and literary criticism.

For instance, in his *Postcolonialism: A Very Short Introduction* (2003), Young, by using the musical form of "rai" as an analogy, argues that, in addition to subject matters, styles, and form of music, this genre itself is a representation of hybridization and can engender new meanings:

"A hybrid genre of this kind (referring to 'rai') says something about contemporary social problems, social contradictions: its politics are in its articulations, even its articulations of inarticulate states of being—it has no quick solutions, and may well have no immediate solutions at all. Like post-colonialism itself, it offers challenge rather than solution in the first stance, and allows its audiences themselves to interpret its new spaces with relevant meanings of their own. It does not arrive at delivering its meaning already fully-formed—rather it enables new meanings to be created and projected in dialogic encounters" (Young *Postcolonialism* 74).

The rai music first appeared in the 1970s in Algeria as a result of migration throughout Algeria to the cities, a process of modernization. The emergence of this musical form, therefore, involves "much more than a process of fusion, synthesis, or intermixture" (Young *Postcolonialism* 70) in terms of culture, politics and history. Being a product of construction as well as deconstruction, the rai music is an integration of the Western rock and "its haunting self expression of reggae and African-American blues" (Young *Postcolonialism* 70). It is often described as defiant, spontaneous, flexible and inclusive, all of which makes it an "independent form and force, breaking established conventions within the musical and social culture of Algeria" (Young *Postcolonialism* 72). Due to these characteristics, Young finds the rai music helpful in his interpretation of hybridity.

Young sees constructiveness as the strength of hybridity, and transforms its meaning from something impure, infertile, unnatural, and inferior in the 19th century science of species and race to one of power of subversion celebrated by the post-colonial theory in the late 20th century. Besides, he agrees with Bakhtin and Bhabha on the point that a hybrid genre calls for reinterpretation of any old signs rather than simply acknowledging their "already full-formed" old meanings. Thanks to the dialogic mechanism brought forth by this hybrid genre, new meanings will be created within the single and same text by its readers with various social background. To put it simply, Young tries to prove that genre itself, if highly hybridized, will be creative and constructive as can be manifested in the literary production and therefore is one of the effective strategic rhetorics in writing.

As it has been mentioned above, Mikhail Bakhtin first applies this notion to his interpretation of polyphony. In *The Dialogic Imagination* (1975)[1], Bakhtin declares that hybridization is "a mixture of two social languages within the limits of a single utterance, an encounter, within the arena of an utterance, between two different linguistic consciousnesses, separated from one another by an epoch, by social differentiation or by some other factor" (Bakhtin 358). According to Bakhtin, language is not self-sufficient in itself, for it has to be examined in relation to its usage in specific contexts. It is social by nature since it represents different consciousness and speaks out for particular groups of people. Such mixing of two social languages within the boundary of a single utterance, he explains, is a strategy used in novel writing, a rhetorical device aimed at dissolving the dominant discourse. The co-existence of two

---

1 *The Dialogic Imagination: Four Essays* (1975) introduces the concepts of heteroglossia, dialogism and chronotope. In one of the four essays entitled "Discourse in the Novel", Bakhtin points out the hybrid nature of language and claims that hybridization is an effective measure against the single utterance or dominant discourse. Bakhtin is the first to apply hybridity to the study of polyphony, dialogism and heteroglossia. Originally a music concept, "polyphony" is borrowed by Bakhtin to refer to a diversity of points of view and voices which he defines as an indispensible feature of the novel. He takes Dostoevsky's prose as an example to prove that conflicting voices and views help to enrich the meaning of the text by breaking the singularity of vision. The term "heteroglossia" is used to describe the combination of different types of speeches co-existing in the novel, including the speech of the narrator, the character and the author. Bakhtin argues that heteroglossia is a manifestation of the author's strategy of making his intrusive voice "heard" in the disguise of a multi-voiced text. Both polyphony and heteroglossia are effective means in constructing a dialogue among a multiplicity of voices and their agents.

languages, set apart by their differentiation, shares the power within the text and therefore diminishes the power of any single language.

Bakhtin further classifies this rhetorical device in the novel into groups of "intentional hybridity" and "unconscious organic hybridity" (Bakhtin 358). While the former is consciously used as a strategy of subversion in the novel, the latter plays a more significant role in the evolution of all languages, for it is achieved by a mixing of various languages that facilitate the development of language. Bakhtin's confirmation of the productive power of hybridity in the historical development of language echoes that of Daniel Defoe, which holds that "the productive of strength, creativity and courage in the English" owes a lot to what is implied in hybridity (Guignery *et al.* 14).

Believing in the culturally productive effect of hybridization, Bakhtin, on the one hand, confirms the constructiveness of hybridity; on the other hand, he declares that, by replacing the single-voiced authority with a double or multi-voiced one, hybridity becomes an effective strategy in unmasking or undermining authoritative discourse. Robert Young later reinterprets this view on hybridity as follows:

Hybridity is itself an example of hybridity, of a doubleness that both brings together, *fuses*, but also maintains *separation*. For Bakhtin himself, the crucial effect of hybridization comes with the latter, political category, the moment where, within a single discourse, one voice is able to *unmask* the other. This is the point where authoritative discourse is *undone* (Young *Colonial Desire* 21, emphasis added).

Young explains that, for Bakhtin, authoritative discourse may be challenged by a new voice that emerges from within a work. Being double-voiced, the authoritative discourse can hardly maintain its position of authority and has to face the risk of being unmasked. In addition to being a strategy of deconstruction, hybridity can also be perceived as a process of integration since it allows for the fusion as well as interdependence of each voice within a single discourse, thus maintaining the integrity of all voices involved.

Later, Homi Bhabha borrows the term from Bakhtin and amends its core implication of productivity and subversion[1]. Bhabha examines the concept of hybridity in his essay entitled "Signs Taken for Wonders: Ambivalence and Authority Under a Tree Outside Delhi, May 1817", which is later collected in *The Location of Culture* (1994). The following is the definition of hybridity given by Bhabha:

> Hybridity is the sign of the *productivity* of colonial power, its *shifting* forces and *fixities*; it is the name for the *strategic reversal* of the process of domination through *disavowal* (that is, the production of discriminatory identities that secure the 'pure' and original identity of authority). Hybridity is the *reevaluation* of the assumption of *colonial identity* through the repetition of discriminatory identity effects. It *displays* the necessary *deformation* and *displacement* of all sites of discrimination and domination. (Bhabha *Location* 112, emphasis added)

As defined by Bhabha, hybridity is related to such actions as reversal, reevaluation, and relocation. By saying no to the pure or original identity of any prejudicing authority, the discriminated, with the help of its hybridized identity, will be able to challenge. In other words, to get one's identity redefined is one of the premises in deteriorating and deconstructing

---

1 Bhabha's contemporaries, such as Stuart Hall, Edward Said, Terry Eagleton and Toni Morrison, have praised Bhabha for his contribution to the extent to which the concept of hybridity can be applied. For example, Terry Eagleton puts Bhabha on top of the most remarkable post-colonial writers: "Few post-colonial writers can rival Homi Bhabha in his exhilarated sense of alternative possibilities—of a world in which 'hybridity', 'in-betweenness', a culture in permanent transition and incompleteness, may be embraced without anxiety or nostalgia" (Eagleton 12). According to Eagleton, Bhabha stands out in post-colonial studies partly because of his exploration of hybridity. *The Location of Culture* is regarded as "a milestone in the development of post-colonial critique" (Sheng Ning 93) for its theoretical contribution to such key issues as negotiations between heterogenous cultures, hybridity, rewriting of identity.

the power of domination. For Bhabha, since hybridity is used to refer to a mixture of races, groups, ideological systems, cultures, and languages, and it can be represented in multiple forms, hybridization may create an anti-colonial space to dismantle the dominant colonial discourse. It is interesting that both Bhabha and Bakhtin agree that language can hardly be divorced from the specific context which it grows out of and lives in. But Bhabha highlights the confrontation of races and cultures in hostile situations.

According to Bhabha, to relocate the position of a different culture without prejudice, one needs to find a new space for the relocation of meaning. This new "in-between space" (Bhabha *Location* 38) is defined by Bhabha as the Third Space which leaves little room for direct contradiction, absolute negation or binary opposition. Bhabha believes that the power or constructiveness of hybridity lies in the fact that it gives full play to this Third Space enunciation, a precondition for the articulation of cultural difference. He elaborates on the function of hybridity and its relation to the Third Space enunciations as follows:

> It is significant that the productive capacities of this Third Space have a colonial or postcolonial provenance. For a willingness to descend into that alien territory—where I have led you—may reveal that the theoretical recognition of the split-space of enunciation may open the way to conceptualizing an *inter*national culture, based not on the exoticism of multiculturalism or the *diversity* of cultures, but on the inscription and articulation of culture's *hybridity*. To that end we should remember that it is the 'inter'—the cutting edge of translation and negotiation, the *in-between* space—that carries the burden of the meaning of culture (Bhabha *Location* 38–39, italics original).

Bhabha regards the Third Space as an outcome of the colonial society or the mixture of various cultures which endows it with productive capacities. If the colonial authority is produced by the difference between the colonizer and the colonized, then anti-colonial discourse[1] can hardly be articulated without the participation of an interaction between colonial and anti-colonial discourses, an interaction mobilized by a newly derived Third Space. Growing out of hybridity, Third Space enunciations make it possible for the Other within the same culture to have their own say to or negotiate with the dominant discourse. Since the Third Space can create a contradictory or ambivalent context for the interpretation of meaning and culture, it leaves little room for the existence of any primordial, fixed, or pure meaning. Rather, the meaning of a culture may be derived from reinterpretations, translations, and negotiations arising from the Third Space, which is always already blended, depending heavily on both the authoritative and the non-authoritative languages. As Bhabha explains, "It is that Third Space, though unrepresentable in itself, which constitutes the discursive conditions of enunciation that ensure that the meaning and symbols of culture have no primordial unity or fixity; that even the same signs can be appropriated, translated, rehistoricized and read anew" (Bhabha *Location* 37). In other words, thanks to Third Space enunciations, the interpretation of any culture can become dynamic and flexible since it depends on interpreters with different historical, social, and educational backgrounds.

In the Third Space, the disputed parties are supplementary to each other, without one being superior to or replaced by the others. The contradiction will be less intensive and consequently a much gentle process of reconciliation will give birth to "a new Other characterized by harmony, unity and equity" (Li Xinyun 66). In other words, hybridity can bring about peaceful co-existence of different participants and says no to supremacy. Consequently, in the post-

---

1   The "discourse" in Bakhtin's interpretation of hybridity refers to the "contrary voices representing opposed social, political, and cultural viewpoints or perspectives often compete within polyphonic works" (Murfin & Ray 115), that is, within one single utterance, namely the single literary text. It consists of the voices of both the characters and the author which makes possible the establishment of dialogism within the literary text. Unlike Bakhtin, Bhabha applies this to his post-colonial study, and his "discourse" here refers not only to the voices of but also to the way both the colonizer and the colonized articulate in their negotiation. The post-colonial discourse then is characterized by both the strategy and the specific context of its articulator.

colonial society, hybridity may serve as a strategy to resist the dominant mode of colonial discourse—fixity—especially in depicting the marginalized, such as the colonized, the female, or the East other. It is an articulation of displacement and dislocation:

> An important feature of colonial discourse is its dependence on the concept of 'fixity' in the ideological construction of otherness. Fixity, as the sign of cultural/ historical /racial difference in the discourse of colonialism, is a paradoxical mode of representation: it connotes rigidity and an unchanging order as well as disorder, degeneracy and daemonic repetition (Bhabha *Location* 66).

If fixity leads to stereotype, hybridity goes the other way. While it is almost impossible for colonial discourse to offer a faithful representation of the East due to this fixity, hybridity offers alternative possibilities and breaks new paths. As Bhabha demonstrates, hybridity serves as a bridge to create an in-between channel for cultural negotiation rather than polarization. Furthermore, it is a strategy to reverse, for the "other 'denied' knowledges [to] enter upon the dominant discourse and estrange the basis of its authority—its rules of recognition" (Bhabha *Location* 114). To Bhabha, hybridity stands in opposite to the production of any unified cultural identity by projecting individuality, in particular, the presence of the discriminated. It therefore makes it possible for the "denied" knowledge to re-emerge and thus deform the basis of its authority. Since the "denied knowledge" may become counter authoritative, it is more difficult to make a straight judgment. This puts into question the standard set by the dominant discourse, even temporarily, rendering it semi- or pseudo-authoritative.

Bhabha further explains that due to the emergence of these "denied knowledges", binary representation is losing ground in the negotiation mobilized by Third Space enunciations:

> Such negotiation is neither assimilation nor collaboration. It makes

possible the emergence of an 'interstitial' agency that refuses the binary representation of social antagonism. Hybrid agencies find their voice in a dialectic that does not seek cultural supremacy or sovereignty. They deploy the partial culture from which they emerge to construct visions of community, and versions of historic memory, that give narrative form to the minority positions they occupy; the outside of the inside: the part in the whole (Bhabha "Culture's In-Between" 58).

Being a platform for negotiation among parties with unequal power, Bhabha argues, hybridization calls for "neither assimilation nor collaboration" of all those involved. No matter how large the social gap between them, each participant of the dialogue enjoys the same right of articulation. Thanks to this kind of team work with each member presenting its own culture in their own voice, visions of community and versions of historic memory are constructed.

While Bakhtin emphasizes the co-articulation of voices, each identifying with a specific social background within one utterance, Bhabha stresses the significance of an "interstice" (Bhabha *Location* 2), a brand-new space open to fair play of all participants. While Bhabha believes that the subversive power exists on the border, Bakhtin argues that deconstruction may take place from within, even a dismantlement from the center. It seems that while the Bakhtinian hybridity foregrounds contradictions and "contrary voices" "compet[ing] within polyphonic works" (Murfin & Ray 115), Bhabha's is more likely to achieve subversion through negotiation.

Unlike Bakhtin and Bhabha, Robert Young defines the meaning of hybridity by using an analogy:

At its simplest, hybridity, however, implies a disruption and forcing together of any unlike living things, grafting a vine or a rose on to a different root stock, making difference into sameness... Hybridization can also consist of the forcing of a single entity into two or more parts, a severing of a single object into two, turning sameness into difference... Hybridity thus makes difference into sameness, and sameness into difference, but in a way that makes the same no longer the same, the different no longer simply different. In that sense, it operates according to the form of logic that Derrida isolates in the term 'brisure', a breaking and a joining at the same time, in the same place: difference and sameness in an apparently impossible simultaneity (Young *Colonial Desire* 24–25).

Young notices the extension of this term from a racial theory to a cultural critique, a process characterized by "disruption", "grafting" and "breaking and joining at the same time". Furthermore, hybridity is neither a simple mixture nor combination of things with a difference, but a binary process in which different things integrate into each other without losing much of their own distinctive features, or to quote Bhabha, there is "neither assimilation nor collaboration" (Bhabha "Culture's In-Between" 58). Therefore, hybridity thus understood is an effective means for producing multiplicity, complicity, ambivalence, or ambiguity in the context of socio-cultural or literary communication. It resists the simple replacement and dislocation of forms, styles, or identities and gives rise to more openness, an openness growing out of either integration or subversion or both of them. While taking sides with both Bakhtin and Bhabha, Young further emphasizes the productivity or fertility of hybridity, a fact that can be manifested in many different fields of study.

Apart from the above mentioned three, the discussion of hybridity has been extended by other scholars and researchers, including May Joseph, Pnina Werbner, Edward Said, Jennifer Natalya Fink, Marwan M. Kraidy, Sten Pultz Moslund, Anjali Prabhu, and Shirley Anne Tate. In a 1998 book co-edited by May Joseph and Jennifer Natalya Fink, *Performing Hybridity*, hybridity is discussed from the perspective of performance studies and cultural studies. A collection of poems, essays, case studies, and photographic works, the book sets out to demonstrate how artists articulate hybrid identities as a way of reconsidering questions of sexuality, social agency and national affiliation. In other words, hybridity is now perceived as a more convenient strategy in redefining meanings, identities, and forms of knowledge, a perspective echoing the views of Bakhtin and Bhabha. May Joseph also claims that "postcolonial scholarship has stressed the growing relevance of hybridization in understanding contemporary cultural practice", including "cultural performance that drew on theater, dance, ritual, folklore, religious and linguistic practices" (Joseph 7–8). Similarly, Pnina Werbner and Tariq Modood, in *Debating Cultural Hybridity: Multicultural Identities and the Politics of Anti-Racism* (1997), suggest that hybridity can be regarded as a "theoretical meta-construction of social order" (Werbner & Modood 1), and agree with Bhabha that hybridity functions as a constructive strategy of subversion in the sense that it contributes to the diversification of identities as presented by various forms of culture, races, religions or literary practices.

Likewise, in *Culture and Imperialism* (1994), Edward Said addresses the hybridity of post-colonial culture, claiming that "all cultures are involved in one another, none is single and pure, all are hybrid, heterogeneous, extraordinarily differentiated, and unmonolithic" (Said *Culture and Imperialism* xxv). He further elaborates on the "oddly hybrid" nature of historical and cultural experiences, reminding the reader of the fact that hybridized experiences emerge from "many often contradictory experiences and domains, cross national boundaries, defy the police action of simple dogma and loud patriotism" (Said *Culture and Imperialism* 15), so that they are inevitably "out of place"[1].

Shirley Anne Tate in *Black Skins, Black Masks: Hybridity, Dialogism, Performativity* (2005) uses the daily talks of 36 women, all of Caribbean

---

1   *Out of Place* (1999) is the title of Edward Said's memoir and the label he gives to public intellectuals, including himself. Being a well-acknowledged literary theorist and cultural critic, Said frequently crosses "national boundaries" (Said *Culture and Imperialism* 15), both in life and mind. It is due to his own hybrid experience that he is so concerned about the issue of the East and the West, which he discusses in depth in *Orientalism* (1978). He himself is a good example of the "oddly hybrid" who spares no effort in defying "simple dogma and loud patriotism" all his life (Said *Culture and Imperialism* 15). As an exile most of his life, Said takes advantage of his position both inside and outside, believing that the unique perspective and status help in observing the world in a cool-headed manner.

heritage, who live in three geographical areas of Britain to theorize hybridity[1]. Influenced by Bhabha's interpretation of mimicry and Stuart Hall's theory of "new ethnicities", Tate identifies hybridity as a "strategic identificatory performance that arose in the talk" of these women (Tate *Black Skins* 163). Later, in her essay entitled "Foucault, Bakhtin, Ethnomethodology: Accounting for Hybridity in Talk-in-Interaction" (2007), Tate elaborates on her view that hybridity addresses the ongoing assemblage of identities in speech, demonstrating that "talk-in-interaction" results from "the negotiation of discourses of identity positionings that constitutes *a hybridity of the everyday*" (Tate "Foucault, Bakhtin" 16)[2]. After tracing hybridity back to its ancient sources, she "highlights the conceptual and empirical inadequacy of the theory of hybridity and the third space" (Acheraïou 8) in a postcolonial context.

Inspired by these studies as much as Bakhtin and Bhabha's interpretation of hybridity in the study of language, postcolonial culture, and literature, this study examines Lessing's body of work for the purpose of illustrating the function of hybridity when it comes to narration, to show the power of hybridity when used as "a strategic rhetoric" to "subvert dominant discourses" (Kraidy 58). Lessing's hybridized narrations are both deconstructive and constructive, actualized by her flexible handling of key narrative elements as well as a mix-match of different styles, genres, and subject matters. Like two sides of a coin, constructiveness and deconstructiveness allow hybridity

---

1   The title of this book is taken from Frantz Fanon's *Black Skin, White Mask* (1952), which probes into the position and identity of the Afro-Americans in the world of white men and serves as his "weapon" in the anti-colonial struggle. Through this empirical study on black women's spoken language and so-called "everyday" hybridity, or "hybridity-of-the-everyday", Tate "examine[s] how Blackness is transformed and reformed in women's talk and through their social actions" (Osler 293). Her aim is to show how the identity of black women can be reconstructed with the help of hybridized language.

2   Although criticized as ill-organized, for she "does not make the most of her own data in illustrating her theoretical insights" (Osler 295), this book is still worth mentioning since the study she conducts is based on an analysis of language that offers insight into Lessing's works, especially those concerning colonial issues.

to become an effective strategic rhetoric or a sort of "hybrid vigour" (qtd. in Pieterse 226). With the help of hybridity, Lessing finds it convenient to follow tradition while making conventions anew.

A brief look at recent articles and monographs related to this topic shows that the study of hybridity has been extended to many fields and concepts. Against the background of trans-culturation and globalization, hybridity involves identities, languages, cultures, politics, forms of arts, and genres. Since diversified hybrids can be concretized, literary works serve as significant medium for the study of hybrid expressions. In this respect, Lessing is a good case in point since her writing, as this book will show, is highly hybridized. This study of Lessing's strategic use of hybridity will focus on the hybrid construction of Lessing as a single speaker on the one hand, and her dialogic encounters with others on the other hand, both of which can be proved by her flexible handling of narrative elements, her mastery of highly hybridized genres, styles and subject matters, and the differences as well as similarities between her and several other writers and theorists.

For more than two decades, Lessing scholars have noted the features of hybridity in her narration, offering discussions on the points of view, narrators, voices, perspectives, and styles in several of her masterpieces. What makes Doris Lessing unique among, if not superior to, other contemporary writers is her extended horizon as a result of hybridity. Roberta Rubenstein comments that "the broad range of issues that occupy the center of her canon demands that she be addressed critically as one of the significant writers of this (20th) century" (Rubenstein *Novelistic Vision* 3). A wide range of subject matters is just one aspect of Lessing's hybridity, which will be discussed in detail in the following chapter. Indeed, hybridity can be shown in her handling of diversified narrative voices, narrators, and perspectives, and in her styles, genres, and subject matters as well. Up to now, however, only a few scholars have established a link between Lessing's narrative and the theory of hybridity, and few monographs have offered a comprehensive study of this particular aspect of her work. Lessing herself mentioned the idea of hybridity in a 1990 interview, and she has elaborated on this issue from time to time, without recognizing the organic relations and implicit influences of this strategy on her writing philosophy.

Although scholars and critics have noticed the hybridized features of Lessing's narrative, they do not go further enough, and the texts they tend to choose have not effectively demonstrated this distinctive feature of hers. For instance, in the special Lessing issue of *Contemporary Literature Studies* and a collection entitled *Rereading Doris Lessing*, scholars have analyzed various kinds of narrative techniques in Lessing's novels, but few of them have interpreted these techniques from the perspective of hybridization. In other words, while there have been studies addressing narrative issues in Lessing's works, few of them have addressed these issues in terms of hybridity.

It is not until the 1980s that Eve Bertelsen, a significant Lessing scholar, explicitly pointed out that there is a "hybrid" in Lessing's *Canopus in Argos* series:

> Here she takes on a new genre, that of science fiction, but characteristically exploits it to her own ends, developing a portmanteau form which is forced to accommodate any number of perspectives and styles, sometimes alternating in dizzying succession, at others producing an infuriating longueur. Even her most dedicated readers have been confused by this *hybrid*... It is as if Lessing's lifelong questioning of boundaries is given at last free play, and her contempt for a single personal perspective and a single style has reached its apotheosis (Bertelsen *Doris Lessing* 22, emphasis added).

Bertelsen notices that in these five novels spanning from 1979 to 1982, Lessing resorts to multiple points of view and alternates between different styles, adopting a narrator who feels free to forget about his time and space. Hence, Bertelsen argues, Lessing, in this period, was "developing a portmanteau". Bertelsen attributes this diversification of perspective and style to Lessing's steadfast pursuit of freedom and her fight against imprisonment. While this point is valid, a hybrid narrative voice does not just characterize

Lessing's latest work: it can be found in her earlier writings as well. For instance, *The Golden Notebook*, one of her earliest works and superficially a naturalistic or chronological story, turns out to be a novel putting together elements of realism and (post-)modernism without being limited by time and space. It is well-known that, in this narrative, the complicated and purposefully designed structure plays an important role of "showing" and "telling" the reader the ultimate meaning of the story, which means that its so-called sophistication comes not only from its complicated structure, but also from its mixture of narrative skills. Therefore, it provides an integration resulting from compartmentization, or a unified meaning deriving from a hybridized way of narration.

Some studies have noticed Lessing's experiments with narrative voice and point of view. Jeannette King (1989), for example, analyzes the internal and external focalization in *The Grass Is Singing,* pointing out the contradictions and biases caused by blended and biased points of views, which not only complicates the narrative voice but also invites the reader to work out the meaning of the work from different perspectives. According to King, the two focalizations refer to the inside view of the white community in Africa for "the narrative voice speaks from outside the African experience, but from within that of the white community" (King 5), and the outsider's view of Tony Marston, a young British male and newly arrival on the colony who makes his own judgment on the whole event: "Marston articulates those questions and criticisms which we would expect of an outsider, thus acting as a focal point for the European reader" (King 5). Due to the ambiguity arising from the shifted viewpoints, the judgments offered by the "omniscient" narrator may not be the most justifiable one and it is up to the reader to make the final evaluation. King also calls attention to the "silent" narrative of Moses, which reflects the White instead of the Black point of view. King emphasizes that by adopting this narrative method, Lessing "works against any final, closed reading, any authoritative sanctioning of a single attitude as 'correct'" (King 7). Taking *The Good Terrorist* (1985) as an example, the irony in the narrator's voice undermines the credibility of authoritative voice, thus creating "'openness' of meaning" in the story (King 104).

Andrzej Gasiorek, in his *Post-War British Fiction: Realism and After* (1995), has called attention to hybridity in Lessing's narrative structures which are usually regarded as realism-oriented yet postmodern in nature. "Doris Lessing 'produces texts in which realism splinters into a wide range of alternative narrative modes' without abandoning the traditional narrative contract between text and context, artifice and reality'" (qtd. in Visel 62). Gasiorek notes that Lessing has experimented with various modes of writing without confining herself to any one "-ism", even the realism for which she shows great admiration.

Another reference to hybridity in Lessing appears in an article by Christine W. Sizemore entitled "In Pursuit of the English: Hybridity and the Local in Doris Lessing's First Urban Text", submitted to the Second Conference on Doris Lessing (2008), which declares that Lessing's hybridized vision of England is a result of her hybridized identity as a colonizer in Africa and at the same time, "her continuing status as an outsider in the culture of the West" as pointed out by Michael Thorpe (Thorpe x).

Chinese scholars, compared with their counterparts in Western countries, have paid even less attention to hybridity in Lessing's narrative. Lu Jiande, analyzing the narrative features in *GN* in *Post-Modernism: Realism and Experimentation: A Study of British Novels Since 1945* (1997), notices the complexity and contradiction in Lessing's novels which results in the tension and openness of her narrative space. A doctoral dissertation by Lu Jing—*The Artistic Forms of* The Golden Notebook *and Lessing's Life Experience* (2008)— devotes one chapter out of six to a discussion of narrative skills in *GN*, but the discussion does not touch upon hybridity. Similarly, although many Chinese graduate students have chosen to discuss narrative features in Lessing's writing, few of them have addressed the relationship between Lessing's narration and her hybridity. Generally speaking, few Chinese scholars have made hybridity in Lessing's works the focus of their studies.

Lessing herself has noticed the "juxtapositions" in her works. In a 1969 interview in which she was asked about her view of *The Four-Gated City*

(1969), Lessing answered, "I do think perhaps that I'm better at putting facts together; I think I'm quite good at seeing things in juxtaposition" (Terkel & Lessing 21). This is one of the earliest explicit statements Lessing made confirming her literary modes of "putting facts together" and "seeing things in juxtaposition". In fact, there is not only a juxtaposition of things, facts, subject matters in her writing, but also of narrating voices, perspectives, styles, and genres, which she obviously fails to explicate.

Later, in a 1990 interview "A Writer Is Not a Professor", Lessing declared that the novel "is a complete hybrid, full of influences (film, myth, music, and pictures), prodigiously adaptable" (Montremy & Lessing 196). There are two layers of meaning in this statement: First, the novel is a complete hybrid because it may borrow from many artistic forms such as film, myth, music, painting, photography, and newspapers. Second, due to this formal hybridity, the novel may become informative and all embracing, hence flexible and adaptable. While Lessing has made no explicit reference to Bhabha's theory of hybridity, this 1990 statement does resonate with Bhabha, who did not elaborate on his theory of hybridity until four years later in *The Location of Culture*.

Two more points need to be clarified concerning the theory of hybridity. First, is it reasonable to discuss Lessing in a post-colonial context given the post-colonial tint of hybridity? Critics disagree on this point. Some prefer to take her as a realist writer: "Yet critics have been, until comparatively recently, reluctant to see Lessing as a postcolonial writer or to read her work in relation to postcolonial theory and criticism" (Watkins & Chambers 3). However, this study will argue that Lessing's hybridity, both her hybrid identity and her hybridized narratives, qualifies the post-coloniality in her. Second, is the hybridized narrative a constant practice through Lessing's writing, or in other words, is there any mixture of perspectives, tones, voices, or styles in her works of different periods, especially the earliest ones, which are often grouped into realism? The answer is also affirmative, since a closer look at her works at different periods prove that her experimentation with different styles and strategies—be they realistic, modernist, or post-modernist—is a strong proof of her consistent hybridized narration[1].

This study will focus on the following two questions: (1) how Lessing resorts to the strategy of hybridity and (2) why she chooses this strategy? While Chapter One and Chapter Two deal with the first question, Chapter Three tackles the second. Chapter One demonstrates Lessing's hybridized narrative approach by examining three key elements in the study of narration: voice, narrator, and perspective. The analysis starts from an examination of the fourfold-voice narrative in *Love, again* (1996) and the multiplied narrators in *The Diaries of Jane Somers* (1984)[2]. In *Love, again*, the reader hears four different voices or narrators, including the omniscient narrator and the first-person narration, through the free, indirect speech and the first-person revelations of the characters' journal and letters. In *The Diaries of Jane Somers*, the dominating first-person narration is frequently "interfered" with an omniscient third-person narrator and the interior monologue of some characters. Thus, the diversified narrators combine to comprise a hybridized, yet organically unified, narration. There will also be a close look at the retrospective perspective in *The Diaries of Jane Somers,* the white-focused

---

1   Alongside the theory of hybridity, narratology serves as the other theoretical framework for this study, which will frequently resort to some of the classical works in narrative studies. Among these, the most helpful are *The Rhetoric of Fiction* (1983) by Wayne Booth, *The Art of Fiction* (1994) by David Lodge, and *Western Narratology: Classical and Postclassical* (2010) coauthored by Shen Dan and Wang Liya. The general rules governing narration, as deciphered by Wayne Booth in detail, are enlightening to our understanding of narration and, therefore, helpful in a discussion on Lessing's narrative skills. Similarly, Shen Dan's *Western Narratology: Classical and Postclassical* briefs the author on the development of narration and some of the core concepts in this field, with clear explanation and demonstration.

2   *The Diary of a Good Neighbour* by Jane Somers was first published in 1983 in England. "Jane Somers" was a pseudonym taken by Doris Lessing and is also the first-person narrator in the story, a well-known woman journalist. In the following year, this same Jane Somers published another novel entitled *If the Old Could*, the sequel to *The Diary of a Good Neighbour*. In the same year, *The Diaries of Jane Somers* (1984), which put the above two books into one volume, appeared for the first time under Doris Lessing's name, together with a new preface by the author. All the quotations from this book used in this study come from the 2005 edition published by Foreign Language Teaching and Research Press.

perspective in *The Grass Is Singing,* and the internalized patriarchal perspective in *The Golden Notebook.* Thanks to the "intentional" and the "unconscious" hybridity, a polyphonic narrative is constructed inside and outside the text.

Chapter Two further examines Lessing's hybridity in her choice and flexible use of different "-isms", genres, and subject matters as well as her resemblances to and differences from several other writers and theorists. Some of her works boast the distinctive features of her literary forefathers—the great realists—and her contemporaries, the modernists and post-modernists. Two cases in point are *The Grass Is Singing* and *The Summer Before the Dark.* A discussion of the blurring of fiction and non-fiction in *The Memoirs of a Survivor* (1974) and *Alfred and Emily* (2008) helps to show her bold practice of remixing genres. In addition, it is interesting to hear what Lessing says about the advantages of space fiction and to examine her experiments in this genre, such as *The Marriages Between Zone Three, Four, and Five* (1994). Apart from an open stance towards various "-isms" and genres, Lessing's adoption of a juxtaposition of subject matters, which can be roughly categorized into travel narratives, female narratives, narratives of growth, and narratives of trauma, makes her writing even more hybridized. Since travel narrative and female narrative appear in most of her writings and are most supportive in demonstrating her hybridity, they form a large part of the chapter. The flexibility and diversity in Lessing's writing shows that she is good at both inheriting and innovating, which adds up to the hybridity in her own writing and integrates her discourse into a heteroglossia.

Chapter Three traces the causes of Lessing's hybridization, or the sources of the constructiveness and de-constructiveness in her writing, showing that it is both natured and nurtured. Lessing's spirit of resistance, her awareness of tradition and innovation all encourage her to use hybridity as a strategy in her search for an effective discourse. Evidence for this can be found in her complaint about the philistinism of British literature, her protest against conventions and labelling, and the early formation and gradual evolution of her rebelliousness. Most important of all, Lessing constantly revises her views on the author's function, the moral issue in the literary work and the author-text-reader relationships. This evolution in her writing philosophy has a direct bearing on her choice of narrative skills and patterns. It seems that there is a retrospective Lessing and an experiencing Lessing negotiating with each other, hence a self-reflective dialogue. To conclude, the dialogues at various levels, conducted among different agencies within the single text, or among the author, text and reader, or between Lessing and other writers, or within the author herself all contribute to the construction of the dialogic mechanism inside and outside the text. These dialogues are produced and produce in turn the effect of hybridity which becomes a powerful rhetorical strategy in Lessing's writing.

Chapter One
Polyphonic Narrative out of Intentional or Unconscious Hybridity

In relation to narrative, heteroglossia stands as the appearance in real life of that plurality of languages of class, gender, region, or ideology which enter the novel in the form of dialogism, resulting—in Bakhtin's most praised authors such as Dostoevsky—in a polyphony narrative.

—David Herman

This chapter will focus on Lessing's handling of hybridized narrative: her narrative voice, narrators, and perspectives. It will analyze the multi-voiced narration in *Love, again* and the diversified narrators in *The Diaries of Jane Somers* and elaborate on the relationship between the author's voice and its communicative function in these novels. In addition, a look into the shifting perspectives in three of her novels—the retrospective perspective in *The Diaries of Jane Somers,* the white perspective in *The Grass Is Singing,* and the internalized patriarchal perspective in *The Golden Notebook*—will demonstrate how flexible Lessing is in terms of narrative strategy.

Lessing seems to have a tighter control of the narrative voice in her early writing because of her belief in the educational and didactic function of literature. With this belief becoming less solid, she loses confidence in authorial interference in her later works. In spite of her increasing doubt about the writer's superior position and moral power, she tends to more willingly offer her own authorial guidance and judgment to the reader, a stance not quite in line with her identity as a "silenced" and marginalized writer or as one fond of change of narrative voices, shift of perspectives, and blended styles and subject matters in narration. The ambiguity and complexity achieved by these tactics often overshadow her strong intention to provide authorial instruction, as she becomes a more manipulating author over time.

To delve into shifting perspectives in Lessing's narration, it is necessary to distinguish between *voice* and *perspective/point of view*, with *perspective* and *point of view* being used interchangeably both in Chinese and English. The concept of *voice* in a narrative was put forward by Genette in *Narrative Discourse: An Essay in Method* (1983) firstly published in French in 1972. Genette, as pointed out by Jonathan Culler in the foreword to this book, argues that some people have mistaken *voice* for *point of view*, for "they have failed to distinguish properly between '*mood* and *voice*, that is to say, between the question *who is the character whose point of view orients the narrative perspective?* and the very different question *who is the narrator?*'" (Genette 10). For Genette, *point of view* has something to do with focalization while voice is a matter of "who speaks" (Fludernik 162), a question to which the answer may be concreted as the first-person, second-person, third-person narration and several other complicated forms of narration. Genette (1983) classifies *point of view* into three types: zero focalization (similar to third-person omniscient narration), external focalization, and internal focalization which can be fixed, variable or multiple. While *voice* is critical in the discussion of the distance issue between the author and the text for it can identify the "the degrees of narratorial mediation in speech and thought representation (minimal distance in interior monologue, maximal distance in speech report)" (Fludernik 162), *persective/point of view* gives clues to both the narratorial mediation, that is, the author-text relationships, and the narrator's identity. Besides showing the reader whether the viewpoint is an outside or inside one, *persective/point of view*, a term used to "describe the different kinds of access readers have to the consciousness of a novel's protagonists" which mainly consists of the "traditional visual (point of view) and psychological perspective (representation of consciousness)" (Fludernik 159), reveals more about the narrator's identity, worldview and motivation instead of those of the author, or as defined in *Routledge Encyclopedia of*

Narrative Theory (2005), it may reflect "a character's or narrator's subjective worldview" insofar as

> the factors that determine a character's worldview are his/her knowledge and abilities, psychological disposition, system of norms and values, belief sets, attitudes, motivations, needs and intentions as well as his/her sex, gender, sexuality, ethnic identity, and the general economic, political, social, and cultural conditions under which s/he lives (Herman *et al.* 424).

Perspective here means "whose eyes we see through—the angle of vision" (Martin 124). Since each character and narrator possesses a distinctive identity and takes a specific position, the angle of vision the character provides varies. Whenever there is a change of narrator, perspective changes accordingly. As a study of narrator can disclose the author's degree of intrusion on the one hand, and explains for the ambiguity of the text narrated by various characters with distinctive characteristics and identities on the other, a look into the shifting or (more typically) conflicting perspectives helps to understand Lessing's competence in constructing a hybrid text.

In one sense, the contradiction or ambiguity resulting from hybridized perspectives can produce effects similar to that of the strategies such as Bakhtin's "polyphony" or "heteroglossia": "In relation to narrative, heteroglossia stands as the appearance in real life of that plurality of languages of class, gender, region, or ideology which enter the novel in the form of dialogism, resulting—in Bakhtin's most praised authors such as Dostoevsky— in a polyphony narrative" (Herman *et al.* 213). Originally a musical concept, "polyphony" is borrowed by Bakhtin to refer to a diversity of points of view and voices that he defines as an indispensible feature of the novel. He takes Dostoevsky's prose as an example to prove that conflicting voices and views help to enrich the meaning of the text by breaking the singularity of vision. He uses the term "polyphony" and "heteroglossia" interchangeably to describe the combination of different types of speeches co-existing in the novel, including the speech of narrators, of characters, and of the author. Such a mixing of speech, further complicated by the background of the class, gender, locality, or ideology of the speaker, makes the text inevitably multi-voiced. To Bakhtin, polyphony or heteroglossia is on the one hand the author's strategy of making his intrusive voice heard in the disguise of a multi-voiced text and on the other hand, allows for the co-existence of voices presenting a diversified rather than unified worldview:

> If the perspective can be integrated into a unified worldview or if a single point of view is privileged, the narrative text has a "closed" perspective structure. If the perspectives contrast and contradict each other and if there are unresolved differences between conflicting world-models, the perspective structure of the text remains "open". In the latter case, the absence of any prefabricated solutions or of an authoritative, dominating perspective reveals a plurality of conflicting moral and ideological views which are granted equal validity within the text, a scenario typically characterizing what Bakhtin terms polyphony or heteroglossia (Herman *et al.* 424).

Accordingly, conflicting perspectives tear the text "open", with the "authoritative, dominating perspective" being supplemented by "a plurality of conflicting moral and ideological views". Frequent switches between different perspectives may confuse the reader and reduce his trust in the author, and the reader then has to decide by himself whether or not the narrator is reliable. He has to ask himself whether the author purposefully makes the perspective fluctuate and, if he does, for what reason. Hence, reading becomes a demanding process which invigorates critical thinking.

Thanks to this mixing of perspectives, the author's voice becomes less arbitrarily intrusive and the omniscient narrator tends to recede from the story, for just as David Lodge points out, there can and should be no omniscient narration in fiction:

> Totally objective, totally impartial narration may be a worthy aim in

journalism or historiography, but a fictional story is unlikely to engage our interest unless we know whose story it is. The choice of the point(s) of view from which the story is told is arguably the most important single decision that the novelist has to make, for it fundamentally affects the way readers will respond, emotionally and morally, to the fictional characters and their actions (Lodge 26).

Lodge believes that however hard a writer tries to hide himself from the text, his choice of point of view reveals the authorial intention, being his "most important single decision" to make when writing. This choice will have an inevitable influence on the reader's interpretation of the text, the characters, and their actions, since it is what the author wants his reader to "see" and accept. Since Lessing is good at making her "voice" heard through masterful use of shifting perspectives, a manifestation of her hybridized narration, a close examination of this aspect of her writing is worthwhile.

1.1 Multi-voiced Narration in *Love, again*

In *Love, again*, Lessing integrates the story of Julie Vairon into that of Sarah, bringing about an inter-textuality of the past and the present as well as a double narrative pattern achieved through intertwining the omniscient third-person narrator and first-person voice[1]. She charges both of the two heroines in the story with the task of first-person narration so that the voices within the text belong to different characters or the same character at different ages, a strategy that complicates the narrative voice. Let's first have a look at the shift between

---

1 Claire Sprague has conducted an in-depth discussion on Lessing's narrative patterns of doubling and repetition in her monograph entitled *Re-reading Doris Lessing, Narrative Patterns of Doubling and Repetition* (1987). Sprague argues that Lessing tries to make the most of the doubling and repetition in characters, naming, numerological patterns, environments and narrative forms in most of her works, so as to show her questioning of and protest against "the singleness and stability of personality—especially for women—and of narrative conventions" (Sprague 5). This study is indebted to her study which sheds light on the multi-voiced narration in this part.

the third-person voice and Sarah's focalizing voice.

The story begins with an omniscient narrator calmly describing the details of the scene and the heroine:

> Easy to think this was a junkroom, silent and airless in a warm dusk, but then a shadow moved, someone emerged from it to pull back curtains and throw open windows. It was a woman, who now stepped quickly to a door and went out, leaving it open. The room thus revealed was certainly over-full. Along one wall were all the evidences of technical evolution—a fax machine, a copy machine, a word processor, telephones—but as for the rest, the place could easily be some kind of theatrical storeroom, with a gold bust of some Roman female, much larger than life, masks, a crimson velvet curtain, posters, and piles of sheet music, or rather photocopies that had faithful reproduced yellowing and crumbling originals (*LA* 1).

In this opening paragraph, a camera-like view presents details to the reader by showing static objects and then the movement of a woman. The simple and direct presentation of the physical environment provides the reader with some information about the woman, such as her career, habits, and identity. "A fax machine", "a copy machine" and "a word processor" reveal her profession while the "gold bust of some Roman female" and "piles of sheet music" indicate that it may have to do with art. Guided by the omniscient third-person narrator, the reader knows that she is a "woman of a certain age, as the French put it, or even a bit older, and not dressed to present herself, but wearing old trousers and shirt" (*LA* 2).

On the next page, however, when the woman sits down and turns off the music she has just listened to, she falls into a deep thought:

> Silence. She sat breathing it in. She was altogether too much affected by this old troubadour and trouvere music. She had been listening to little else for days, to set the tone of what she had to write... she was restless, and she was feverish. When had the music affected her like this before?

She did not think it had. Wait, though. Once she had listened to jazz, particularly the blues, it seemed day and night, for months. But that was when her husband died, and the music had fed her melancholy. But she did not remember… yes, first she had been grief-ridden, and then she had chosen music to fit her state. But this was a different matter together (*LA* 2–3).

Here, the narrator enters into the consciousness of the heroine so that the reader can "hear" the flow of the woman's thoughts and feelings without narrative interference. However, unlike stream-of-consciousness or interior monologue, this revelation of her inner activities is made by the third-person narrator instead of a first-person voice, so that it may be defined as *free indirect discourse* or *narrated monologue*.

Free-indirect-discourse (FID), a form of reporting speech and thought of the character in the text, is often put in contrast to the direct one. Dorrit Cohn names it as the "narrated monologue" (Cohn 99), claiming that this form of reporting, together with the other two forms, namely, the psycho-narration and quoted monologue, is responsible for presenting the consciousness in third-person context[1]. Similarly, in *The Art of Fiction* (1992), David Lodge clarifies the differences between *free indirect speech*, *stream-of-consciousness*, and *interior monologue*:

There are two staple techniques for representing consciousness in prose fiction. One is *interior monologue*, in which the grammatical subject of the discourse is an 'I', and we, as it were, overhear the character verbalizing his or her thoughts as they occur… The other method, called *free indirect style*, goes back at least as far as Jane Austen, but was employed with ever-increasing scope and virtuosity by modern novelists like Woolf. It renders thought as reported speech (*in the third person, past tense*) but keeps to the kind of vocabulary that is appropriate to the character, and

---

1 For detailed discussion on "narrated monologue", see Cohn: 99–142.

deletes some of the tags, like 'she thought', 'she wondered', 'she asked herself' etc. that a more formal narrative style would require. This gives the illusion of intimate access to a character's mind, but without totally surrendering *authorial participation* in the discourse (Lodge 43, emphasis added).

To Lodge, free indirect speech is conducted "in the third person, past tense" and it is called "free" because it is indirect speech without such grammatical patterns as "'she thought', 'she wondered', 'she asked herself' etc.". Taking advantage of this technique, the author can convey the thoughts of the character "without totally surrendering authorial participation" since the reader can hear two voices simultaneously: one of the narrator and the other of the character. It is called "free", as compared with ordinary indirect speech, in the sense that it "is characterized by the freedom of its syntax and the presence of deictic and expressive elements reflecting the perspective of the original speaker or of the consciousness being portrayed" (Fludernik 154). Therefore, free indirect speech, as "a vehicle of dual-voice discourse" (Herman *et al.* 189), is conductive to polyphony or heteroglossia, which is an effective strategy of letting more voices heard.

As the story progresses, numerous "she thought" "she knew" and "she said" constructions appear apart from the omniscient third-person narrative, with the former indirectly speaking the mind of the heroine and the latter telling her story from an outsider's viewpoint. The frequent switch between the outside voice and the inside within a short paragraph shows that Sarah is extremely "busy" with inner thoughts:

Sitting there, the word processor pushed to one side, for she was still at the stage of words scribbled on loose sheets with a Biro—yes, pretty old-fashioned, she knew—she thought, That's something of a claim I'm making... conceited? Perhaps. But I think it's true. This young woman hasn't understood the first thing about Julie... I care very much that her translation is flat, no effervescence. *I care too much.* I am altogether too much involved in this business. Yes, of course you have to be totally submerged in what you are working on, even if a week after it's finished you've forgotten it... What is it about that bloody Julie: she gets under people's skin; she's under mine. Look how this thing takes off, spreads itself about—she's blowing us all apart, and we know it. I really am intoxicated— probably all these months of listening to the music. Well, I have to listen to it this week... I'm making everything too complicated: I've spent years and years weighted with Duty, working like a madwoman, and if I don't watch out I'll go sailing off into the sky like a hydrogen balloon (*LA* 46, italics original).

In this monologue, delivered through a mixed voice composed of both third-person and first-person narration conducted either loudly or silently, Sarah shows her anxiety over the translation of Julie's journals: she knows that she is "too much involved in this business" and complains about those "years and years weighted with Duty, working like a madwoman". By opening Sarah's inner world, Lessing manages to shorten the distance between the heroine and her "listeners" who may find themselves involved in the story and eager to know more about this "madwoman".

Apart from the co-existence of the two (internal and external) voices, the narration is made more complicated since the first-person narration is provided by different heroines. There are two heroines in *LA*: one is the sixty-five-year-old writer Sarah Durham, who falls in love with three men, and the other is Julie Vairon, the French girl who has a tragic love affair and commits suicide in 1912. Several decades later, Sarah is working together with her friends on a play based on Julie Vairon's journals. During her preparation for the play about Vairon's love affairs with the three men, Sarah keeps journals and letters which become her first-person narration. Meanwhile, the journals of Julie Vairon serve her as first-person voice. In a broad sense, the journals can be regarded as a type of autobiographical narrative, while letters (like those in an epistolary novel) may have the same narrative effects: since both the journals and letters are presented in the first-person voice, they directly speak the mind of its writer and may arouse more easily the reader's sympathy than a third-person observer's voice can do. Taking into consideration the context of this story, Julie's journals may be seen as playing a more complicated narrative role than Sarah's journals and letters. Unlike Sarah, Julie the dead person and her "past" journals with first-person voice bring about a new perspective in re-evaluating her personality and character. The supposed-to-be silenced voice of a dead person therefore gets revitalized in the story with the help of silent words and revises or even subverts people's original views, be it just or prejudiced, on this girl.

To bring Julie the dead heroine back to life, Lessing resorts to Julie's journals and letters as a form of interior monologue so that the reader can "listen to" the inner voice of Julie and pass their own judgments on her personality. In contrast to the public remarks and rumors that present an outside view of her, Julie's self-portrayal acts as her self-defense and her confession, "discovering the real, her hidden nature" (*LA* 18). For instance, she reflects upon her love relations and complains about the injustice done to her: "*I like him so much, and everything about this proposition is sensible. Why then does it lack conviction?*" (*LA* 24, italics original). She also describes, in a calm and sensible tone, her dreams of a marriage life with her future husband:

I shall wake up in that comfortable bed beside him, when the maid comes in to do the fire. Just as his wife did. Then I will kiss him and I will get up to make the coffee, since he likes my coffee. Then I shall kiss him when he goes downstairs to the shop. Then I shall give the girl orders. At last I will go to the room he says I can have for myself and I shall paint. Oils if I like. I will be able to afford anything I like in that line. He usually doesn't come to the midday meal, so I shall ignore it and walk in the gardens and make conversations with the citizens, who are hanging to forgive me. Then I shall play the piano a little, or my flute... (*LA* 24–25)

In this journal entry, Julie describes an imagined day from morning to night. Her plain words and calm narration depict a girl who is deeply in love and aspires to nothing but a normal married life. Instead of a "vagabond and disturber of minds" who does harm to the community for being "both illegitimate and coloured" (*LA* 23), Julie with her love for painting and music proves to be a talented girl with good taste who is "more intelligent" (*LA* 16) than that of those clever girls from the rich family.

Lessing makes no comment on this entry but lets the third-person narrator tell the reader about the girl's financial condition in the next paragraph:

> Not once is there a suggestion of a financial calculation. Yet she was quite alone in the world. Her mother had been killed in the Mount Pelee earthquake, having gone to visit a sister living at St. Pierre, which was destroyed. It is not recorded whether Julie ever asked her father for help (*LA* 25).

This detail, added by a detached third-person voice, reveals another side of Julie as a poor motherless girl who strives to make a living on her own, deserving more sympathy than the "Julie" whose portrayal is circumscribed by public remarks and rumors. By integrating the first-person narration of Julie's journal with third-person narration, Lessing informs the reader of the struggles and suffering of a socially disadvantaged girl. This implicit authorial intrusion is more likely to gain credibility and the reader may feel freer to pass judgment on both the younger Julie and the elder Sarah.

Julie's journals not only play the role of self-defense of the girl, but also help present a portrait of Sarah who holds a different attitude towards love. In contrast to Julie's courageous search for freedom and love, Sarah finally chooses to give up. With two lovers leaving her and one committing suicide, Sarah, by the end of the story, is an even older woman who "has aged ten years" (*LA* 349), living in anguish, grief, and loneliness:

> Months have passed. Sarah is looking into her mirror, just as on the evening when we first saw her. At first glance she has not much changed, but a closer look says otherwise. She has aged by ten years. For one thing,

her hair, which for so long remained like a smooth dulled metal, now has grey bands across the front. She has acquired that slow cautious look of the elderly, as if afraid of what they will see around the next corner. Sarah has changed, and so have the rooms she lives in (*LA* 349).

Echoing its beginning, the story ends with an omniscient narrator calmly describing the details of the scene and the heroine without any of the authorial interference. The author once again retreats from the story and the reader is encouraged to discover the meaning underneath. The polyphony of the novel, as achieved by an integration of omniscient third-person narration, free indirect speech, and the first-person voice of the two heroines not only diversifies the narration of the story, but motivates the reader to interpret without feeling manipulated by the author.

1.2 Diversified Narrators in *The Diaries of Jane Somers*

Compared with the younger Lessing, who has confidence in authorial power and tends to be more intrusive in her narration, Lessing in her later years of writing becomes a more distanced author, a fact that can be seen in her handling of narrative strategy due to a change in writing philosophy, which will be discussed in the last part of this chapter. This is evidenced, for example, in *The Diaries of Jane Somers*[1] in which the heroine, Janna Somers, an intelligent fashion magazine editor, finds herself a lonely and detached person after the death of her mother and husband, and is sometimes tortured by her guilty conscience of negligence of and indifference towards them. One day, she meets Maudie Fowler, an old woman in her nineties, in a chemist's shop. From then on, the two women become friends and this friendship changes Janna. While taking care of Maudie, Janna gets to know other old women such as Eliza Bates, and gradually finds more of herself which enables her to undergo

---

1 *The Diaries of Jane Somers* consists of two stories published separately in two consecutive years, *The Diary of a Good Neighbour* (1983) and *If the Old Could* (1984) which were put into one volume in 1984. The following analysis on the multiplied narrators focuses on the first story.

a mental transformation as she changes her attitudes toward the old age, death and life.

The narration in this story is even more complex than the multi-voiced narration in *LA*. Since the story takes the form of a diary, Janna shows every detail of her life and reveals the subtle thoughts on her mind. In addition to this dominant first-person narration, however, there is an omniscient third-person narrator telling the reader about a whole day's life of Maudie and Eliza Bates. Yet this omniscient narrator is none other than Janna herself, who turns out to be the real author of their stories. In addition to keeping a diary, Janna writes a book in her spare time, adding to her diary as "Maudie's Day" and "Eliza Bate's Day" which is told in an omniscient third-person voice. Within these two stories, meanwhile, there are the third-person narration and interior monologues of the old people interwoven. The following, for example, is the first paragraph of "Maudie's Day":

> She wakes inside a black smothering weight, she can't breathe, can't move. They've buried me alive, she *thinks*, and struggles. The weight shifts. Oh, it's the cat, it's my pretty, she *thinks*, and heaves. The weight lifts, and she hears a thud as the cat arrives on the floor. Pretty? She *asks,* for she is not sure, it is so dark and her limbs are so stiff. She hears the cat moving about and knows she is alive. And warm... and in bed... Oh, oh, she *says* aloud, I must go to the toilet or I'll wet the bed again. Panic! Have I wet the bed already? Her hand explores the bed. She *mutters*, dreadful, dreadful, dreadful, dreadful, thinking how, a few days ago, she had wet the bed, and the trouble and difficulty of getting everything dry (*DJS* 113, emphasis added).

In describing how Maudie takes cares of herself at night, the third-person narrator uses a series of verbs: she "thinks", she "asks", she "says", and she "mutters". With Maudie muttering to herself or "speaking out" her mind, Lessing creates a kind of interior monologue by letting Maudie tell her immediate thoughts. Throughout the nine pages devoted to "Maudie's Day", this first-person telling is woven into the third-person narration, presenting both the outside world and the inner activities of this old woman.

By providing what Wayne Booth calls a "sustained inside view" of Maudie, Lessing makes Maudie a first-person narrator, and a change of identity naturally occurs since:

> … narrators who provide inside views differ in the depth and the axis of their plunge… We should remind ourselves that any sustained inside view, of whatever depth, temporarily turns the character whose mind is *shown* into a narrator… (Booth *Rhetoric* 172–174)

Booth argues that this "inside view", whether deep or superficial, temporarily turns the character whose mind is shown into a "telling" narrator. While Maudie is telling her own story in this way, Lessing hides herself behind the story. In contrast to such a response-inviting first-person narrator, the third-person narrator seems to make observations in a more detached way. Thus, a balance is created between an interfering and a distanced authorial voice.

In "Maudie's Day", Lessing directly tells the reader that the omniscient third-person narrator is Janna; yet, in the following part entitled "Janna's day", Janna denies this identity and confesses to the reader that "I wrote Maudie's day because I want to understand. I *do* understand a lot more about her, but is it true? I can only write what I have experienced myself, heard her say, observed…" (*DJS* 126, italics original). In this confession, Janna tries to play the role of a third-person narrator whose job is to put down what she has "experienced", "heard", and "observed" without offering her own personal judgment. Later though, in "Eliza Bate's Day", Lessing reveals that the observations have been made from within the internal focalization of Janna:

> Eliza, disliking television, will go across the road to watch Upstairs, Downstairs. This makes me cross; but then I ask myself, Why then am I into writing romantic novels? The truth is intolerable, and that is all there is to it! (*DJS* 151)

Here, the "I" is Janna and, consequently, the judgment is also made by her. Since the focalization belongs to Janna, it is inevitably influenced by her personal stand and viewpoint. By emphasizing the importance of Janna, the seemingly "real author" within the story, Lessing manages to make herself a detached observer who seems to be innocent of any authorial intrusion.

This strategy of diminishing the actual author's "presence" in the story is revealed in another example from "Janna's day", which occurs immediately after "Maudie's Day" and is told in the first-person voice of Janna. What makes this section different from most of others is its extremely frequent use of the first-person pronoun "I", especially in the opening paragraph:

> The alarm makes me sit up in bed. Sometimes I switch it off, sink back, today not: I sit in the already bright morning, five o'clock, and look through the day ahead: I cannot believe that by the time I end it I shall have done so much. I make myself jump out of bed, I make myself coffee, I am at my typewriter ten minutes after I am awake. I should have put in: I emptied my bladder, but I am still "young" and do not count that among the things that have to be done! But today I shall write down the visits to the loo, otherwise how can I compare my day with Maudie's? The articles I wrote, so tentatively, and without confidence, last year, have become a book. It is nearly finished. I said it would be done by the end of this month. It will be. *Because I said it would be.* That I do what I say gives me such strength! And then, there is a project no one knows about: a historical novel. It was Maudie gave me the idea. I think of that time as quite recent, my grandmother's; but Vera Rogers speaks of it as I might speak of, I don't know, let's say Waterloo. I plan a historical novel, conceived and written as one, about a milliner in London. I long to begin it (*DJS* 123, italics original).

This intensive use of the first-person voice, with 24 occurrences of "I" in the above quote, enhances the existence of the narrator (Janna) while the simple, short sentence structure quickens the pace of the narration. Compared with the first-person narration in other parts of the story, which is conducted in a comparatively distanced manner, its use here appears to be more personal and sentimental. The quickened pace and self-centered tone typical of the quick-tempered and impatient Janna at the beginning of the story make the reader even more conscious of Janna's first-person narration to the effect of weakening the voice of Lessing the real author.

Due to Lessing's effort to conceal her own presence, the middle-aged Janna seems to have a strong desire to communicate with the reader, showing and telling details about her life, including her editorial work, living conditions, habits, likes and dislikes, friendships with the old women, and thoughts. The narrator, apparently, hopes to bridge the gap between herself and readers, to share what she has experienced and her reflection upon these experiences, and ultimately, to obtain the latter's trust so that they will not only see what she sees but also believe what she believes. While the narrator gets the upper hand in this guiding or preaching, the author recedes. In the so-called pure observation of "Eliza Bate's Day" as well as in the sentimental telling of "Janna's day", the "loud" voice of Janna enlarges the role of the real author within the story while disguising the authorial intrusion, thus lending credibility to the story.

Bearing this concern with credibility in mind, Lessing, especially in her later period, chooses to be a detached observer rather than an intruding author, with the former trying to keep the distance from the story while the latter tending to be more manipulating. In fact, the key to distinguishing between these two kinds of author is "distance", which plays a decisive role in the author-reader relationships. What makes a detached observer different from, if not better than, an intrusive author is the fact that the former shows more respect to the reader by showing them facts, while the latter appears to be more interfering or even arbitrary in the telling of the story. This intrusive author, on the other hand, by making comments on the character and action, by showing his "telling" of the story, makes himself "a highly audible and visible" (Herman *et al.* 364) narrator, hence, the authorial narrator. Taking the perspective of an omniscient third-person narrator, the intrusive author "tells the story from on high, as it were, in full knowledge of the outcome of the complications that exist on the plot level, and has access to the thoughts and minds of the characters whenever s/he wishes" (Fludernik 150). The intrusive author then creates an "authorial narrative situation" where, as the Austrian narratologist Franz Stanzel says, "a third-person narrative [telling] an intrusive and (usually) omniscient narrator" (Herman *et al.* 34).[1] The opposite situation is the distanced author. According to Booth, the first to have emphasized the importance of "distance" in narrative modes, the author's objectivity and impartiality has to do with "the amount of detachment" (Booth *Rhetoric* 82). The detached author manages to lower down his voice or erase his presence in the story by providing the reader with a diversity of perspectives to conceal his intention of intrusion in a superficially cool-headed manner.

As many critics and scholars have argued, however, no matter how hard the author tries to be detached or involved, there is always a dominating authorial voice hidden behind or between the lines. In the case of *DJS*, a transcending authorial voice, in the disguise of different narrators, both tells and shows her understanding and recognition of her ever-changing attitude toward the seniors. In *DJS*, by switching between the first-person and third-person narrator, by intertwining omniscient third-person narration and interior monologue, and by confusing the real author within the story with the one outside of the story, Lessing renders her narration hybrid. Meanwhile, the complexity and ambiguity arising from this ever-changing narrative voices call for more active participation on the part of readers who, due to their differentiated backgrounds and experiences, are invited to provide interpretations.

Having discussed the diversified narrators in *DJS*, the discussion now turns to the issue of authorial intrusion and Lessing's dynamic view of this strategy in different stages of her writing. The above examples show that Lessing keeps making adjustments in selecting the most appropriate narrator for each of her novels, be it an implied narrator, a third-person omniscient narrator, a first-person narrator, or an intrusive narrator, or by overlapping

---

1   Franz Stanzel divides the narrative situations into three types, the other two are: the first-person narrative and the figural narrative.

different types of narrators. However diversified the narrators are, though, there is always the real author's voice behind them. "The author's voice is never really silenced", as Booth points out in *The Rhetoric of Fiction*:

> It is easy for us now to see what was not so clear at the beginning of the century: whether an impersonal novelist hides behind a single narrator or observer, the multiple points of view of *Ulysses* or *As I Lay Dying*, or the objective surfaces of *The Awkward Age* or Compton-Burnett's *Parents and Children*, the author's voice is never really silenced. It is, in fact, one of the things we read fiction for, and we are never troubled by it unless the author makes a great to-do about his own superior naturalness (Booth *Rhetoric* 59).

Booth holds that disguised as a single narrator, in multiplied points of view or in objective observation, the author always makes her voice heard, either consciously or unconsciously; consequently, authorial interference is always there to be felt, whether overtly or implicitly. The reason sometimes the reader feels free from a sense of being manipulated is that the author "makes a great to-do about his own superior naturalness"; in other words, the author makes effort to conceal his transcending manner by offering a seemingly objective presentation.

It is true that "while the presence of the implied author pervades the text and controls the reader's response, at any and every given moment it is the author who 'speaks'" (Wall 8). Consequently, "the narrator is variously described as an instrument, a construction, or a device wielded by the author" (Abbott 63). Since there will always be an "all-informing authorial presence, the 'face behind the page'" (Wall 6), the author inevitably writes out of his own experience. However, this does not necessarily mean that authors will put things down as they happen in life. An experienced writer knows how to artistically make use of lived experience, and Lessing has explained in detail how she draws from her real life and makes it anew in her writing.

For example, Martha Quest, the heroine of *Children of Violence* series, is based on Lessing and several of her friends. Mary, the white girl who marries a poor white in Africa in *The Grass Is Singing*, is drawn from two of Lessing's friends, while many of the details in *The Golden Notebook* are based on Lessing's personal experiences, either in Africa or in London. Even when dealing with things biographical, Lessing feels free to travel between the real world and the imaginative. This is why the story in *Alfred and Emily* turns out to be partly fictional and partly biographical, making a hybridized narration in terms of its genre (i.e., fictional or biographical). Instead of objectively presenting the world around her as it is, as a distanced observer should do, Lessing prefers to represent it in a way that retains her personal traits and styles, so that there is always her voice and "face behind the page" (Wall 6).

Lessing's awareness and adoption of this strategy, however, changes over time, a dynamic process that should be observed in connection with her understanding of the writer's function[1]. Generally speaking, in the earlier period, she prefers to use the intrusive authorial voice and, later, cares more about the significance of detachment, claiming that if one is too much involved in writing, one would spoil the work. In a 1989 interview, confronted with her own claim that she "wrote *The Fifth Child* out of a rage" (Thomson & Lessing 191), Lessing replied, "No, that was the fuel; that's a different thing. Yes, the 'fuel' is the accurate word, for the fuel for that book was frustration and rage—the total intransigence of our helplessness in the face of terror and horror" (Thomson & Lessing 191). For her, strong feelings as fury and frustration serve as a sort of stimulus or catalyzer. However, in the process of writing, she holds that one has to remain cool-headed and distanced in order to take control of the whole work, which she claims is a prerequisite for more objective observations.

Although there is an obvious transition in the later stages of her writing, Lessing does not thoroughly break away from the intrusive author, even when she no longer has confidence in the instructiveness of the writer for reasons

---

1 For a detailed discussion on Lessing's Writing philosophy which has a direct bearing on her choice of narrative techniques, see "The Fluidity in Writing Philosophy" in Chapter Three.

similar to those that, as David Lodge has explained, motivate other writers as well:

> Around the turn of the century, however, the intrusive authorial voice fell into disfavour, partly because it detracts from realistic illusion and reduces the emotional intensity of the experience being represented, by calling attention to the act of narrating... Modern fiction has tended to suppress or eliminate the authorial voice, by presenting the action through the consciousness of the characters, or by handing over to them the narrative task itself (Lodge 10).

To Lodge, the intrusive voice interferes with readers' involvement in the story, reminding them of the "making" of the story and thus destroying its sense of authenticity. Therefore, in the modernistic period, when people have less trust in the conventions and rationality of pre-modern fiction, the intrusive voice becomes less powerful. If modern fiction resorts to this voice, it is mostly for the purpose of achieving irony. Indeed, Lessing sometimes reminds readers of the artificial making of the story by intentionally drawing their attention to the existence of a manipulating author and, consequently, to the discrepancy between the real and the fictional. This kind of authorial intrusion distracts readers' attention from the story proper and arouses their suspicion about the authenticity or realness of the novel. This is precisely what Lessing intends to achieve by foregrounding the construction or making of the story, rendering the text ambiguous and multivalent, which she believes best mirrors the real life in modern society.

Although the author's voice can never be "silenced" in the text, it is better not to make it dominating. Lessing tries to keep a distance from the explicit presence of an author by diversifying the voices in her stories, although she sometimes fails to achieve this goal and can hardly become invisible in the story. She was once praised by Per Wästberg, chairman of the Nobel Committee for Literature, for her skillful handling of the author-text distance in the Award Ceremony Speech: "Lessing has the ability to freely move into and away from herself, to barge in and become an invisible lodger. She often begins by observing her characters from within and then moving outside them, to strip them of their illusions from an objective distance" (Wästberg Para.11)[1]. Indeed, in both *Love, again* and *The Diaries of Jane Somers* Lessing seems to be able to move into or keep a distance from the story, to make the authorial voice either intrusive or detached according to specific contexts, a strategy that adds to the hybridity of her narration.

1.3 Mixed Perspectives in *The Diaries of Jane Somers*, *The Grass Is Singing* and *The Golden Notebook*

The Retrospective Perspective in *The Diaries of Jane Somers*

Along with the multi-voiced narration in *DJS*, the "retrospective" perspectives of Janna Somers and Maudie are also worth examining. The middle-aged editor Janna keeps looking back to her youth, making judgments on her former experiences and reflecting upon her occasional immaturity and indifference. Through a distanced viewpoint, she gradually gets to know her true self and achieves spiritual growth. Likewise, Maudie, the old woman in her nineties, always looks back to her youth, contrasting her imagined past with the cruel present. Either consciously or unconsciously, Maudie tries to heal her wounds in reality by constantly resorting to a self-deceiving perception.

At the beginning of the story, Janna is tortured by her former carelessness towards her mother and husband. She often reflects upon her younger self and the time she spent with her family:

> It was a year after she came she got sick. I said to myself, Now, this time you aren't going to pretend it isn't happening. I went with her to the hospital. They told her it was cancer... It was the first time in my life I wanted to be like her. Before that I had always found her embarrassing,

---

1   For the complete script of Per Wästberg's presentation speech made on Dec. 10, 2007, see http://www.nobelprize.org/nobel_prizes/literature/laureates/2007/presentation-speech.html.

her clothes, her hair. When I was out with her I used to think, no one would believe I could be her daughter, two worlds, heavy suburban respectable—and me. As I sat there beside her and she talked about her forthcoming death with the doctors, so dignified and nice, I felt awful. But I was scared witless, because Uncle Jim died of cancer, and now her—both sides. I thought: will it be my turn next? What I felt was, it isn't fair (*DJS* 7).

A casual reading of the above paragraph could confuse the reader. Obviously, this is Janna recalling her life in the past year told in the past tense. However, the present tense is also used in two occasions. The first one is at the beginning of the paragraph: "I said to myself, Now, this time you aren't going to pretend it isn't happening." The second one is at the end of the paragraph: "What I felt was, it isn't fair." Why is there a blend of both past tense and present tense? What kind of perspective is being offered?

To answer the above two questions, it is necessary to classify the two "selves" in the first-person narrative, particularly the ***first-person retrospective perspective*** as interpreted by Shen Dan in *Narratology and Post-Classical Narratology*. She points out that, in first-person narrative, the "self" can be either an ***experiencing self*** or a ***retrospective self***. In first-person retrospective narration, there is usually a switching between these two perspectives, one coming from the narrating or acting "self", who is recalling a past experience, and the other belonging to the retrospective "self", who is in the midst of the experience or who is experiencing "right now". The former perspective is a commonly used device in the retelling of a story, while the latter can be regarded as a rhetorical device similar to the ***third-person limited perspective***, which is conductive to suspension or dramatic effects. This limited point of view and resulting suspension or dramatic effect is designed by an author who hides behind the narrator to make her voice heard in an implicit way. According to Shen's interpretation on the ***experiencing self*** and ***retrospective self***, the above two sentences, though grammatically wrong, are purposeful "mistakes" made by the author to achieve an intentional rhetorical effect.

Furthermore, this switched perspective between the experiencing "self" and the retrospective "self" is used throughout the story. By creating a hybrid tense and presenting discrepancie between observations made at different time or by people at different ages, Lessing encourages the reader to pass their own judgment on the characters and their deeds.

Similarly, Janna's good friend Maudie Fowler offers a retrospective perspective that adds to the complexity of the novel. Maudie's perspective, belonging to that of the old people, differs from that of Janna's in that it turns out to be an ironic one that arouses sympathy in the reader. Maudie's recollection of her past is presented in the direct speech of the ask-and-answer model. She tells Janna about her past experience in a way that is self-deceiving. For example, she tries to convince Janna that "she had a lovely childhood, she couldn't wish a better to anyone, not the Queen herself" and she "keeps talking of a swing in a garden under apple trees, and long uncut grass": "I used to sit and swing myself, for hours at a time, and swing, and swing, and I sang all the songs I knew, and then poor Mother came out and called to me, and I ran into her and she gave me fruit cake and milk and kissed me, and I ran back to the swing" (*DJS* 29).

Janna, however, doubts the authenticity of the lovely picture Maudie draws for her:

> None of it adds up. There couldn't, surely, have been a deep grassy garden behind the hardware in Bell Street? And in St. John's Wood she would have been too old for swings and playing by herself in the grasses while the bird sang? And when her father went off to his smart suppers and the theatre, when was that? I ask, but she doesn't like to have a progression made, her mind has bright pictures in it that she has painted for herself and has been dwelling on for all those decades (*DJS* 29).

The truth is: Maudie "has painted for herself" a beautiful picture of a lovely childhood. In addition, she describes to Janna the "great plates of porridge and real milk", the "big late supper", and the "wonderful" days when she worked as a maid in somebody's house (*DJS* 33). In reality, she has intoxicated herself with imaginative memories over the years. Being a poor, old woman deserted by her husband and robbed of her only son, Maudie has had a hard life. Now in her nineties, she has no other friends to talk to except Janna and no other place to go except the shabby little room she pays for with almost all of her pension. Compared with Janna's perspective, which draws a picture of personal development and growth, Maudie's retrospective picture reveals the miseries of old people in a cold world. By trying to "sweeten" her past so as to forget about the bitter "Now", Muadie presents a distorted retrospective perspective that consists of nothing but fancy and imagination. This is, perhaps, the only way she has to maintain her dignity and keep the courage to move on in face of a harsh and cruel reality. Ironic as it is, this "false" retrospective perspective protects her against the indifferent world. In a sense, it is Muadie the marginalized who tries to have her own say in a world negligent of the old and disadvantaged. No matter how feeble the voice or how false the perspective is, it nevertheless becomes part of the heteroglossia and gets heard by the outside world.

If Maudie's look back to past arouses sympathy for the old in the reader, Janna's younger perspective is concerned with spiritual growth, in particular with her understanding of old age and death. Her first impression of Maudie, for example, is an unpleasant one:

Saw her as I did the first day: an old crooked witch. Quite terrifying, nose and chin nearly meeting, heavy grey brows, straggly bits of white hair under the black splodge of hat. She was breathing heavily as she came up to me. She gave her impatient shake of the head when I said hello, and went down the steps without speaking to me (*DJS* 30).

Maudie terrifies her at first sight, due to her unpleasant appearance and manner. Although she cares about this bad-tempered poor woman, she confesses to "all the shifts of liking, anger, [and] irritation" in both of them (*DJS* 31). Over time, though, Janna begins to see the loveliness in Maudie and discovers that, occasionally, Maudie "has a young fresh laugh, not an old woman's laugh at all" (*DJS* 34). As their friendship deepens, she understands Maudie's helplessness, miseries and untold wishes and says to herself, "I like her. I respect her" (*DJS* 79). As a result, she tries to keep company with this old woman until the last days of her life. For Janna, the friendship between herself and Maudie and her acceptance of old age make her more deeply involved in life. Having a different understanding of life and death, and the importance of love between friends, she finally reconciles with her family and her younger self, thereby growing mentally and morally.

By using the retrospective perspective and having Janna discover a new view of her past, Lessing presents the inner journeys of her character:

These inner journeys occur at different levels of development and reach different stages of self-awareness, revealing not only the challenges and difficulties of the older years for women but also the unique opportunities that such challenges provide to acquire a new perspective on one's self and one's life—to find (or make) a place or space, a vantage point, from which to view one's past, one's sense of self, even the workings of one's mind (Perrakis 2).

Perrakis's interpretation here coincides with Lessing's opinion that one of the advantages of old age is that it enables one to observe the younger self in a detached manner: "You float away from the personal. You have received that great gift of getting older—detachment, impersonality" (*TB* 92). Experienced old people, she suggests, tend to be more rational when evaluating their past, and meditation and reassessment give rise to a different understanding of the younger self. No wonder, then, that some old people like Maudi in *DJS* become less sensible and avoid facing reality by indulging in imagined memories of the past. As Perrakis points out, looking back to one's past provides "a new perspective on one's self and one's life" with which one can enter a new stage of development. So is Lessing who keeps revising her views on writing philosophy and making adaptations in practical writing accordingly.

The newly formed perspective derived from life experience presented by the old women and Janna in *DJS* has characteristics that can be described with such words as tolerating, forgiving, comprehensive, retrospective, and introspective. Apart from these, this new perspective also shows is the spirit of resistance. By looking back to their pasts and contrasting them with current society, the aged in this story not only complain about the maltreatment imposed upon them and the marginalized status from which they have suffered, but also protest against the younger generation for their misinterpretation of the world and experience of the disadvantaged old. In addition to venting the anger and dissatisfaction of the old by way of a retrospective perspective, Lessing takes advantage of this perspective to inform the reader of the tragic existence of some physically deteriorating people while elevating the mental status of the whole group, which is implied in their understanding of life, their perseverance, and their aspirations. Weakness, disease, and death are not the only experiences inscribed on the old, who also aspire for happiness, dreams, and dynamic experiences, a fact that dawns on Janna as she becomes increasingly involved in Maudie's life. This subversion of her previous understanding brings about Janna's transformation toward a more objective understanding of the world.

The perspectives in *DJS* show that compared with the "younger" perspective, the retrospective perspective of the senior group counts more in one's inner journey and mental growth. The "new perspective" (Perrakis 2) acquired in these inner journeys, together with the old perspective of the younger self, provides the reader with a more comprehensive perspective that is effective in the showing and telling of the story.

The White-Focused Perspective in *The Grass Is Singing (GS)*

Unlike the retrospective perspective in *DJS,* which is a carefully designed strategy, the shifted point of view in *GS* turns out to be more complicated and even contrary to Lessing's expectations. Lessing tells the story from an omniscient third-person perspective without being aware of the fact that sometimes the point of view may become white-focused, even though she is capable of producing both the white and black experiences. The biased white perspective, together with that of an omniscient third-person narrator, gives rise to the ambiguity and complexity of a hybrid text.

GS is about poor whites in colonized Africa and their contact with native black people. The Turners, a white couple, are detested by the other white colonizers because they "kept themselves to themselves" (GS 2). However, due to a bad harvest, they can only afford to live in "that little box of a house" (GS 3) no better than those of some natives, which is an embarrassment to many of the colonial whites. Although a hard-working man, Dick suffers one defeat after another because of his stubbornness, pride, and inappropriate way of farming. In his wife's eyes, this "tall, spare, stooping man" is "a swaggering little boy, trying to keep his end up after cold water had been poured over his enthusiasm" (GS 96). Mary Turner has never imagined that she would have had such an unhappy, lonely, and wretched married life in a shabby country house where she is constantly terrified by the natives. She hates Dick for trapping her in this nightmare and gradually turns to violence out of anger and despair. However, her maltreatment of the black people does not save her from her suffering. At the end of the story, she is murdered by her black servant Moses.

In GS, the omniscient third-person perspective is supplemented by the limited third-person perspective of Mary. The former, which is supposed to be an objective "all-knower"[1], turns out to be a limited and intrusive one incapable of showing and telling in an objective "all-knowing" manner. Free as the characters are, they can never rid themselves of the control of the author, which, as has been mentioned above, usually falls into two types: an intrusive author who takes the disguise of an omniscient narrator, and a detached observer who seems to keep the distance from any direct comment on or

---

1　Such a narrator "knows everything that needs to be known about the agents, actions, and events, and has privileged access to the character's thoughts, feelings, and motives; also that of the narrator is free to move at will in time and place, to shift from character to character, and to report (or conceal) their speech, doings and states of consciousness" (Abrams *Literary Terms* 232).

evaluation of the characters. In the case of *GS*, the reader will soon discover Lessing's white-focused perspective in disguise of an omniscient third-person narrator, similar to Mary's limited third-person perspective which tends to be "white" as well.

In one paragraph from the story, for example, when Mary is found murdered and the police are called upon, Charlie Slatter, the rich white who lives nearby, comes to the site to help handle the situation.

> Charlie walked up to the policemen, who saluted him. They were in fezzes, and their rather fancy-dress uniform. This last thought did not occur to Charlie, who liked his natives either one way or the other: properly dressed according to their situation, or in loincloths. He could not bear the half-civilized native. The policemen, picked for their physique, were a fine body of men, but they were put in the shade by Moses, who was a great powerful man, black as polished linoleum, and dressed in a singlet and shorts, which were damp and muddy. Charlie stood directly in front of the murderer and looked into his face. The man stared back, expressionless, indifferent. His own face was curious: it showed a kind of triumph, a guarded vindictiveness, and fear. Why fear? Of Moses, who was as hanged already? But he was uneasy, troubled. Then he seemed to shake himself into self-command, and turned and saw Dick Turner, standing a few paces, covered with mud (*GS* 9).

In this paragraph, the observation of the black policemen should have been neither "white" nor "black" for the omniscient third-person perspective. However, a careful study of the text reveals that the observation is made through the focalization of Charlie Slatter, the white colonizer, because the adjectives used are all racially biased. It is through the eyes of Charlie Slatter that the black people, "half-civilized natives", are dressed in "rather fancy-dress uniform" which is "damp and muddy". The emphasis on their "physique" and "shade" is a particularly racist representation: black people are physically strong and sexually threatening, usually depicted as ugly, stinky, numb, ridiculous, and disgusting. Their "shifty and dishonest nature" makes them untrustworthy (*GS* 72); or, in Mary's words, "they were such cunning swine" (*GS* 73). Even in the eyes of the more tolerant and kind white farmers such as Dick Turner, the natives "are nothing but savages after all" (*GS* 84). No wonder "most white people think it is 'cheek' if a native speaks English" (*GS* 133). Given these assumptions, white colonizers often feel unsafe and terrified in their relations with the natives, the way Charlie feels "uneasy" and "troubled" when confronting Moses and is forced to overcome his "fear" and "shake himself into self-command". In fact, the "fear" of the black natives and the land as well tortures most of the white colonizers, especially Mary Turner.

The ostensibly objective omniscient third-person perspective is very likely affected by the author's white perspective. For instance, "Charlie stood directly in front of the murderer and looked into his face. The man stared back, expressionless, indifferent" (*GS* 9). The word "indifferent" carries with it a prejudice against Moses and black people as a whole by impressing the reader with a stereotypical image of black violence and cold-bloodedness. Believing that black people are inborn killers or murderers, Slatter takes it for granted that Moses, the murderer, is "indifferent" to his white hostess.

Throughout the story, whenever narration concerning the black is made by a white colonizer, it is humiliating and insulting. For instance, when the white farmers gather together, they discuss nothing but the shortcomings and deficiencies of the natives: "They never cease complaining about their unhappy lot, having to deal with natives who are so exasperatingly indifferent to the welfare of the white man, working only to please themselves. They had no idea of the dignity of labor, no idea of improving themselves by hard work" (*GS* 82). With this biased view, the white colonizers can hardly treat them as equals, a fact that has made young Marston, the newly arrived white assistant on Turner's farm, feel shocked and uncomfortable: "They were revolted a hundred times a day by the casual way they were spoken of, as if they were so many cattle; or by a blow, or a look. They had been prepared to treat them as human beings. But they could not stand out against the society they were joining. It did not take them long to change... One never knew them in their own lives, as human beings" (*GS* 11–12). Surprised as he is, though, Marston becomes one of the white settlers who expect nothing but violence and ugliness on this land: "Anger, violence, death, seemed natural to this vast, harsh country" (*GS* 13).

Newcomers from the continent such as Marston at first believe in the principles of equality and justice, hoping to show their decency and goodwill in their relations with the natives. It does not take long, however, for them to get accustomed to the mindset of the old settlers in their integration into the local white community. Marston comes to feel deeply annoyed by his lack of knowledge about these native people and "could not even begin to imagine the mind of a native" (*GS* 24). Ignorance, prejudice, and a stereotyped way of thinking characterize a white perspective.

Meanwhile, the black murderer Moses in the story is always seen through the eyes of the whites, whether Mary Turner or Marston, manifesting Jeannette King's view that "white readers—of character or of fiction—are not capable of interpreting black experience" (King 7). Despite her anti-colonial stance, Lessing turns out to be a spokesman of the white, a fact that can be proved by more evidence from *GS*. The following paragraph, for instance, is full of stereotypical descriptions of the black image:

> She used to sit quite still, watching him work. The powerful, broad-built body fascinated her. She had given him white shorts and shirts to wear in the house, that had been used by her former servants. They were too small for him; as he swept or scrubbed or bent to the stove, his muscles bulged and filled out the thin material of the sleeves until it seemed they would split. He appeared even taller and broader than he was, because of the littleness of the house (*GS* 161).

In this paragraph, the observation is made from the viewpoint of Mary, the white hostess whose focus is on the physical body rather than the consciousness of Moses. What impress her most are his "powerful, broad-built body" and the "muscles" which seem to diminish the house. Mary also sometimes catches a glimpse of Moses' naked body while he is taking a bath at the back of the house: "Remembering that thick black neck with the lather frothing whitely on it, the powerful back stooping over the bucket, was like a goad to her" (*GS* 164). In contrast to her white husband's weakness and sickness, Moses' "taller" and "broader" body "fascinated" her, and this is held accountable for their intimate relations and the tragedy in the end. Although Moses is frequently on the scene, especially in the second half of the story, most of the attention is given to his physical appearance instead of his emotions or his experiences with his white host and hostess while the mental activities of Mary are described in detail. The fact that the observations of Moses are made by Mary, the female white colonizer who neither knows nor cares much about her black lover, turns Moses into an object of seeing like an orient, "Orientals are rarely seen or looked at; they were seen through, analyzed not as citizens, or even people, but as problems to be solved or confined or—as the colonial powers openly coveted their territory—taken over" (Said 207).

Said pierces to the truth that the colonized can only be "seen through" and treated like the property "taken over" by the white colonizer. Observed from a white perspective, Moses and the colonized blacks are backward, uncivilized, emotionally and intellectually retarded, and sexually appealing: they are never individuals. For example, in telling the story of *GS*, Lessing purposefully avoids informing the reader of the background details of the characters, such as the sexual relations between Mary Turner and Moses or the motive behind Moses' murder. Due to the ambiguities in the plot and the mixed perspectives in *GS*, readers may feel confused or find it hard to catch up with the story. But this outcome is what Lessing expects and this kind of implicitness is consistent with Lessing's understanding of the African context and the codes of behavior of the whites in the colonized Africa. Lessing even grew angry when asked to make changes to the story:

> The whole point of *The Grass Is Singing* was the unspoken, devious codes
> of behavior of the whites, nothing ever said, everything understood, and

the relationship between Mary Turner, the white woman, and Moses, the black man, was described so that nothing was explicit. This was only part of literary instinct (*WS* 7–8).

Lessing believes that there must be something "unspoken" yet well "understood" in literature. She regards using ambiguity—accomplished by multiplied voices and narrators—as the most appropriate strategy for telling her story. For Lessing, this strategy is a shared knowledge among those familiar with the "codes of behavior of the whites" and the color issue. Lessing tries to defend her orientalist perspective. She once admitted that she regretted having handled Moses the way she does, but later claimed that this intentional minimization of the black character was a right choice, for only in this way could she foreground the unfair treatment of the black people:

> You know I'm not aware of it. There was a long time when I thought that it was a pity I ever wrote Moses like that, because he was less of a person than a symbol. But it was the only way I *could* write him at that time since I'd never *met* Africans excepting the servants or politically, in a certain complicated way. But now I've changed my mind again. I think it was the right way to write Moses, because if I'd made him too individual it would've unbalanced the book. I think I was right to make him a bit unknown (Bertelsen 133, italics original).

Black people have to remain, like Moses in this story, "a distant and amorphous Orient" (Said 22). Lessing believes that by purposefully telling the story from a white perspective, she can better arouse the attention of the reader to the fact that the colonized black are anything but independent individuals in the eyes of the white colonizer, a manifestation of racism that she personally hates and fights against all her life.

Lessing also argues that the cure for racism is to treat everybody in the same way, whatever the color of their skin. It is possible, however, to treat black "others" empathetically while still regarding them as inferiors. As

Lessing writes,

> I remember once how I realized that I really was on my way to being
> cured from color feeling when an Indian turned up in my flat unannounced
> and asked me to do something. I disliked him as a person, and I said, 'Get
> out' and I thought, My God, I'm cured because it never crossed my mind
> that I mustn't be unkind to a dark-skinned person (Thorpe 101).

For Lessing, relief comes when she simply treats the "dark-skinned"
"as a person". The right way to deal with racism, she comes to believe, is to
treat everybody as one's equal. There is no need to adhere to an anti-colonial
viewpoint—sometimes, a straight white focus may be more faithful and
convincing. To treat the black as the white's equal does not necessarily mean to
deny the differences between them. Therefore, it is up to the author to decide
on the perspective issue, as long as he achieves the goal of raising people's
awareness of anti-colonialism.

Lessing's paradox in *GS* has been noticed by critics such as Joy Wang
who points out that while exposing the white postcolonial guilt in *GS*, "Doris
Lessing's double experience of working-class struggles and also of the
oppressiveness of family structures very much inflected her stance against
racial apartheid" (Wang 44). But Wang is wrong in concluding that Lessing
"provides a unified voice against gendered and economic forms of oppression"
(Wang 44) in this novel. Instead, while condemning the colonialist white, her
voice is somewhat weakened by her blindness to color. Just as she once said
in one of her essays that "people in groups we now know are likely to behave
in fairly stereotyped ways that are predictable" (Lessing *Prisons* 20), Lessing
sometimes unfortunately falls victim to this stereotyped ways of representation.
Her criticism then, like most of the post-colonial scholars and theorists, is still
"targeted at the internal problems of the Western culture" (Sheng Ning 89).
This incongruity in intention and action no wonder leads to the ambiguity in
the text. An apparently anti-colonial story aiming at the exposure of white's
indifference, cruelty and suppression turns out to be a white story with the poor

white as her subject of sympathy.

Lessing is a black-and-white writer and her motivation for writing is more complicated than that of either black or white writers. The perspective in *GS*, which superficially belongs to an omniscient third-person narrator, turns out to be constantly interfered with the white perspective whenever it turns to a depiction of the black characters. Whether this is a strategy, as Lessing claims, or a result of her white identity, the intermingled perspectives prove to be a supporting evidence of Lessing's complex and hybridized narration.

The Internalized Patriarchal Perspective in *The Golden Notebook*

Besides the retrospective view in *DJS* and the white-focused perspective in *GS*, there is an internalized patriarchal perspective in *GN*. Though determined to dismantle the patriarchal discourse, Lessing sometimes falls into this group, a fact that can be seen in *GS* and *GN*, both of which resort to an internalized patriarchal perspective. It should be noticed that Lessing is keenly aware of the issue of sex relations. As early as the 1950s when Lessing was working on *GS* and some of her other African stories, she was bothered by the relationships between men and women:

> Why does a woman always risk losing her identity for good when she loves a man? If it goes bad, she hardly recovers from it. Whereas after spectacular shipwrecks men are able to find their places again quickly. Yes, why can't women, in the depth of their being, do without men? Whereas men, once they regularize the sexual problem, manage quite well in the end: the job, ambition, metaphysics, sport or automobiles allow them to keep aloof in their relationships with a woman (or women) (Montremy & Lessing 195).

Why can't women do without men? Why is it harder for women to recover from hurts and loses? Why can't women "manage quite well in the end", as men do whenever stuck in the same difficult situations? Lessing weaves her concern and reflection on these issues into the story of *GN,* which is regarded as one of her representative works dealing with male-female relations.

In a 1990 interview, Lessing once again expounded her views on sex relations and the so-called feminism: "As time passes, moreover, I see one source of feminism in that fixation of women on men. In the end, it is something that could be labeled grotesquely as feminism" (Montremy & Lessing 195). Perhaps this fixation is a problem with most women, including Lessing herself. In her earlier years of writing, Lessing is unaware of the impact of her internalized male-supremacist perspectives, which has prevented her from creating real, independent women characters. Some of her female characters are presented from the perspective of a male, with their identity and happiness defined by their relationships with men. Although Lessing tries to be a New Woman[1] herself, her vision of and insight into the issue of the male-female relationship is somewhat blurred or misguided by her internalized patriarchal perspective.

But critics have pointed out that both Mary Turner in *GS* and the so-called New Women Ann and Molly in *GN* have suffered from alienation within a male-dominant society, no matter how hard they try to live an independent life, with man or without. To escape from this dilemma, women have to realize their own fault by changing themselves internally and outwardly. Lessing sometimes seems to be trapped in this dilemma as well without knowing or acknowledging it. On the one hand, she claims that women, especially middle-aged housewives, are not inferior to working women or men: "They can cope with God-knows-what human situations with tact and patience" (Bikman & Lessing 59), as can be seen from the heroines in some of her writings,

---

1 New Woman is a reversal of the Victorian Woman who has to be confined to domestic life or a small circle of intimate friends. This New Woman owns the right to make her own choices about love, marriage, and life and plays an active role on the public stage. She is "independent, educated, (relatively) sexually liberated, oriented more toward productive life in the public sphere than toward reproductive life in the home" (Marianne 174). Therefore, she is capable of committing "the murder of the 'Angel in the house'", which is "Victorian nurturant-domestic femininity" (Marianne 174). Lessing's *GN* is commonly acknowledged as a New Woman story. For a brief introduction on New Women and their fiction, see Showalter: xxi–xxvii.

including *SBD* and *GN*. On the other hand, she sometimes unconsciously makes her heroines inferior to men, when men become the deciding figures for the so-called independent women. For instance, in *GN*, almost all women, either in the main story or in the story within the story, depend for their happiness on their relationships with men or identification by men. Anna and Molly are supposed to be spiritually and economically independent and want to make their own choices about love, marriage, and profession. Instead of simply focusing on domestic life, they would prefer to play an active role in the public sphere. However, their success in profession and independence does not bring them safety and happiness as they have expected. They seem to be forever annoyed with their relations with men. Lessing does not realize that even within these New Women novels, the viewpoints and structures remain male-dominated. The roles men play in women's careers, love affairs, and family lives seem to be the deciding factors in their evaluations of life.

In other words, however well-intentioned Lessing is to create New Women in *GN*, there seems to be no real New Woman in this novel. Critics have already drawn the conclusion that the so-called Free Women in *GN* are actually still assuming a subordinate position to men: "Men are thus depicted in the novel as 'naming' women, using the language of the patriarchal order to define and thus limit women, and the ideological process described in Chapter 1 of this study ensures that women, in turn, collaborate in this process" (King 40). It is true that sometimes the observations on or judgments of women in this story are made from the viewpoint of men. The first-person narrator sometimes turns into an omniscient one, not just observing from the perspective of the narrating character Anna Wulf, but also that of the real author Lessing who would assume a male perspective without her being aware of it. As a result, there seems to be a mixed voice coming out of both sexes. Due to this ambiguity in voice, the narrator's personality, disposition or attitude is also to some extent ambivalent.

In *GN*, the seemingly self-sufficient women find their relations to men problematic. No matter how successful they are in the public arena, they have experienced loneliness, unhappiness or a sense of insecurity in their private life. This sense of insecurity may have to do with their fear for aging since most of these successful new women, such as Anna and Molly, are in their midlife, a turning point either towards "progress" or "decline" (qtd. in Rubenstein "Feminism, Eros, and the Coming of Age" 4). Some of them are elderly women who have suffered more intensely from aging, like Sarah in *LA*, the successful woman playwright in her sixties and Kate Brown in *SBD*, a housewife in her forties. They may become less confident in their power for love, like Sarah. Or they may become disappointed with life for their husband's indifference and coldness, like Brown in *SBD*. The lack of men's love and care, plus the fear for the advancing age, undermines the sense of fulfillment of these once self-sufficient women. Though successful economically and professionally, these women feel at a loss or even desperate either sexually or emotionally.

Just as Lessing shifts between her white colonial viewpoint and the anticolonial one, she constantly changes her viewpoint from female to male, to the effect that she sometimes is unconsciously collaborative in neglect and suppression of women, as noticed by Elaine Showalter, since the so-called free women in *GN* are "not so free after all" (Showalter 301), for these women are "still locked into dependency upon men" (Showalter 301).

Critic Ellen Morgan, in her essay entitled "Alienation of the woman writer in *The Golden Notebook*", declares that "the overriding weakness of the Golden is alienation from the authentic female perspective, a perspective which repeatedly is clearly sketched in and then smeared by the censor in Lessing" (Morgan 480). The complicated personality or the contradiction in their thoughts and action, as can be seen by a penetrating reader, owes to its creator—Doris Lessing. The so-called "discrepancy between the perceptions and the alien standards", therefore, should hold Lessing accountable because of her careful design of narrative skills such as the integration of various narrators, as well as her internalized patriarchal perspective which is applied in this story out of her own awareness.

However, this blended perspective of male and female, if interpreted appropriately, helps to raise people's awareness of women's predicament and the roots of their problems, problems that not only come from the outside but also from within. Women, in their strive for freedom and equity therefore, should first of all be introspective and rid themselves of the patriarchal thoughts rather than simplistically put the blame on the prejudicing male. Mentally weak and dependent as they are, Lessing's free women sometimes appear to be more powerful than men. Lacking a sense of security, the women usually become protectors of their men. For example, Anna tends to take care of Saul who seems to be a fragile and powerless child suffering from insecurity, a weakness shown completely when asleep, which arouses Anna's sympathy and love. Lessing just shows that perhaps there are no fixed roles of men and women.

But when the female point of view in this blending of perspectives is frequently interfered with the internalized patriarchal one, problems will ensue. The white-focused perspective in *GS* and internalized patriarchal perspective in *GN* fall into either "intentional, conscious hybridization" or "unconscious organic hybridity" (Bakhtin 358–359). In the intentional one, "there are always two consciousnesses, two language-intentions, two *voices* and consequently two accents participating in an intentional and conscious artistic hybrid" (Bakhtin 360). The purpose of integrating the two independent voices into one utterance is to compare and to contrast, with one of them performing the function of satirizing and exposing the other. While the intentional hybridization aims at showing difference and contradiction, the unconscious and organic one which is usually a natural mixture of different languages or discourses is capable of "emphasizing sameness and integration" (He Yugao 43). The two modes of hybridization, put into one, may more effectively actualize hybridity, in a way that "difference and sameness in an apparently impossible simultaneity (Young *Colonial Desire* 24–25).

In the above mentioned two novels, Lessing's seemingly single-voiced discourse in fact consists of two voices. In *GS*, in the disguise of an omniscient third-person narrator, the anti-colonist Lessing speaks out while the other Lessing assumes a tone with white supremacy without her own awareness providing her perception from time to time. The black are perceived from a white-focused perspective which seems to go against the author's intention.

Lessing the author wants to show the evilness of racial discrimination and colonialism in this African story. But the interwoven black and white tone makes the text ambiguous and ironic. Likewise, in *GN*, besides the voice of Anna and Molly, there seems to be once in a while a male perceiving the two women and posing his influence on the heroines. A penetrating reader would doubt the real independence of the New Woman in the story and the intention of Lessing the author behind the story.

The multi-voiced narration, diversified narrators and mixed perspectives are evidence of Lessing's strategic use of hybridity. Thanks to the carefully designed narrating voices, narrating agents and perspectives, a polyphonic narrative comes to the fore, posing a challenge to the authoritative discourse. This authoritative voice could be the advantaged group in the story, for instance, the middle-aged Janna in *DJS*, the living heroine Sarah in *LA*, the privileged white in *GS*, the so-called New Woman in *GN*, or even the real author Lessing in contrast to her reader. They are more privileged in making their articulations. According to Bakhtin, a narrative depending on a co-existence of various levels of speech "makes it a supremely democratic, anti-totalitarian literary form, in which no ideological or moral positions immune from challenge and contradiction" (Lodge 129). To be specific, multiplied voices can more effectively create contradictions and bring about a literary form which tends to be more democratic in the sense that each member will have his own say, a premise for dismantling established systems and fixed identities. A polyphonic narrative, therefore, gives full play to the agencies involved in a single text on the one hand, and on the other, it puts all of them to test, including both the dominating and the marginalized.

Take the author as an example. Being the creator of the text, the author who should have been superior to the reader can no longer feel safe with his manipulating power and guidance. Like the characters he creates, he is confronted with "challenge and contradiction" since he becomes one of the articulators in the dialogue. As Bakhtin declares, be it hidden or real, the author can hardly maintain the position of authority in a polyphonic context. It should be kept in mind that one of the major characteristics of polyphonic text is that "the author's voice is not superior to that of the major characters" (Lin Jianhou 68). In Lessing's artistic handling of the narrators and perspectives, the voices of the old woman Maudie as well as her middle-aged companion Janna are equally heard and judged by their audience, with neither of them taking the supremacy.

Under the surface of co-articulation, there is an effort at personal enunciation rather than a write-off of one's individuality, for "the independence of the protagonist is fundamental in the polyphonic theory" (Song Datu 44). A polyphonic narrative therefore, consists of voices each speaking out freely in its own manner. The character within the novel, upon being triggered off between the lines, may grow out of the author's expectation. The author, either by letting loose the control of his character or interfering in one way or another, also wants to make his presence. But it does not follow that the author will have to give way to its character and he will become less active. In contrast, his initiative is demonstrated in his dialogue with his character which enjoys the same right of speaking out and freedom of becoming himself. This author-character relations, if perceived from the dialogism, confirms both the author's and the character's initiative in their communication. The inter-dependence between the author and his character as well as the freedom each enjoys, though to different extent, brings liveliness to the narrative and makes the characterization convincing.

While enabling a fair play of voices at different levels, polyphony in the meanwhile engenders more initiatives on the part of the reader. Having received the diversified messages delivered by various speakers within the text, the dialogic listener outside the text may "spare no effort in responding to what he has heard from the text. He may choose to analyze or to evaluate, to accept or to contradict, to revise or to make further explanations" (Bai Chunren 165). If the communication between the speaker and listener can be conducted in such a manner, the production of meaning consequently will be more individualized, for the increased layers of interpretation inevitably lead to the enrichment of meaning.

When the reader becomes active in this dialogue, the author will find it likely to be challenged, doubted or even contradicted by the reader. Based on his own judgment and observation, the reader is able to free himself from the manipulation of the author. For instance, the white-focused perspective in *GS* presented by the "white" Lessing, or the internalized patriarchal perspective in *GN* provided by the "female" Lessing, though presented without Lessing the author's own awareness, proves the author's limitation at least in delivering the appropriate message. Fortunately, a cool-headed and unbiased reader may realize this fault in the author and make adjustment accordingly rather than putting all his trust in the author, thus finding his way out of a hybrid of voices.

A polyphony resulting from the diversified narrating voices, narrators and perspectives, however, does serve the author well in hiding his own voice, but whenever the authorial interference in this kind of intentional covering becomes unwittingly visible, a more active response from the reader is called for. It is therefore up to the reader to see through the trick of the author and to decipher the text. A dialogue would inevitably involve an exchange of views so that more interactions and communications may occur among various characters within the text, and between the characters and reader outside the text. For example, while old Maudie is telling her story with the help of interior monologue, Janna is one of her audience. Getting to know Muadie in this way and making her own judgment of the authenticity of Maudie's so-called sweet memory, Janna gradually revises her views on the disadvantaged old and the world as a whole. To some extent, the subsequent growth and maturity is an outcome of the silent dialogue between Janna and Maudie. In this case, dialogue does not lead to contradiction, but rather, reconciliation or sympathy which gives rise to a new interpretation of the meaning shared by both the character and the reader.

Apart from these dialogues, the characters within the text are constantly talking to themselves, hence a hidden and individualized dialogue within the multi-leveled polyphony. A case in point is Janna in *DJS*. With the help of an intermingling of the retrospective perspective and the experiencing perspective, the middle-aged Janna frequently looks back and "talks" to the young Janna. As she grows old, Janna gradually becomes aware of the innocence, indifference or even coldness in the young Janna and decides to make some change. Keeping the distance from the past and observing herself in a detached manner, Janna gets to know more about herself and the outside world. As long as this dialogue goes on, her insights into and understanding of both the people and the world keep growing, a process denying any definite or ultimate interpretation. What's more, during the process of reading, the reader, like the characters within the text, also has to be retrospective in the sense that he may constantly revise his former perception and reorient his vantage point. Consequently, "the act of reading is a project in which one receives back one's own response from the other (the text) in transfigured or de-familiarized form" (Eagleton 187). Whenever the dialogic mechanism is built up in a text, the interaction between author, text and reader becomes more frequent and dynamic. That's why dialogism, being one of the indispensable elements in Bakhtin's theory of hybridity, as observed by Wu Xiaodu, is a "constructive way of thinking" due to the "incompleteness" (Wu Xiaodu 45) in the interpretation of meaning.

As has been discussed in the introductory part, hybridity as a "strategic identificatory performance" (Tate *Black Skins* 163) in a multi-cultural talk can be one of the "strategies of subversion" (Bhabha *Location* 112), just as Terry Eagleton explains in *The Event of Literature* (2012), "Strategies, then, constitute the vital link between work and reader, as the cooperative activity which brings the literary work into being in the first place" (Eagleton 186). If properly handled, strategies can provide the reader with necessary clues in the interpretation of the text. In Lessing's case, the production of meaning becomes a complicated yet challenging task for the reader because of the strategic rhetorical of hybridity.

If Lessing's flexible handling of "voice" such as the narrating voice, the narrator and the perspective serves to construct a polyphonic narrative, mixed styles, genres and subject matters help to deliver a voice deliberately distanced from singularity or dominance. Lessing constantly warns herself against the "provincialism" of British literature and tries to make her own writing more inclusive[1] so that more voices can be heard. A steadfast supporter of England's literary tradition, Lessing yet does not hesitate to show her appreciation for newborn literary ideas and modes. Her openness in writing makes her a border-crossing writer who is willing to experiment with various modes of writing with a hybrid of styles, genres and subject matters.

---

1 Lessing's complaint about "provincialism" in British literature and her protest against labelling will be discussed in detail in Chapter Three.

Chapter Two
Heteroglossia Inside and Outside the Text

We stroll through the great library of her work, where all sections are unmarked and all genre classification pointless. There is life and movement behind the broad or narrow spines of the books, resisting categorisation and the imposition of order.

—Per Wästberg

Being a steadfast follower of 19th century realists while at the same time open to new concepts and modes of writing, Lessing integrates different elements into her writing as her writing becomes more and more diversified, especially in her later period. During the early period of writing, she is often criticized for being too committed and serious to be objective in conception. James Gindin once made such a comment on her:

Miss Lessing's kind of intensity is simultaneously her greatest distinction and her principal effect. She produces an enormously lucid sociological journalism, honest and committed, but in much of her work she lacks a multiple awareness, a sense of comedy, a perception that parts of human experience cannot be categorized or precisely located, a human and intellectual depth. Intense commitment can cut off a whole dimension of human experience (Gindin 85–86).

Lessing seldom admits any effectiveness of such criticism and there seems to be complaints whenever she comes up to this topic. But evidence shows that she does try to integrate into her writing "a multiple awareness" so that the universal human experience can be conveyed to the reader.

Having drawn lessons from her own experience, Lessing mocks at herself for being committed to single convictions. If "intense commitment can cut off a whole dimension of human experience", then the practice of being committed to single ways of writing, for instance the narrative pattern, stands in the way of a truthful representation of human experience as a whole. But that is not all. The mixed forms of writing not only help to deepen and broaden the connotation of words, but also add up to the artistic value of the work. Yet Lessing is frequently blamed for lack of such a value. For instance, Water Allen regards GN as a sociological work which is too honest to be artistic:

> As a work of art, *The Golden Notebook* seems to be to fail. The structure is clumsy, complicated rather than complex. But all the same it is most impressive in its honesty and integrity, and unique... Its main interest seems to be sociological; but that said, it must also be said that it is essential reading for anyone interested in our times... (Allen 276–277)

According to Allen, the structure in *The Golden Notebook* [1] is "complicated rather than complex" which may lead to confusion rather than exquisiteness. It is less attractive in terms of artistic fulfillment for its strong sense of social awareness. Allen's evaluation is typical among Lessing criticism on GN, a viewpoint which arouses strong resentment from Lessing. Lessing believes in the expressiveness of the structure of the story which she has carefully

---

1   In GN, the heroine Anna keeps four diaries colored black, red, yellow, blue and golden each. The black one recalls her experience as a writer in Southern Rhodesia, touching upon the theme of colonialism and racism. The red one tells about her involvement in political activists, together with a group of left-wing intellectuals in the 1950s' London. In the yellow notebook, Anna writes a story entitled "Free Women", a love story partly based on her own experience. She keeps a record of her current life, memories and dreams in the blue notebook. At the end of the story, there comes the golden notebook which centers on Anna's reflection on life and the mental growth. Lessing uses five notebooks to depict a multi-facet Anna.

designed so that it becomes part of the text, as she explains in her preface to
the second edition of *GN*.

As for the form or "shape" of the story, Lessing regards it a good practice
to construct a hybrid text, which turns out to be her way of going beyond
and showing "her dissatisfactions with the limits of existing forms, with the
limits of writing itself" (Sprague 10–11). In her essay entitled "A Reissue of
The Golden Notebook", Lessing tries to explain for the success of the book,
of which one of the secrets is the vitality and energy deriving from a conflict
between the form and content:

> I reread the novel the other day and remembered the fury of energy
> that went into it. Probably that is why the book goes on and on as
> it does—because of its 'charge'. It does have a remarkable vitality.
> Some of it is the energy of conflict. I was writing my way out of one
> set of ideas, even out of a way of life, but that is not what I thought
> while I was doing it. Inside that tight framework is an effervescence.
> Sometimes the energy in a book contradicts it apparent message (*GN*
> 140).

Admitting that she does not confine herself to just one set of ideas or
one way of life, Lessing tries to incorporate into the text various kind of
philosophies, concepts and a diversified way of life by means of a carefully
designed framework. She claims that "shape" speaks out the truth and her
major aim in writing is to "shape a book which would make its own comment,
a wordless statement: to talk through the way it was shaped" (*GN* 14). The
"shape" of a book, she believes, will have its own say in a "wordless" way. The
superficial rigidness in form and underlying flexibilities in content, as obvious
in *GN* therefore, seem to contradict with each other with a tension created
around "words". But this tension allows for a dialogue among various agents,
which is an inborn characteristic of hybridity in Bakhtin's interpretation.
Diversification, flexibility as well as contradiction help the text to be "charged"
with energy and vitality, a construction or reconstruction with new power as

defined by Bhabha.

Wayne Booth (1983) believes that a great artist knows well to "do justice to the complexities of the world" and the secret to his greatness lies in "not genuine ambiguity, but rather complexity with clarity" (Booth *Rhetoric* 135) in the text. Lessing's text, therefore, often leads to ambiguity and confusion, yet speaks out her mind explicitly if read with a keen observation and reflection. Her self-defense for the carefully designed structure of the story of *GN* is a case in point, indicating that, rhetorically speaking, structure or form of the story-telling has its own say similar to other narrative strategies. By making use of the story-within-story structure, by interweaving into the story realistic and modernistic techniques, and by dividing the story into five notebooks each with a different color, Lessing manages to make *GN* extremely hybridized in terms of structure, a structure that is self-supplementary by the internal formal elements. Yet all this complexity, as explained by Lessing, while creating a sense of ambiguity, is meanwhile delivering the message that neither single standard nor binary judgment is applicable in getting to the truth of real life. Lessing, to quote Booth, by doing justice to "the complexities of the world" (Booth *Rhetoric*135) with her hybrid text, makes her voice heard in her own way. By using mixed forms in the story-telling, she creates an effective strategy to counter the narrowness of British literature and the practice of labelling, a steadfast stand that she has reiterated all her life.

What's more, Lessing regards *GN* as a novel free from ambiguity for its readers. Feeling confident that her reader is capable of understanding her, she claims that the interaction among author, text and reader, the process of identifying authorial intention, and a carefully-designed structure make reading a challenging task. Although she does not consciously adopt hybridity as a strategy or declares openly any relation with it, she nevertheless becomes a master of this strategy.

Critics have long noticed Lessing's special attention to the issue of shape: "Thus, *Love, Again* and *The Sweetest Dream* in addressing the complexities of contemporary narratives expand Lessing's assertion in the 1972 introduction to *The Golden Notebook* that 'shape' is a narrative in and of itself" (Raschke *et al.* 5). It seems that after the success of *GN,* Lessing keeps experimenting with "shape" in some of her later works. That's why Roberta Rubenstein compares her to a mythological figure Proteus[1]: "A different figure from Greek mythology might also be instructively used to describe Doris Lessing: Proteus, the shape-lifter who, when caught, metamorphosed into multiple other shapes. Lessing is one of the literary world's most accomplished shape-lifters" (Rubenstein 11). Rubenstein notices Lessing's changeability and puts her on top of the list of "shape-lifters". By comparing Lessing to Proteus, the sea-god in Greek mythology good at changing shapes, Rubenstein affirms Lessing's flexibility and adaptability achieved through constant changing shapes in her writing.

Believing in the power of structure, shape or forms of literature, Lessing has made efforts in experimenting with styles, genres and subject matters, an attempt that has effectively diversifies her writing and distinguished her in terms of multiplicity, innovation and inclusiveness. The discussion in this chapter, therefore, will focus on the mixed styles, composite genres and the multi-dimensional subject matters in her works. It will cover five of Lessing's works with a focus on the following aspects: the different styles in *The Grass Is Singing* and *The Summer Before the Dark*, the integration of fiction and non-fiction in *The Memoirs of a Survivor* and *Alfred and Emily*[2], Lessing's trials on the space fiction *The Marriages Between Zones Three, Four, and Five* as a transcendence over her former realistic novels, and the wide range of subject matters.

Lessing has addressed quite a few critical issues in her writing, among

---

1 Proteus is one of the early sea-gods in Greek mythology. He foretells the future and is capable of changing shapes. As a result, he is often associated with flexibility, versatility and adaptability.

2 Among the four works, *SBD* is acknowledged as a milestone in Lessing's writing career after *GN* and is praised by *The New York Times* as the best novel since Gabriel Garcia Marquez's *One Hundred Years of Solitude* (1967), partly for its innovation and inheritance of the literary tradition. Similarly, *MS* is another typical example demonstrating Lessing's innovative competence.

which the most frequently discussed are the experience and status of being exiled, either forced or voluntary, the trauma caused by war, racialism, natural disasters and terrorism, personal growth in individual-collective relationship, child-parent relationship, the experience of old age and death, and feminist issues in her so-called New Women narratives. Therefore, her writings can be roughly divided into narratives of travel, feminism, trauma, and growth. Both her fiction and her non-fiction, including her autobiographies, memoirs and journals are heavily embedded with these themes. Since the travel and feminist narratives are the two most frequently discussed, they will be the focus of this chapter.

If Lessing's experiments with styles, genres and the choice of subject matters help to bring forth a highly individualized hybrid text, her correspondence with other writers and theorists enables her to "discuss" or "debate" with them so that she, together with her dialogic partners, gets involved in a heteroglossia which turns out to be a collective effort in the development of literary production. Her participation in the construction of this heteroglossia, like in her personal polyphonic narrative production, proves in a different light the effectiveness of the strategic rhetoric of hybridity.

2.1 From Realism to Post-Modernism: *The Grass Is Singing* and *The Summer Before the Dark*

Lessing protests against being labelled as any specific type of writer, although people usually prefer to divide her writing career into three principal phases according to the distinctive features of each stage: the earliest period for realism, the turn to modernism and post-modernism, and finally the turn back to realism. However, these phases overlap and frequently co-occur in her writing, leading to a hybridization of "-isms". Lessing's mastery of various styles is most apparent in her handling of time issue, her balance and juxtaposition of "showing" and "telling"[1] and her concern for individual-universal dichotomy.

Generally speaking, her works in the 1950s and 1960s including *The Grass Is Singing* (1950), *The Golden Notebook* (1962), and *The Children of Violence* (1952—1969) series, fall generally into the category of realism. The 1970s saw Lessing begin to experiment more frequently with modernistic and post-modernistic ways of writing, producing such works as *The Summer Before the Dark* (1973) and *The Memoirs of a Survivor (1974)*. After the four-volume *Canopus in Argos*: Archives (1979—1983), starting from the end of the 1970s, Lessing returned to realistic style in the following decade, with the publication of *The Diary of a Good Neighbour* (as *Jane Somers*) (1983) and *The Good Terrorist* (1985). During this period, she favors "smaller, practical aims: things that can be done" (Upchurch 222), a turn which can be best shown in her collection of short stories, *The Real Thing* (1992) (British version: *London Observed*). This small book consists of 18 sketches and stories. As praised in one book review, it "showcases the uncompromising realism that first won Doris Lessing fame" and is "A real treat for Lessing fans" (Lessing *Real Thing* back cover). One critic once comments that the book uses "a straightforward, I-am-a-camera approach to give a lucid depiction of time and place" (Upchurch 221). Being a showcase of realism, as noted above, all the stories in this collection are told from an outsider's viewpoint and in a chronological order. Lessing the author tries to distance herself from the text rather than getting involved in the story. The detached observer or the omniscient narrator offers a comparatively

---

1   "Showing" and "telling" are two terms coined by writers and literary critics including Walter Scott, Percy Lubbock, Wayne C. Booth and Gerard Genette to show the differences between two ways of presentation: "Showing is relatively unmediated enactment or dramatisation of events, while telling is a mediated report on them" (Herman *et al.* 531). These two terms are closely related to the discussion on the distinctions between imitation and narration, between objectivity and partiality, between the "showing" character who faithful presents whatever he sees and feels and the "telling" narrator who is a spokesman for the hidden author. Writers and theorists dispute over the effectiveness of these two modes of presentation which will be discussed in the following parts of this chapter. For detailed discussion, see Herman 530–531.

objective view of the "real thing". Instead of focusing on the dark side of society or of human beings, a common practice in realism, Lessing chooses to depict the bright side of human nature and metropolitan London, recommending it as a perfect place to live, at least for most people, which is contradictory to her former cynical attitude toward London and human nature.

In the 1990s, *The Marriages Between Zone Three, Four, and Five* (1994), a piece of science fiction, and *Love, again*, a typical modernistic production, show Lessing's preference for (post-)modernistic modes of writing. In 2001, she published *The Sweetest Dream*, which indicates a return to realism. Several years later, in the epic-story *The Cleft* (2007) which tells the history of the Clefts, a pre-historic community of women living in wilderness, Lessing resorts to (post-)modernistic narrative again.

Critics have long noticed Lessing's bold experiments with styles or "-isms", claiming that she is "unpredictable, consistent only in her readiness to take risks" (Bertelsen 16). *The Golden Notebook* is a typical example since its style has long been subjected to heated discussion. Some define it as naturalistic or realistic while others speak of it for its modernistic elements. Still others conclude that it represents a paradoxical quest for both realistic effect and the transcendence of realistic narrative. Generally speaking, in this carefully structured masterpiece, especially in "Free Women", a novel-within-the-novel, Lessing is comparatively realistic, while the four notebooks with four different colors consist of both modernistic and post-modernistic elements. The story of "Free Women" is told in traditional chronological order and emphasis has been put on the description of external environment. In contrast, the four notebooks explore into the mind of the characters with the help of meta-fiction, stream-of-consciousness, montage, news clippings, and diary entries. The interwoven of both realistic and (post-)modernistic elements, the clashes between the traditional and modernistic factors, the dilemma, confrontation as well as conflict coming thereafter correspond with the theme of the story, hence, a correspondence not only in idea but also in form.

Like *GN*, most of Lessing's works can hardly be labelled with any single "-ism". *The Grass Is Singing*, for instance, with its overlapping of chronological and psychological time, penetration into the characters' consciousness, and combination of both telling and showing, proves Lessing to be a master of the realistic style and modernistic strategies. Although *GS* is not a typical psychological novel, it shares some of the features of psycho-narration[1] as much hailed by modernistic writers. Alongside its chronological order, it uses a flashback, newspaper clippings, diaries, news reports, and dreams, and totally "disorders" chronological time for psychological time, which is quite avant-garde at the time.

The story is told through a flashback, beginning with the murder scene and a brief introduction to the background as "told" by an omniscient narrator. The flashback arouses a sense of mystery and curiosity in the reader, which leads to suspense; and it is not until the second chapter that Lessing begins to tell the story of Mary in a chronological order, from her early days in South Africa to her happy single life in town and, at last, to her tragic married life on a farm. As the story of Mary progresses, increasing attention is given to her mental activities, which takes the reader back and forth with Mary on her journey, switching among her past, present, and future. For instance, disillusioned by her life on the farm and with no one to turn to, she can only depend on daydreaming, which brings her back to "that beautiful lost time" and forward to an illusory better future:

In the afternoon, these days, she always slept. She slept for hours and hours: it was a way to make time pass quickly… It was during those two hours of half-consciousness that she allowed herself to dream about that beautiful lost time when she worked in an office and lived as she pleased, before 'people made her get married'. That was how she put it to herself.

---

1   "Psycho-narration" is a term coined by Dorrit Cohn (1978) in her analysis of the modes of presenting consciousness in third-person context, together with the other two forms "the quoted monologue" and "narrated monologue". It is the thought of the character reported by the narrator about the character's mental processes. It can also be called "narratised speech, internal analysis, narratorial analysis, omniscient description, and submerged speech" (Herman 604). For detailed discussion on this term, see Cohn: 21–45.

And she began to think, during those gray wastes of time, how it would be when Dick at last made some money and they could go and live in town again; although she knew, in her moments of honesty, that he would never make money. Then came the thought that there was nothing to prevent her running away and going back to her old life; here the memory of her friends checked her: what would they say, breaking up a marriage like that? The conventionality of her ethics, which had nothing to do with her real life, was restored by the thought of those friends, and the memory of their judgments on other people (*GS* 106–107).

The description of this day dreaming covers almost two pages and this kind of daydreaming occurs frequently as the story progresses. Only by lingering in these self-deceiving fantasies can Mary, though just for a while, forget about her miseries in the present life and imagine "how it would be when Dick at last made some money and they could go and live in town again", although she knows this outcome is impossible "in her moments of honesty". Memory or fantasy, this is the only way for Mary to "cease" her miseries. Just as in the above quoted paragraphs, specific moments in Mary's life are discussed in detail and at a slow pace. These moments, or instants, are lengthened to a great extent, giving the reader sufficient time to probe into the character's mind, "seeing" and sharing her agonies, sorrows, and fears. If the flashback at the beginning of the story creates suspense, the later intensive delineation of Mary's inner activities offers clues about, and directs the reader to, the truth of Mary's tragedy. By "showing" instead of "telling" the consciousness of the character, Lessing allows the reader to gradually become involved in the story. By taking advantage of psychological time, Lessing manages to reduce direct authorial intervention.

Compared with *The Grass Is Singing*, *The Summer Before the Dark* is an even more hybridized text with regard to time. The five chapters of the story are arranged in a chronological order, revealing Kate's life, work, and journey in one particular summer. At the same time, Kate's interior monologue runs through the story, along with the first-person and third-person narration. Lessing's emphasis on Kate's inner activity, which switches back and forth, brings about a juxtaposition of physical time and psychological time as well as a mixing of past and present, creating a sense of chaos which Lessing believes to be closer to the nature of inward and outward reality.

In *SBD,* the heroine Kate Brown dreams frequently about a seal, a dream that varies each time and appears throughout the story:

> The poor seal had *scars* on its sides: it had been bumping overland to reach the sea, and had torn itself on rocks and on stony soil. She was worrying that she did not have any ointment for these wounds, some of which were fresh and bleeding. There were many scars, too, of old wounds. Perhaps some of the low bitter shrubs that grew from the stones had medicinal properties. She carefully laid down the seal, who put its head on her feed, off the stones, and she reached down and sideways and put some ends of the shrub. There was no way pulp this green, so she chewed it, and spat the liquid from her mouth onto the seal's wounds. It seemed to her that these were already healing, but she could stop to do any more, and she again picked up the seal and struggled on with it (*SBD* 54).

The seal comes back to Kate's dream more than ten times. Each time, Kate tries her best to save or heal the wounded seal; for instance, finding water for the seal to keep him from drying out in the sun. She dreams of entering an arena with the seal one hot afternoon. While chased by lions, wolves, tigers, and leopards, she climbs up onto the edge of the arena, "trying to lift the seal up and away from the fangs and claws" (*SBD* 144). Another day, she carries the weak seal in the snowy, cold weather. It seems to her that "walking into the winter that lay in front of her, she was carrying her life as well as the seal's—as if she were holding out into a cold winter her palm, on which lay a single dried leaf" (*SBD* 145). In these dreams, Kate has always been deeply concerned about the safety and liveliness of the injured seal. It is not until the end of the story, when Kate decides to start a new life on her own, that she ceases to dream of the seal. When she last "sees" the seal, she is not worried about his safety and liveliness as before:

> She was no longer anxious about the seal, that it might be dead or dying: she knew that it was full of life, and, like her, full of hope...There, on a flat rock, she let the seal slide into the water. It sank out of sight, then came up, and rested its head for the last time on the edge of the rock: its dark soft eyes looked at her, then it closed its nostrils and dived. The sea was full of seals swimming beside each other, turning over to swim on their backs, swerving and diving, playing. A seal swam past that had scars on its flank and its back, and Kate thought that must be her seal, whom she had carried through so many perils. But it did not look at her now Her journey was over (*SBD* 266).

At last, the seal recovers from his wounds and is strong enough to save himself from possible injures and threats. Life comes back to him, together with hope. Kate is no longer worried about the seal, and her journey ends at the same time.

It is not difficult to connect the meaning of the seal dream with Kate's life. Lessing explains that she uses dreams to indicate that Kate finds way out "in fact through her dreams of this magical seal that she found on this hillside" (Hendin & Lessing 54). These dreams are a reflection of her confusion, confinement, and suffocation, of her subconscious desire to escape from her bondages. Believing in depicting the mental problems of a human being through dreams, Lessing frequently resorts to it, which as in the case of *SBD*, places her writing in both the realistic and modernistic category. What's more, Lessing's favor for a seemingly chaotic presentation of time either physically or psychologically gives rise to the ambiguity or uncertainty shared by her contemporary readers in a chaotic after-war world.

In addition to the time issue, Lessing's flexible use of "showing" and "telling" provides glimpses into her hybridized narrative style. "Showing" and "telling", as two approaches to plot development, have long been under heated discussion. At the beginning of the 19th century, the Scottish novelist Walter

Scott pointed out that a novelist was double burdened with "showing" and "telling":

> … all must be told (in the novel), for nothing can be shown… Thus, the very dialogue becomes mixed with the narration, for (the novelist) must not only tell what the character actually said, in which his task is the same as that of the dramatic author, but must also describe the tone, the look, the gesture, with which their speech was accompanied, —telling in short all which, in the drama, it becomes the province of the actor to express (qtd. in Booth *Rhetorics* 2).

Scott offers a comparison between the novel and drama and claims that it is necessary for a novelist to accomplish the task of describing "the tone, the look, the gesture" to the reader directly, a task which, in a drama, can be fulfilled by an actor's speech. The novelist, by contrast, is charged with the dual task of telling and showing, which can be achieved by way of authorial intrusion as well as presenting things and characters as they are. For a novelist, Scott holds, the tasks of "showing" and "telling" are equally important.

Later, Percy Lubbock elaborates on the distinction between these two different ways of presentation, arguing that "showing" means to dramatize events while "telling" to describe events: "showing is a relatively unmediated enactment or dramatization of events, while telling is a mediated report on them" (Herman *et al.* 530). According to Lubbock, dramatic showing is superior to descriptive telling: "Other things being equal, the more dramatic way is better than the less. It is indirect, as a method; but it places the thing itself in view, instead of recalling and reflecting and picturing it" (Lubbock 149–150). However, this interpretation is not universally accepted. Booth argues that "the 'omniscient' techniques of Fielding or Thackeray, with their chatty addresses to the reader, were not intrinsically inferior to the seemingly objective techniques favoured by James or Hemingway" (Herman *et al.* 58). Booth praises both of these modes of narration for their effectiveness, with each carrying its own rhetorical strength if used appropriately. Likewise,

Genette (1980) declares it is unnecessary to make the distinction between these two terms.

The dispute over the two terms has to do with the interpretation of literary realism and the "real"[1]. Literary realism reached its heyday at the end of the 19th century and early 20th century. One distinctive feature of the early realism is its objectivity thanks to the realist's "very close attention to the surfaces of everyday life" (Barrish 5). To turn its back to Romanticism which enjoyed popularity until the mid-19th century, realist authors assumed a down-to-earth manner by presenting physical details, everyday experiences and activities in a photographic way, hoping to provide the reader with a sense of "impartial fidelity" in their writing (Barrish 5)[2]. In this sense, "showing" becomes a more qualified technique than "telling" if understood in their narrow sense. But in the broad sense, there is no distinction between these two modes of presentation. Or as Genette argues, "narrative is by its very nature always telling and that in narrative showing is therefore always an illusion" (Herman *et al.* 531). This negation of the distinction between "showing" and "telling" finds a more justifiable explanation in Ian Watt's relevant statement.

Ian Watt (1957) discusses the differences among realists in *The Rise of Novel: Studies in Defoe, Richardson and Fielding* (1957). He defines Richardson's realism as *the realism of presentation* while that of Fielding as *the realism of assessment.* According to Watt, the former focuses on external description while the latter delves into the internal self [3]. While *the realism of presentation* tends to make an external description of the physical world like the above mentioned "showing", *the realism of assessment* aims at an internal observation of the character similar to the technique of "telling". Watt's classification on these two kinds of presentation, especially his second term, corresponds to some extent with Henry James's definition on psychological

---

1   For detailed discussion on the "real" issue, see McGowan 102–118.

2   For detailed discussion, see Barrish 1–7.

3   Fro detailed discussion, see Watt 290–296.

realism[1]. James believes that it is more important for a writer to focus on the conscious experiences rather than simply depicting the external world, for "if the novel is a mirror in a roadway, it reflects not only the panorama of existence, but the countenance of the artist in the very act of experiencing the world around him" (Edel 6). James revises the definition of realism, by extending the concept into the consciousness and experiences of the character. James' advocacy for a turn from "emphasizing the accuracy of external detail to reporting internal detail, the thought process of human mind or consciousness" (Murfin & Supryia 398) foresees modernist writers' experiment with stream-of- consciousness.

Since the debate on the two terms is still going on and there is no ultimate solution to the dispute, the present author prefers to use the two terms in their narrow sense, that is, "showing" refers to the photographic depiction of the external details, a common practice among the early 19th realists while "telling" refers to the intrusive reporting of the inner world of the character which is more popular among writers afterwards. Lessing adopts a two-in-one strategy, alternating between the two preferences. In some of her novels such as *The Grass Is Singing, The Memoirs of a Survivor* and *The Cleft,* the external description is endowed with heavy metaphorical implications, while in such novels as *The Summer Before the Dark, The Diaries of Jane Somers* and *Martha Quest,* the delineation of the internal activities of the character is given priority, which seems to be more in line with the modernistic way of narration.

The interpretation of Booth and Genette on this issue sounds more reasonable, for Lessing takes the advantage of both "showing" and "telling" as long as they help to achieve the expected artistic purpose, an attitude that is accountable for the mixed forms and styles in her writing. Whenever she wants to become an outside observer, keeping an eye on her characters and listening

---

1 Henry James, though recognized as a realist, stands out of his contemporary realists by his brilliant interpretation on "phychological realism" and is therefore regarded as "one of the first modern psychological analysts" who has great influence on the modernistic writers in the 20th century (Edel 7–8). James talks about the responsibility of the artist and the approach he adopts in "The Art of Fiction" (1984).

to what they say without commentary, she turns herself into an "eavesdropper", as she once explains about her writing of *The Good Terrorist*: "What fascinated me while I was writing was something that I had never sensed so distinctly: I was in the position of an eavesdropper, and a whole cluster of details from my own life coming back to me were determining the form of the book" (Rousseau 149). She finds it fascinating to make the most of "showing", providing readers with enough information and details for textual interpretation. For instance, in *GS,* Lessing shows Mary's disappointment in, and fear of, her new life when she first follows her husband into their shabby house on the farm:

> The moon had gone behind a great luminous white cloud, and it was suddenly very dark—miles of darkness under a dimly starlit sky. All around were trees, the squat, flattened trees of the Highveld, which seem as if pressure of sun has distorted them, looking now like vague dark presences standing about the small clearing where the car had stopped. There was a small square building whose corrugated roof began to gleam whitely as the moon slowly slid out from behind the cloud and drenched the clearing with brilliance (*GS* 53).

In contrast to hope, delight, and excitement, Mary sees only "darkness" and "a dimly starlit sky". The trees seem to be "distorted" by the sun. Nothing is cheerful to the eye. The house "looked shut and dark and stuffy, under that wide streaming moonlight" (*GS* 53). Even worse, nothing is cheerful to hear. The strange, wild, nocturnal sounds make her "suddenly terrified, as if a hostile breath had blown upon her, from another world, from the trees" (*GS* 53). "Showing" like this, supported by detailed descriptions of the environment, occurs throughout the story so that at first sight, the technique used here reflects that of the realistic description. Yet a further look into the text, in particular, the choice of words, will lead to a different answer. This short paragraph is heavily embedded with words and phrases like "darkness", "dimly starlit", "vague dark", "gleam whitely" and "brilliance", drawing attention to a sharp contrast between brightness and darkness. The word-picture drawn by Lessing creates a sense of uncertainty, insecurity or confusion, similar to the mentality of the newly-married Mary who first sets her foot on this farm. Instead of a new life with hope, Mary sees nothing but vague darkness waiting for her. A careful reader therefore will hear what Lessing "tells" between the lines, for what is shown is also the "telling" conducted by Lessing the interfering author. The tone and atmosphere created by the well-chosen words save Lessing the trouble of managing to tell something without making direct comments.

But Lessing is not content with this, for she prefers mixed forms in her writing. She feels free to make her presence, putting emphasis on authorial commentary alongside the detailed presentation of details. At the beginning of *GS,* when the omniscient narrator begins to tell the story of the Turners, there seem to be hidden authorial comments made by the narrator. When people keep silent about the murder of Mary Turner, the narrator comments: "The most interesting thing about the whole affair was this silent, unconscious agreement. Everyone behaved like a flock of birds who communicate—or so it seems—by means of a kind of telepathy" (*GS* 2). The critical tone seems to belong more to Lessing than to the otherwise objective omniscient narrator. When introducing Charlie Slatter to the reader, the narrator comments again: "He was still a proper cockney, even after twenty years in Africa. He came with one idea: to make money. He made it. He made plenty. He was a crude, brutal, ruthless, yet kindhearted man, in his own way, and according to his own impulses, who could not help making money" (*GS* 6–7). Although a "kindhearted" man, Slatter later forces the Turners to leave their farm, which leads to the final mental corruption of the couple. As the story progresses, the reader comes to realize the meaning of "kindheartedness" and becomes aware of the one who is speaking behind the lines.

Lessing, in other words, tries to achieve a flexible balance between authorial intrusion and mere description of incidences and characters so that readers are given more freedom to interpret the text on their own. Noticing this balance in Lessing's work, Michael Thorpe argues that "there are authorial comments that do point up the social and racial issues for the uninformed reader, but one of the chief strengths of *The Grass Is Singing* is that it is not an attitudinizing work. Lessing's method is to present relationships and an episode and allow readers the liberty of their own interpretation" (Thorpe 11). Thorpe praises Lessing for her wise handling of both "showing" and "telling" without which the story will become "attitudinizing".

For Lessing, to let loose her control of the text does not mean forgetting the task of moral teaching and guidance. It does not mean that she puts into the hands of the reader the entire task of interpretation. By showing details about the characters and the things around them so as to obtain the reader's trust, and by adopting a seemingly detached tone without direct judgment, Lessing builds up a not-so-obvious guide-and-accept link between herself and the reader, taking control of her characters and readers while, at the same time, keeping a distance from both.

Lessing's flexible handling of the time issue and her balance between "showing" and "telling" indicate her openness toward different ways of writing. In general, Lessing is a steadfast practitioner of realism who, at the same time, experiments with modernistic techniques. Since she is a fan of the 19th century realism—like that of Flaubert who is also adept at showing and presenting, or Henry Fielding who takes delight in speaking his own mind to the reader, or Henry James who believes in the moral power of the novel but protests against authorial intrusion, or Defoe who advocates direct authorial intrusion—a hybrid of these realistic elements can be found in most of her writing. Lessing repeatedly declares her admiration for the great realists, in particular, Turgenev and Chekhov whom Harold Bloom praises for his skillfulness in story-telling and his explicit detachment. Lessing, like these literary idols, consciously handles her narration in a detached tone in some of her best works, gradually turning from a manipulating author-narrator to a detached storyteller.

Lessing likes to experiment with new styles. A glance at the list of her favorite writers shows her interest in and admiration for the modernistic and post-modernistic writers. Claiming that she is influenced by many modernists in one way or another, yet Lessing can not tell definitely which one has the most impact on her writing. While talking about D. H. Lawrence and Virginia

Woolf, she admits, "I suppose they influenced me. The thing is I read so much then, you see. Because I was very isolated, I read day and night. Luckily I read very fast. It'd be very hard to say what influenced me and what didn't" (Bertelsen 127). She praises Stendhal, T. S. Eliot, W. B. Yeats and Bill Hopkins for their distinctive features.

Among the favored British modernists, she puts Lawrence on top of the list, emphasizing that it is not the ideas but the liveliness in Lawrence's writing that impresses her: "He was among the first of the modern writers I read. His writing had an enormous effect on me because of the vitality of the man… I never read him for his ideas, you know; I don't think that's his virtue. I read him for his vitality—unforgettable scenes, one after another (Ingersoll & Lessing 231)." For Lessing, "vitality" is the word that best characterizes Lawrence, and "vitality" is one of the distinctive features of Lessing's work as well. As Lawrence is skilled at injecting vigor and liveliness into trivial matters; so is Doris Lessing. For instance, *The Diaries of Jane Somers* shows the daily routines of her heroines during a span of two years. Trivial details, subtle feelings, and things of insignificance are all presented in such an intricate way that the reader is touched by the experiences of the characters.

Lessing also shows admiration for American modernists. She "felt a kinship with Norman Mailer" (Oates & Lessing 37), for instance, and believes that he did not get the proper treatment from his critics at his time. She admires Vonnegut and regards "*Slaughterhouse-Five* as an especially impressive book of his" (Oates & Lessing 37). She also regards Marcel Proust, together with Norman Mailer and Carson McCullers, as one of her favorite authors, claiming, "I'm quite sure that at one time I must have been one of the world experts on Proust" (Thorpe 98).

Due to her admiration for both the great realists and modernists, Lessing integrates into her writing both realistic and modernistic elements so that her text becomes a platform for sameness and difference, which makes possible a dual-process of infusion and separation, a manifestation of hybridity as defined by Bhabha. This hybrid of styles, together with the mixed genres which will be the focus of discussion immediately afterwards, "on the one hand generates new literary or artistic forms, but on the other hand, blurs the distinction between original genres and ultimately threatens the very notion of genre" (Guignery *et al.* 61). While confirming the generating power of hybridity, Guignery at the same time shows his doubt about this strategy, for fear that it may give rise to ambivalence or ambiguity robbing the original genres of their purity.

Guignery is not alone in being worried about the emergence of a "cross-breeding" genre. That's why Lessing's practice of "cross-breeding" is not always appreciated. She has been criticized for her mixed practice or hybridized way of narration, which some critics believe makes her work "puzzling" or "chaotic" (qtd. in Bertelsen 19). But Lessing is not discouraged by these negative or even hostile reviews and criticisms. Instead, she doubles her efforts to combine conventional ideas with new practices and concepts. Therefore, her later works become even more hybridized in terms of narrative. To put it simply, there may be disruptive elements in her writing, but one thing that characterizes her works from the beginning to the end of her career is her consistency in producing a mix of narrative styles. Lessing, as noticed by Robin Visel, frequently "travels back to realism through modernism and postmodernism" (Visel 61) and this tracing back to the 19th century realism on the one hand, and moving ahead of her time on the other, add up to stylistically hybridized flavor in her writing.

2.2 Experiments with Genres: *The Memoirs of a Survivor*, *Alfred and Emily* and *The Marriages Between Zone Three, Four, and Five*

In addition to mixing of styles, there is in Lessing a mixture of various genres, such as novels, short stories, fairy tales, autobiography, and drama. Furthermore, Lessing freely incorporates into her writing materials such as news reports, films, diaries, poetry, music, drama, and literary reviews. By putting all of these together, she provides the reader with a hybrid genre that "is used to designate works of art which transgress genre boundaries by combing characteristic traits and elements of diverse literary and nonliterary genres" (Herman *et al.* 226–227). Like a shifting perspective, which is used to achieve the effect of heteroglossia, hybrid genres help Lessing to attain the goal of border crossing in a manner designed to subvert dominant discourses:

> By transgressing genre boundaries, hybrid genres aim at distancing themselves from the homogeneous, one-voiced, and "one-discoursed" worldview conventional narratives seem to suggest, a notion which is closely related to Bakthin's concept of dialogic imagination. Moreover, hybrid genres are intricately linked to the notion of hybrid identity, which is fluid, unstable, incessantly in search of and transforming itself (Herman *et al.* 227).

As interpreted by David Herman, hybrid genres as achieved by diversified forms or technique challenge the authority of the conventional ways of writing. It injects new vitality into literary production. With regard to Lessing's hybridity in terms of genres, her handling of fiction and non-fiction is particularly interesting, as she purposefully blurs the distinction between them. In recent years, her interest in space fiction, which she claims to be more autobiographically true than her autobiographies, makes her hybridity in genres even more complicated.

Lessing has written two autobiographical volumes: *Under My Skin: Volume One of My Autobiography, to 1949* (1994) and *Walking in the Shade: Volume Two of My Autobiography, 1949 to 1962* (1997). Before these two books, she published a collection of essays entitled *Going Home* (1957), which is a journal describing her seven-week trip back to Africa. It not only features Central African politics and significant public figures, but also keeps a record of her personal experiences during her short visit there. Another collection entitled *African Laughter: Four Visits to Zimbabwe* (1992) primarily focuses on her memories of her second homeland, Southern Rhodesia, which she revisited four times—in 1982, 1988, 1989, and 1992. She recalls in this book what she saw and experienced during the four visits, touching upon such pressing issues in Africa as the menace of AIDS, the extinction of wildlife, the deterioration of the bush, the corruption of politics, and the success of communal enterprises.

In addition to these non-fiction works consisting of autobiographies and collections of journals and memoirs, Lessing also writes several autobiographical novels. The earliest one is *In Pursuit of the English* (1960), which recalls her first return to London with her one-year-old son, and her struggle there as a single-parent and independent writer. Later, the *Children of Violence* series, which is to some extent autobiographical fiction, tells about the growth and life experience of Martha Quest and covers a time span of almost two decades[1].

That series, with Martha Quest in the role of a young Doris Lessing as its central figure, discloses her growth from adolescence to adulthood, her maturity through sex and marriage, her choices between having a social platform and maintaining a family, and her escape from her mother's control. As the series progresses, Martha Quest retreats from the forefront and is no longer the center figure, but this matters little. The reader can still find Lessing in characters besides Martha Quest, and Lessing admits that she is drawing a map of herself through the different characters. For example, in the last volume of the series, *The Four-Gated City*, "various aspects of myself were parceled out between the different characters. They were a fairly interesting map of myself, that roll of characters, actually" (Bertelsen 143). This makes it justifiable for this study to have a close look at her personal experience in the discussion of the resources of Lessing's narrative features, a detailed discussion which will be carried out in the first part of Chapter Three.

According to Lessing, among the five volumes in *Children of Violence* series, the first two are more autobiographical than the following three:

> The first volumes of *Martha Quest* are the most autobiographical. I put in my autobiography what is and what isn't. It's certainly true about the emotions—these abrasive, adolescent emotions. They are all truer than anything I can possibly say now. But the facts are not necessarily true,

---

1 The whole series is composed of five books published in separate years, extending from 1952 to 1969, including *Martha Quest* (1952), *A Proper Marriage* (1954), *A Ripple from the Storm* (1958), *Landlocked* (1965), and *The Four-Gated City* (1969).

because I change things around. *Proper Marriage* is more or less true, with differences, and I've said what the differences are. *A Ripple from the Storm* is very autobiographical—of course, people are always fitted together to make a composite (Ingersoll & Lessing 229–230).

As explained in this interview, Lessing believes that what matters is the truth about emotions rather than the truth about facts. Regardless of how many details are invented in a story, as long as they reveal emotions, which are "truer" than anything else, the story can be deemed realistic. She, on the one hand, puts the five books in the category of autobiography while, on the other, declares that they are realistic in one way or another, with the only difference lying in the percentage of truth revealed through facts.

Lessing's struggle with breaking the boundary between different genres can also be seen in her interpretation of science fiction in *The Memoirs of a Survivor*, which, as she declares, is an attempt at autobiography. She regards it as autobiography based on a combination of reality and dream:

In *The Memoirs of a Survivor,* what the narrator believes that she is seeing behind the wall. That apparent dream world, actually represents her own life, her own childhood. In the tangible world, Emily, whom she sees growing up, represents the image of her adolescence. Thus, reality and dream, marked off by the wall, complement each other to give an all-encompassing vision to the narrator's past. I have said that *The Memoirs of a Survivor* was my imaginative autobiography. Curiously, no one noticed it, as if that precision was embarrassing (Rousseau 148).

Here, *MS* is an "imaginative autobiography" with a "fantastic wall" acting as a magical switch that allows the heroine to move back and forth between "reality" and "dream". She feels embarrassed that the reader has ignored its "precision" about mentality, which is the focus of her autobiographical story and which therefore makes the story non-fictional. The distinction between fiction and non-fiction, for Lessing, lies in the extent to which one is capable of revealing truth—the psychological truth. What's more, Lessing claims that science fiction, traveling between the "dream world" and "tangible world", sometimes offers a more faithful representation of reality. That's why she complains about people's ignorance of the authenticity of this story.

Another example is *Alfred and Emily*, which is a half-biographical fiction, based mostly on the actual experience of Lessing's parents. The novel consists of two parts. While the first part is mostly fictional, imagining the couple's life as it might have been without World War II, the second half is based on the couple's actual suffering in the war, their life on the African farm, and the unhappy child-parent relationship that Lessing frequently examined in her previous works. *Alfred and Emily* is about her painful experience in the past from which she finds hard to recover even several decades later. This half-imaginative and half-factual story serves as a revelation of the spiritual wound of the war victim, including both the crippled child and the incapacitated adults. Therefore, this story turns out to be a hybrid text of non-fiction and fiction in which Lessing intentionally makes vague the difference between reality and imagination. By recalling and revealing the violence and hurt in the past, Lessing in the meanwhile turns her writing to a therapy, or a means of healing.

Perhaps the advantage of revealing in a fictional manner rather than an auto-biographical way is that it is much more convenient for the author to keep the distance, thus making himself a much detached observer and cool-headed judge of the character as well as the story. "Narrative allows us to enter the minds of others in a way that we cannot in real life, and Lessing uses that capacity to great advantage in her autobiographical narratives as in her fiction" (Anderst 275). Lessing seems to have more trust in fiction, given its ability to recall the past through memory and her desire to work through the trauma of her early life. She on the one hand, believes that fiction is no less, if it is indeed not more, authentic than non-fiction. On the other hand, she doubts the reliability of memory as it becomes "fixed" in autobiography and therefore may diminish the authenticity of the story. While she affirms the "truth" of fictional work, she regards autobiography as an interim report: "Once I read autobiography as what the writer thought about her or his life. Now I think, 'That is what they thought at that time.' An interim report—that is what an autobiography is" (Lessing *TB* 92). This comment does not imply that Lessing denies the authenticity of autobiography. What she holds, rather, is that only from a detached and impersonal position can one represent reality or truth in a more reliable way. While it is sometimes difficult for an autobiographer to achieve this since he/she may become personally involved in a story, it is more possible for a writer to do so.

As for the authenticity of the non-fictional writing, Lessing argues that life experiences are floating all the time since one's observations, perceptions, judgments, and, most important of all, viewpoints are always developing. Therefore, it is no easy task to offer a definitive account of one's past unless one obtains a detached position, or unless one is mature enough to look back in a sober way:

> Our own views of our lives change all the time, different at different ages. If I had written an account of myself aged 20 it would have been a belligerent and combative document. At 30—confident and optimistic. At 40—full of guilt and self-justification. At 50—confused, self-doubting. But at 60 and after something else has appeared: you begin to see your early self from a great distance. While you can put yourself back inside the 10-year-old, any time you want, you are seeing that child, that young woman, as-almost-someone else. You float away from the personal. You have received that great gift of getting older—detachment, impersonality (*TB* 92).

According to Lessing, memory, like life experience, is forever changing, and past can hardly be "captured" once for all in words. A writer at an advanced age tends to be more objective in representing the past and reflecting upon reality by keeping a distance from it. Interestingly, Lessing is not the only writer to hold such a position. Virginia Woolf seems to have the same opinion in this regard. Talking about the truthful representation of her mother as well as related memories in her autobiographical essay "A Sketch of the Past", Woolf declares that "if one could give sense of my mother's personality one would have to be an artist" (Woolf 2221). In other words, she finds it hard to fully understand her mother's personality while talking about her identity as a daughter. Instead, she can only get to know about her by keeping a detached stance in writing.

Lessing further argues that novels are more effective at representing the personalities of the author than autobiography, for they are capable of showing different layers of the author's personality through their characters:

> One of the ways one can use novels is to see the different personalities in novelists... Now here is the paradox. It is easier to see this map of a person in their novels than in autobiography. That is because an autobiography is written in one voice, by one person, and this person soothes out the roughness of the different personalities. This is an elderly, judicious, calm person, and this calmness of judgment imposes a unity. The novelist doesn't necessarily know about her own personalities (*TB* 99–100).

For Lessing, the novelist has more freedom in showing and telling the different "selves" through characters in fictional works while the writer of an autobiography has to speak in "one voice" so as to create the autobiographer as unified from the beginning to the end, a reliable narrator of his own story. Meanwhile, the autobiographer is supposed to know his own personalities well enough, to be careful about details and to observe and present himself with "calmness" and fine "judgment". But this is not obligatory for a novelist, whose observation and presentation need not be so cool-headed since his attention should be on truth about emotions rather than facts. Like the shifted and multiplied narrators and perspectives which work together to conspire against any single dominating discourse within the text, the different voices in the fiction and non-fiction are burdened with the task of subverting and constructing, as an indispensible part in heteroglossia.

Due to her belief in the advantages of fiction over non-fiction in representing truth, Lessing tries to integrate these two genres, and her efforts made in this regard, together with her claim that some of her novels are autobiographical, challenge the traditional classification of fiction and non-fiction as distinct genres. Lessing's interpretation and flexible use of both shows, again, her experimentalism with hybridity.

Among her re-interpretation of the genre issue, Lessing has paid special attention to space fiction[1], a genre that she became interested in during the 1970s. Lessing sees space fiction, a product of modernism, not as a break with realistic tradition, but as an inheritance and development of it. By putting both realistic and modernistic elements into space fiction, Lessing makes it a "new mess" (Bigsby & Lessing 83), or a new hybrid.

In the 1950s, Lessing claimed that the 19th century "realist novel, the realist story, is the highest form of prose writing; higher than and out of the reach of any comparison with expressionism, impressionism, symbolism, naturalism, or any other ism" (*ASPV* 4). But three decades later, she changed her attitude by declaring that realism was suitable only for the elementary stage of writing, while a deeper exploration of truth called for more imagination and fantasy: "I think most writers have to start very realistically because that's a way of establishing what they are, particularly women, I've noticed. For a lot of women, when they start writing it's a way of finding out who they are. When you've found out, you can start making things up" (Bikman & Lessing 60). Realism in this sense is the starting point for new writers. Once they are artistically better prepared, they may move on to other forms of writing, which are more flexible and sophisticated in reflecting the realistic world.

Lessing thus began to write space fiction, or "making things up", in the 1970s (Bikman & Lessing 60), with a four-volume series consisting of *Canopus in Argos: Archives: Colonised Planet 5, Shikasta* (1979), *The*

---

1   Instead of "science fiction" which is a more frequently used term, Lessing prefers to call it "space fiction", for she does not feel that she is a qualified writer for science fiction, which is quite demanding in terms of scientific facts and professional knowledge.

Marriage Between Zones Three, Four, and Five (1980), *The Sirian Experiments* (1981), and *The Making of the Representative for Planet 8* (1982). Holding the idea that, compared with realistic writing, space fiction is a better way to represent society and its people, Lessing admitted in an interview that she "turned to space fiction because it alone offered her the opportunity to range freely in time and space and to find metaphors to express her concern with contemporary problems and issues" (Ingersoll X). For her, space fiction with no limit on time and space allows the writer more freedom and flexibility.

Compared with realistic novels often undermined by limitations of locality or provinciality, space fiction is more effective in reflecting universal truth because it facilitates the writer to present reality metaphorically. Lessing defends the benefits of space fiction in her autobiography:

I was excited by their scope, the wideness of their horizons, the ideas, and the possibilities for social criticism—particularly in this time of McCarthy, when the atmosphere was so thick and hostile to new ideas in the United States—and disappointed by the level of characterization and the lack of subtlety (*WS* 30).

Covering a broader scope than realistic fiction, space fiction "mirrors" reality in a more fantastic way. Lessing's interest in fantasy goes hand in hand with her fascination with Eastern religions, especially Sufism. As a fervent follower of Idries Shah, the founder of Sufism, Lessing believes in the perceptive power of the extraordinary sense, the irrational, crazy, or even mystical part of mentality. She declares that space fiction can reflect this preoccupation and disclose of the world of the non-rational.

Having realized both the power and weakness of the genre, Lessing makes efforts to produce better space fiction, for she believes that "a sci-fi novel is yet to be written using density of characterization, like Henry James. It would be great comedy, for a start" (Lessing *WS* 30). Lessing again wants to bring out a "new mess" (Bigsby & Lessing 83) out of its old form by putting emphasis on characterization as Henry James does in his writing, a characterization that cares more about the inner world of the character. But to write a "sci-fi novel", she believes it is better to start with the portrayal of the character realistically rather than depending heavily on imagination which is a common practice with science fiction. The focus of the space novel, Lessing indicates, should still be the concrete and down-to-earth life of the character.

To some extent, Lessing plays down the "fantastic" elements in space fiction because she feels herself to be an unqualified writer for science, but her concern actually goes beyond the mere issue of science. Despite the worry that space fiction may eventually undermine her literary reputation, Lessing enjoys writing space fiction for she believes that "the best social criticism of our time is in science fiction" (Aldiss & Lessing169), since it is the genre more appropriate for a changed social condition.

For example, *The Marriages Between Zone Three, Four, and Five* published in 1994, a hybrid text of myth, fable, and allegory, is deeply concerned with humanistic welfares. In the novel, the Queen of Zone Three is ordered by the Providers, the rulers of all zones, to marry the King of Zone Four. After she gives birth to a baby, she is asked to go back to her own zone again, though she has already been exiled by her own people. Later, King Ben Ata of Zone Four is ordered by the Providers to marry the Queen of Zone Five. Built around these two marriages, the epic-like story tells how women and men get to know each other and how transformation is brought to each zone for the benefit of its people. Although it takes place in a fantastic setting, it is a story about love, marriage, welfare of the people, and the nation as a whole. It demonstrates Lessing's belief that sometimes space fiction is more realistic than realistic fiction, for it offers opportunities to deal with human concerns in a way unimaginable otherwise.

2.3 A Juxtaposition of Subject Matters: Travel Narrative and Female Narrative

As a writer with a strong social consciousness, Lessing integrates into her writing almost all the critical issues of the 20th century, and the wide range of subject matters, therefore, providing further evidence of her hybridity. In the

1950s, colonialism, the color-line, and the misery of the exiled Whites are the central issues in her writings, especially in *The Grass is Singing* and *Martha Quest*. In the 1960s and 1970s, such issues as wars—including political party splits, the cold war, and nuclear war—can be found in *The Golden Notebook* and *The Memoirs of a Survivor*, *The Four-Gated City* and *Briefing for a Descent into Hell*. Meanwhile there are stories about the search for identity and the growth of the self in relation to the community. In the 1980s and 90s, terrorism in various forms and in different parts of the world has aroused Lessing's attention. Entering upon the new millennium, Lessing begins to talk about the Greenhouse Effect, the diminishing rain forests, AIDS and unemployment, especially in her volumes of space fiction, *The Good Terrorist*, *The Marriages Between Zone Three, Four, and Five*, *The Sweetest Dream*, and *The Cleft*.

For Lessing, all that she has experienced would "have its say" in her writing, be it war, colonization in Africa, struggling youth in cities, suburbs and towns, confused middle-age in London, and troubled male-female relationships. Thanks to the diversified "raw materials", Lessing manages to broaden the span of her subject matters. Her first novel, *GS*, is a typical example in that it predicts almost all of her later themes, including colonialism, diasporas, gender issues, and family relationships. Furthermore, her experiments with new concepts and approaches, her broad horizons cultivated by her education and life-long struggles, her keen observations of and meditations on social reality, and her courage of constantly conducting self-criticism all help her transcend daily experience and acquire new insights.

Though each work may provide one or two areas of focus, almost all of the key issues in her day can be found in her writings, including clashes between the city and the veld, conflicts between the White colonizer and the colonized Black, the imprisonment and growth of the self in various forms, the maturity of the female in a patriarchal world, the survival and well-being of humanity, and so on. As she suggests in a central metaphor of *GN*, Lessing seems to have spent all her life pulling a huge stone, a heavy burden of humanistic concerns, up a mountain, never giving up. The belief she holds in a writer's responsibility for social welfare produces in her a deep concern for the struggle and survival of human beings who are each confined to various kinds of imprisonment.

As with her experiments with multiple narrative strategies, the critical themes in her writings advance with time so that their subject matters are inclusive. Unlike the great female writers in the 19th century such as Jane Austen, Emily Bronte, Sharlott Bronte, and George Eliot who could hardly look beyond their family and emotional lives of the middle-class saloon, Lessing tries to transcend her personal experience into broader social context, and her diversified subject matter contributes to her hybridity. These subject matters can be classified into narratives of travel (nostalgia, exile), of feminism (male-female relationships, freedom, independence), of growth (child-parent relationship, individual-collective relationship, old age, death), and of trauma (racism, war, natural disaster, terrorism). Since the first two narratives appear in most of her writings, they deserve more attention in the following parts of discussion.

Travel Narrative

Travel, as "an out-of-ordinary experience and occasion for observations and encounters," has "provided stimulus and material for narrative since ancient times" (Herman 619). It has given rise to many forms of writing, including "the epic, the quest romance, the picaresque novel, the utopian novel and science fiction, the adventure novel, the Robinsonade, and the Bildungsroman" (Herman 619). In a broad sense, travel narrative not only refers to those accounts of travel or exile such as colonization like Lessing's *The Grass Is Singing*, a story closely related to the colonial experiences, but is also used to reflect upon the experiences of self-made exploration and escape, such as running away from one's former environment. The *Children of Violence* series belongs to this group, with the "running away" as one of the recurrent themes of the five stories which tell about the pursuit of freedom from current imprisonments.

Thanks to this running away from one's former environment, travel narrative is often used to "project foreign or alternative, even fantastical, worlds" (Herman *et al.* 146), exploring into something unknown from which new experience is accumulated[1]. Travel narrative can provide "a scenario in which the protagonist's spiritual, sentimental, or other kinds of inner 'journey' can be developed or symbolically mirrored" (Herman *et al.* 146). Most of Lessing's writings, therefore, fall into the category of travel narrative reflecting upon the protagonist's inner journeys along with experiences of real travel, in particular *The Summer Before the Dark, The Diaries of Jane Somers, The Golden Notebook*, and several other novels in which the spiritual growth of the hero or heroine is accompanied by various kinds of travel in their life. Travel narratives can even cover the semi-fiction or autobiographies, including *Alfred and Emily, Walking in the Shade*, and *In Pursuit of the English*, for these works, like the authentic travel narrative, are manifestations of Lessing's mental growth.

But if viewed from a post-colonial perspective, travel narrative often contains a discussion on diaspora, involving such issues as center and margin, identity, resistance and hybridity. In Lessing's case, travel narrative is not only a manifestation of her inclusiveness in subject matters, but also a strategy she purposefully uses in her fight against existing literary tradition, for instance, the "provincialism" in British literature. For by way of travel narrative, she invites the reader to set foot on remote parts of the world and to hear voices from alien groups of people. Being sensitive to "place" in both her fictional and non-fictional writing, Lessing frequently reminds people of her unique position which she defines as thrice-exiled, or to quote Per Wästberg's words, "a poor person in a rich society, a woman among men, a white among blacks" (Wästberg para. 10)[2].

---

1   In this sense, space fiction can be put into this category which opens doors to more of the unknown worlds as well as experiences, such as Lessing's *MS* which tells about two worlds separated by a wall, each representing the real world and the imaginary respectively.

2   Per Wästberg, Chairman of the Nobel Committee for Literature, made this comment on Lessing in his speech at the award ceremony for Lessing's Nobel Prize. For the complete script of this speech, see http://www.nobelprize.org/nobel_prizes/ literature/laureates/2007/presentation-speech. html.

Lessing's concern for place is in fact a concern for identity, an identity that provides her with an insider-outsider perspective which, as she claims, is helpful in her observation and presentation of the life and the experience she knows. Lessing is thus able to make her writing a highly diversified narration. To delve into Lessing's travel narrative, it is first of all necessary to hear her own tale of two cites which is based on her life in London and Africa in different periods, a tale that explains for her life-long dedication towards such issues as colonialism, perspective of observation and presentation, liberation, individual-collective relationships and the gender issues.

Being a multi-fold exile, Lessing claims that London is her homeland and Africa her second homeland, which is why, for a certain period, she finds herself an alien to both, an outside-insider. Naturally, therefore, travel becomes one of her most frequently touched upon subject matters, through which she expresses her nostalgia for both Africa and London and probes into the colonialism she has experienced during her stay in the colonized Africa, through the depiction of the self-made exile of some of her imprisoned characters.

Lessing's simultaneous nostalgia for the African veld and the city of London is one of the most significant themes in her writing, with a primary focus on either of them in different periods. She returns repeatedly to her complicated feelings toward these two places in both fictional writings and non-fiction, especially her two-volume autobiographies. For her, "Africa is an old fever, latent always in the blood" (Bigsby & Lessing 72). Her first novel *GS* has a South Africa setting. Her second book, *This Was the Old Chief's Country* (1951), is a collection of short stories, once again with an African setting which deals with African topics from different perspectives. In 1951, Lessing published the first volume of *Children of Violence* series, *Martha Quest*, which explores Martha's early life in the African countryside and then, later, in town. In 1954, with the publication of the second volume of *Children of Violence* series—*A Proper Marriage*—Martha Quest continues her complicated and disillusioned life in the big city. Martha, like Lessing, travels between Africa and Europe's London to experience the two modes of life. She feels herself, on the one hand, an exile to both places and, on the other hand, attracted by both, no matter how much disillusionment she has derived from them.

In the following years, Lessing continues to write about Africa and London interchangeably. *Going Home* (1957) is a journal about her visit back to Africa in 1956 and *In Pursuit of the English* (1960) recalls her early life in London, which is weighted with unhappy memories. It reads like a novel, yet it is a memoir-like story. Later, she writes a number of African stories that has built her fame as an African writer, some of which are collected into *This Was the Old Chef's Country* (1973) and *The Sun Between Their Feet: Collected African Stories* (1973). Her attitude toward London, which becomes much more positive in the 1990s, can later be seen in *London Observed, Stories and Sketches* (1992). In this collection, Lessing, in an omniscient voice, tells of the loveliness and merits of the city. Meanwhile, in the same year, the public read about her love for Africa in her newly published *African Laughter: Four Visits to Zimbabwe* (1992), in which she recounts her four visits back to Africa after 25-year departure from the continent, providing detailed descriptions of the landscape, the people, and their life with a strong sense of nostalgia. Apart from the above mentioned fictions and non-fictions, Lessing frequently talks about her complicated feeling towards Africa and London in her autobiographies.

Lessing's feeling for these two places is a hybrid of nostalgia and hatred. Chronologically speaking, before 1949 when Lessing was living with her family in Africa, London was her dreamland and "a grail" (Lessing *IPE* 15). She expresses this yearning for London as a teen in *MQ* with a comparison, in one of Martha's daydreams, of small African towns with the metropolises of Europe:

> She looked away over the ploughed land, across the veld to the Dumfries Hills, and refashioned that unused country to the scale of her imagination. There arose, glimmering whitely over the harsh scrub and the stunted trees, a noble city, set foursquare and colonnaded along its falling, flower-bordered terraces. There were splashing fountains, and the sound of flutes;

and its citizens moved, grave and beautiful, black and white and brown together; and these groups of elders paused, and smiled with pleasure at the sight of the children—the blue-eyed, fair-skinned children of the North playing hand in hand with the bronze-skinned, dark-eyed children of the South. Yes, they smiled and approved these many-fathered children, running and playing among the flowers and the terraces, through the white pillars and tall trees of this fabulous and ancient city... (*MQ* 21)

Martha keeps painting the golden city, her idealized four-gated city, in her imagination. She would keep all those people with "pettiness of vision and small understanding" out of the city, including her parents (*MQ* 21). The young Martha is deeply tortured by this aspiration for her promised land, "dreaming of a large city (it did not matter which, for it shared features of London and New York and Paris, and even the Moscow of the great novelists) where people who were not at all false and cynical and disparaging, like the men she had met that afternoon, or fussy and aggressive, like the women—where people altogether generous and warm exchanged generous emotions" (*MQ* 130). She shows her envy for the citizens of Europe who, different from those around her in the small town, enjoy the "freedom of the big cities" (*MQ* 123). Caged behind the desk of a legal office, she feels that "melancholy and envy fused into a bitter, frustrated sadness" (*MQ* 123).

This, however, is just one side of the coin. In addition to Martha's daydreaming about her golden city, there are depictions of the beautiful scenes of the Africa veld:

For it was evening, and very beautiful; a rich watery gold was lighting the dark greens of the foliage, the dark red of the soil, the pale blond of the grass, to the solemn intensity of the sunset hour. She noted a single white-stemmed tree with its light loud of glinting leaf rising abruptly from the solid-packed red earth of an anthill, all bathed in a magical sky-reflecting light, and her heart moved painfully, in exquisite sadness (*MQ* 61).

Here, Lessing uses a series of adjectives for the scenes of a sunset hour, a picture that vividly depicts Martha's love for the land. As a result of this love for both Africa and London, Martha finds herself lost in nameless nostalgia: "She sat there all day, and felt the waves of heat and perfume break across her in shock after shock of shuddering nostalgia. But nostalgia for what? She sat and sniffed painfully at the weighted air, as if it were dealing her blows like an invisible enemy" (*MQ* 32).

The nostalgia of Quest—or the young Lessing—turns out to be bi-directional, and it was not until Lessing had the chance to go back to London in 1949 that her passion for that city somewhat abated: "It was so gray and lightless and grim and unpainted and bombed. It took a lot of getting used to" (Dean 88). She realizes that she has to look at this city and cope with the life there in a different way. Disappointed by London, she feels homesick again for Africa, expressing her preference for the "colorful people" in that wild landscape in a 1964 interview:

People who might be extremely ordinary in a society like England's, where people are pressed into conformity, can become wild eccentrics in all kinds of ways they wouldn't dare try elsewhere. This is one of the things I miss, of course, by living in England. I don't think my memory deceives me, but I think there were more colorful people back in Southern Rhodesia because of the space they had to move in (Newquist & Lessing 3).

Compared with the African people, Londoners are "extremely ordinary" and lack distinct personalities. Initially a dreamland for the young Lessing during her time in Africa—a paradise for a writer like her for its "peace", quietness, and rights to privacy—London now turns out to be a dull place without excitement and liveliness. Lessing once complained that "England is a backwater, and it doesn't make much difference what happens here, or what decisions are made here" (Newquist & Lessing 4). In contrast, Africa produces strong personalities and rich varieties of humanity.

In one of her autobiographies, *Walking in the Shade*, Lessing discusses her unhappy experiences during her early years in London and the extent to which she is "dismayed" at the time, complaining that "the inhabitants of a city cannot share a newcomer's apprehension of it" (*WS* 163). She describes her fear for the future, tolerance of current disappointment and struggle for survival in this enormous place, which is "a conglomeration of villages" (*WS* 164). As a newcomer to London, she feels depressed by its cold exclusion. In Africa, she reiterates, there is "plenty of room for everyone's eccentricities to blossom", but in London, you can only "find people being eccentric behind closed doors. You get to know them, then you find these marvelous maniacs living their quiet, mad lives, but it's not out in the open at all" (Dean & Lessing 88). In contrast to her disappointment with London, Lessing writes, "I miss the Africans so much; they're such beautiful people. They've got this marvelous grace and good humor and charm, and I miss it" (Dean & Lessing 88). Naturally, her travel narratives during this period are mostly about her nostalgia for Africa. It is not until the 1990s, being a well-established Londoner by then, that Lessing finds herself truly in love with the city.

As time transpires, Lessing's nostalgic feelings keep switching between these two lands. Aspiration and disillusionment are the two words that best characterize her feelings for them. Fundamentally an exiled Londoner, she cares most about the big city in which she has spent most of her life, and keeps looking back on and revising her understanding of metropolitans in her fictional writing, autobiographies, critical essays, and interviews. In *WS*, for example, she describes what London looked like upon her first arrival there:

… when I was newly in London I was returned to a child's way of seeing and feeling, every person, building, bus, street, striking my senses with the shocking immediacy of a child's life, everything oversized, very bright, very dark, smelly, noisy. I do not experience London like that now. That was a city of Dickensian exaggeration. I am not saying I saw London through a veil of Dickens, but rather that I was sharing the grotesque vision of Dickens, on the verge of the surreal (*WS* 4).

Here, words such as "oversized", "exaggeration", "grotesque" and "surreal" are used to describe her impression at the time. Perhaps her sense of London as an "exaggeration" results partly from her idealized view of the city during her years of exile in Africa, for she makes the following comment in the same book:

Colonials, the children or grandchildren of the far-flung Empire, arrived in England with expectations created by literature. 'We will find the England of Shelley and Keats and Hopkins, of Dickens and Hardy and the Brontes and Jane Austen, we will breathe the generous airs of literature. We have been sustained *in* exile by the generous airs of literature. We have been sustained in exile by the magnificence of the Word, and soon we will walk into our promised land' (*WS* 22).

According to Lessing, the exiled colonials, on their return to England, will find in their "promised land" a land of despair, for they have been deceived by those great writers and their words. Lessing's mother is a case in point. Her early dreams about London and her real living status in London thirty years later turn out to be a cruel story typical of most white colonials. When she does return to London, she can only afford to live in "a dreary little house, looking after yet another old man, who was not even her relative but my father's" (*WS* 142). Like her mother, when Lessing finally has the opportunity to live in her imagined paradise, she gradually realizes that it is not the city she expected it to be. Still, Lessing tries to discover its merits, as well as those of England in general, despite all of her disappointments with it:

You see, I was brought up in a country where there is very heavy pressure put on people. In Southern Rhodesia it is not possible to detach yourself from what is going on. This means that you spend all your time in a torment of conscientiousness. In England—I'm not saying it's a perfect society, far from it—you can get on with your work in peace and quiet when you choose to withdraw. For this I'm very grateful—I imagine there are few countries left in the world where you have this right of privacy (*ASPV* 48).

Compared with South Africa, England allows her to "detach" herself from what is going on outside and to enjoy privacy, two things that are extremely important to her a as writer. Naturally, Lessing the writer prefers to live in such a place rather than in Southern Rhodesia, where there is a "heavy pressure on people". This may partly explains why she later becomes a fervent lover of London, drawing so many breathtaking sketches of the city in *London Observed*.

Apart from these complicated feelings toward London, Lessing is also deeply concerned with the fate of both the colonized blacks and the colonizing whites, thanks to her early experience in Africa. Therefore, colonialism becomes the second significant topic in her travel narratives and one of the inevitable labels for her writing. She cares about the history, development, and future of this land and frequently reflects upon African issues in her works, even long after moving back to London. Among her major works, *GS* is the most significant narrative about colonialism, but *GN* draws heavily from her experience in colonial Africa as well, as written into Anna's dream. Readers also encounter this topic in her short stories, memoirs, and journals.

While Lessing tends to speak for the African people against colonialism, in her semi-autobiographical writing, written comments, and interviews, including *In Pursuit of English* and *A Small Personal Voice*, most of the time, she holds a white-focused perspective, as in the case of *GS*. Moses, the only black hero in *GS*, does not get enough attention he deserves as a hero but, rather, serves primarily as a human background to the life and struggles of the white colonizers[1]. The seemingly realistic reproduction of black people and

---

1 Lessing's white-focused perspective in *GS* and her self-defense in this respect has been addressed in the third part of Chapter One, entitled "Mixed perspectives in *The Diaries of Jane Somers*, *The Grass Is Singing* and *The Golden Notebook*".

their lives usually turn out to be a story about the self-discovery and struggle of the whites. As one critic comments, "Africans in her work are instrumental to self-discovery in her white characters" (Thorpe ix).

In order to understand Lessing's duality around the issue of colonialism, which adds up to ambiguity and ultimately hybridity in her narration, it is best to "hear" more of what she has to say about the matter: "It is a nostalgia, a hunger, a reaching out for something lost; hard to define but instantly recognizable... All white-African literature is the literature of exile: not from Europe, but from Africa" (as cited in Taylor's preface). Lessing regards herself as one of the white exiles from Africa instead of England. Meanwhile, she cannot erase from herself the inscription of London and keeps aspiring for the life back to this idealized metropolitan during her more than twenty years' stay in Africa. Although she manages to return to London as early as in her twenties and lives there until her last day, it takes her decades to obtain the sense of belonging. Due to this multi-valiant identity and sense of belong-to-nowhere, Lessing sometimes writes in a self-contradictory manner, a fact of which she herself may not have been fully aware.

First of all, no matter how hard she tries to show her understanding of and involvement in African life, she is in essence an exile from white culture. As Michael Thorpe points out in *Doris Lessing's Africa*, "one limit upon her own awareness Lessing scrupulously observes: very rarely does she write from a wholly black viewpoint" (Thorpe 27). Thorpe claims that although a well-intentioned white writer who cares much about colonial issues, Lessing can hardly reproduce the lives of the black inhabitants in her story in an unbiased way, a task that is challenging enough even for black writers who may as well get impeded somewhat in their perspectives[1].

Unwilling to admit as she is, Lessing sometimes unconsciously speaks

---

1　As for the question of representation and misrepresentation of the black people, American literary critic bell hooks holds that it is impossible for the white to present a faithful image of the black. What makes the situation more complicated is that even the black people themselves can hardly reproduce their own image in the right manner if they fall unfortunately victims of the internalized racism.

in the voice of the white colonizer of London instead of the native black underprivileged in the African veld, as in the case of *GS*. This unexpected misrepresentation in the "voice" issue occurs more frequently during the earlier period of her writing when she firmly believes in the authorial power and moral obligation of the writer. She does not hesitate to overtly advocate for and defend those beliefs, a strategy which partly accounts for the criticism on her didacticism. But as time goes on, she becomes more mature and realizes that the hidden author more easily gains trust from the reader. By taking the advantage of an outside-insider and by providing the reader with diversified voices, Lessing gradually gains the fame of a significant African writer rather than the spokesman for the white as she was criticized earlier:

> Her position within both mainstream and marginal British cultural formations was, as has been seen, primarily as a colonial writer, revitalizing, and contributing to, an already dominant set of realist literary conventions: 'Africa' signifying the exotic and the marvelous—a legitimate otherness (Taylor 17).

As Taylor points out, being a "mainstream and marginal British" writer, Lessing is able to perceive Africa from either the perspective of the British white or the colonizing white. Therefore, she achieves "a legitimate otherness", a new identity emerging from her observations of Africa both at a distance and through her intimate relations with it, an identity which plays a key role in her contribution to post-colonial understandings of the African issue as manifested in her travel narratives.

In addition to her writing about Africa and London, there is another kind of narrative that falls into the group of travel narrative: the narrative about the self-made exile "escaping" from the current environment. Due to various kinds of imprisonment caused by patriarchal society, arbitrary parents, disloyal husbands, or restricting socio-political convictions, most of the characters in Lessing's novels try to survive by running away. For example, the Turners in *GS* distance themselves from both the black and white community. Therefore,

Lessing writes, "People spoke of the Turners in the hard, careless voices reserved for misfits, outlaws and the self-exiled" (*GS* 2); Martha Quest wants to move to town to escape from her mother and the tedious country life; the unnamed narrator in *The Memoirs of a Survivor*, together with a twelve-year-old girl and a dog named Hugo, escapes to a flat after a disaster and sees, behind the wall in her flat, a world of the past of which she tries to rid herself.

Almost all the characters in Lessing's work are confronted with the choice between running away and staying on, especially her women who are doubly-oppressed in the patriarchal society. Kate Brown, heroine of *The Summer Before the Dark,* is one typical example. Having devoted herself to family life for almost a quarter of a century, taking care of her three children and her husband, Kate discovers that she is no longer needed by the grown-up children and her husband who has had many extra-marital affairs. Meanwhile, there is the coming threat of her old age and death. Driven by all the confusion, disappointment, and uncertainty, she sets out on a journey of self-discovery one summer, at the end of which she comes to realize the most appropriate thing for her to do and the way to reform her life. Her story, which starts with escaping and ends in an epiphany on-the-road, is a typical example of travel narrative in the sense that a spiritual growth is accompanied, or to be more specific, brought about by a certain sort of on-the-way journey.

Another heroine, Susan Rawling, in "To Room Nineteen", one of Lessing's best known short stories, is trapped in the same predicament. Like Kate Brown, a well-off middle-aged woman, Rawling has been long confined to family life, with four children and husband as the center. Unlike Kate Brown, however, upon knowing her husband's extra-marital affairs, Rawling gradually loses her sanity and finally commits suicide in a hotel room. Having been exiled by society for most of her life and then betrayed by her husband, Rawling cannot recover from the alienation and the hurt enforced on her by a world that ignores her pleas for help. Her journey of self-discovery ends in tragedy.

If the exploration of self by Kate Brown and Susan Rawling are passive, Lessing's lifelong effort to rid herself of her mother's control is, on the contrary, a narrative of more positive exile. Among various forms of imprisonment, the unhappy daughter-mother relationship is one that she keeps fighting against since she is in her teens. Lessing integrates into writing her personal experiences of escaping and struggle for independence, making them a part of the travel narrative. Unwilling to live under the pressure of her mother, Lessing the daughter is forever seeking a way out, declaring that a "powerful" mother is a common phenomenon in her time so that "everyone without exception fought a battle against a mother, who also was a victim, of course, because they're very pathetic people" (Bertelsen "Acknowledging a New Frontier" 136). Having realized that both mother and children fall victim to this unhappy experience, Lessing makes the tense child-parent relationship a crucial topic in her works. The following paragraph in *Love, again*, for instance, shows how Lessing reproduces her unhappy mother-daughter experience through her character. One day Sarah is watching a little girl maltreated by her mother whose attention is all on the baby boy. To gain her mother's attention, the little girl tries her best to "behave" well. Sarah is unhappy while watching this scene and she says to the little girl silently:

Hold on, hold on. Quite soon a door will slam shut inside you because what you are feeling is unendurable. The door will stand there shut all your life: if you are lucky it will never open, and you'll not ever know about the landscape you inhabited—for how long? But child time is not adult time, You are living in an eternity of loneliness and grief, and it is truly a hell, because the point of hell is that there is no hope. You don't know that the door will slam shut, you believe that this is what life is and must be: you will always be disliked, and you will have to watch her love that little creature you love so much because you think that if you love what she loves, she will love you. But one day you'll know it doesn't matter what you do and how hard you try, it is no use. And at that moment the door will slam and you will be free (*LA* 346–347).

This silent address speaks out Lessing's own thoughts. Throughout her childhood and adolescence, she has been tortured by "loneliness" and "grief" due to her parents' indifference to her. No matter how hard she tries to win her parent's love, their attention is always on the younger children in the family, in Lessing's case, her younger brother. Her mother has suffered a lot from her own disillusion with the hard life in Africa and indulged in the dreams of going back to London. Besides, being a manipulating mother and ill-tempered in nature, she wants her daughter to be obedient. But Lessing cannot put up with her mother any longer as she grows up. Feeling pressurized and unhappy, the 14-year-old Lessing quits school on the excuse of eye illness and moves to town by herself, making a living as a typist. This escape from the "hell" of her family, in particular, from the control of her mother, turns a new leaf in her life and is the first experience in her life-long struggle against authority and search for independence.

Along with Sarah in this story who shares part of Lessing's unhappy adolescent experience, Lessing has quite a few spokeswomen in other stories who relate their exile experience, especially Martha Quest. At the beginning of *MQ*, an adolescent Martha overhears her parents chatting with their neighbors and feels extremely annoyed, for she dislikes their mediocrity and arbitrariness: "… the irritation overflowed into a flood of dislike for both her parents. Everything was the same; intolerable that they should have been saying the same things ever since she could remember; and she looked away from them, over the veld" (*MQ* 12). Irritated, she can hardly concentrate on her book: "Perhaps she was so resentful of her surroundings and her parents that the resentment overflowed into everything near her" (*MQ* 13). Her hatred for her mother is so strong that she loses control of herself and says to her, "You are loathsome, bargaining and calculating and… You are disgusting" (*MQ* 171).

As time goes on, Martha's hatred for her parents accumulates and she feels imprisoned. She wants to run away from their pettiness, to "leave her parents who destroyed her" (*MQ* 80). At last, she leaves for town to work as a secretary and feels relieved: "And a door had closed finally; and behind it was the farm, and the girl who had been created by it. It no longer concerned her. Finished. She could forget it. She was a new person, and an extraordinary, magnificent, and altogether *new* life was beginning" (Lessing *CV* 90, italics original). Thus ends *MQ,* the first volume of *Children of Violence.* Series. Young Martha chooses to run away from the African farm and her parents to pursue her idealized city life. The future is unknown for the young Martha, yet the self-exiled girl chooses her road.

To conclude, the travel narrative in Lessing's writing mainly deals with the Africa and London issues, colonialism, and the spiritual journey of various types of exile, all of which contribute to Lessing's hybridity of subject matters. Similar to the diversified narrators, voices and perspectives, this hybridity brings to light mixed experiences from different groups of people and the construction of a heteroglossia text. By resorting to travel narrative which is concerned about the change of place and the transformed status thereafter, Lessing in fact manages to direct people's attention to the identity issue, to the resistance against imprisonment and bondage, which is the fundamental mission as well as the core essence of hybridity.

No wonder Lessing is one of those who are labeled as "By Europe, out of Africa"[1]. They live on the veld of Africa and try to write about their experience there, partly realistic, partly imaginative. Since their feeling towards this land is mixed, their description of the land can hardly be steady. That's why Lessing's travel narrative centering on her experiences in these two different parts of the

---

1 "By Europe, out of Africa" is taken from the title of the doctoral dissertation written by Simon Keith Lewis. The complete title is "By Europe, out of Africa: White women writers on farms and their African invention" (1996). In this dissertation, the author makes a comparative study between Olive Schreiner, Nadine Gordimer, Karen Blixen, Elspeth Huxley and Doris Lessing, focusing on the cultural role of these white women writers on African farms. Later, "Out of Africa" is also quoted by A. S. Byatt as the title of her review on Lessing's second auto-biography *Under My Skin: Volume One of My Autobiography to 1949.* In this essay, Byattt argues that "Lessing is a white writer growing out of Africa who has great concern for the crowds, groups and 'human nature'" (Byatee 16). Like her fictional works, her autobiography is a platform for her to explore into the universality based on her African experience. Her identity as a white writer growing "out of Africa" does not limit her writing to the provincial subjects, but rather, it is one of the subject matters she finds at hand in her presentation of an overall picture of humanity.

world demonstrates a complicated feeling, neither pure white nor anti-white, thus quite supportive in disclosing her hybridity.

Female Narrative

It is believed that Bakhtin never consciously approaches feminist issues in his study of dialogism. More than that, he is even blamed by some for his "glaring omission of any mention of feminist" (Heikinen 114). Nevertheless, he does have a place for feminist studies "for its ability to provide a platform for marginalized feminine voices to be heard above the din of the monologic, authoritative, and hegemonic voice" (Heikinen 114). Lessing is such a case in point.

In a 1966 interview, Lessing expresses her disappointment with the misreading of GN and regards it as a failure, "for if it had been a success, then people wouldn't get so damned emotional when I didn't want them to be... What I wanted was to stand back and look..." (Howe 426). Lessing seems agonized by the public response to this novel, which goes astray from her expectations. She tries to write in a detached manner, hoping that the reader will calmly observe and reflect on what she is writing from a female point of view, but it turns out that most readers put this novel under the category of feminism, even claiming it to be "a kind of banner" for feminism (Howe 426). Lessing can hardly accept such a response, for thus interpreted, "the book was instantly belittled, by friendly reviewers as well as by hostile ones, as being about the sex war, or was claimed by women as a useful weapon in the sex war" (GN 8).

Lessing's protest against this feministic approach to her writing finds support in Elaine Showalter's interpretation of women's writing. Lessing is, as defined by Elaine Showalter, a female writer whose work tries to write from female experience and speak in her own voice. Showalter regards women's writing as the "product of a subculture" (Showalter vii), like other literary subcultures including "the black, Jewish, Canadian, Anglo-Indian, or even American" (Showalter 13) which normally have to move through "phases of subordination, protest and autonomy" (Showalter xiv)[1]. Therefore, she divides women's writing into three stages of development: Feminine, Feminist and Female, each with distinctive features, focuses and representative female writers:

> I identify the Feminine phase as the period from the appearance of the male pseudonym in the 1940s to the death of George Eliot in 1880; the Feminist phase as 1880 to 1920, or the winning of the vote; and the Female phase as 1920 to the present, but entering a new stage of self-awareness about 1960 (Showalter 13).

Generally speaking, the first two groups of Feminine and Feminist writers such as Jane Austen, Charlotte Bronte, George Eliot, and Mrs. Gaskell tend to make compromises with a male-dominated world in which women writers have limited audience. George Eliot, for instance, has to use a man-like penname for better acceptance. Encourage by the progress made in the feminist movement, the success of the suffragist movement in 1920 in the US for instance, female writers began to "believe that they had a moral right to assume leadership" (Showalter 186) rather than put the leadership in the hand of the other sex. As Showalter argues, women's writing, which starts from imitation and protest and gradually finds her own voice in the mainstream culture, has become an indispensible part of the heteroglossia of various subcultures. It turns out that female writers can take the lead as they once aspired for in the 1920s, a fact manifested in Virginia Woolf and Doris Lessing, the former a pioneer in modernistic writing and the latter an avant-garde adept in both realistic and

---

1 Showalter points out that the emergence of a new subculture usually undergoes the following three phases: "First, there is a prolonged phase of *imitation* of the prevailing modes of the dominant tradition, and *internalization* of its standards of art and its views on social roles. Second, there is a phase of *protest* against these standards and values, and advocacy of minority rights and values, including a demand for autonomy. Finally, there is a phase of *self-discovery*, a turning inward freed from some of the dependency of opposition, a search for identity" (Showalter 13, italics original). For detailed discussion on this topic, see Showalter 3–36.

modernistic techniques.

Believing that "after all deep problems very often are expressed through sex" (Howe 426), and that most of the male writers are "anti-women" (Howe 426) in the sense that their portrayals of women can hardly be faithful, Lessing finds it necessary to join hands with her predecessors and contemporaries. But it should be noticed that although she claims to have written from a female point of view, her perspective, hybridized in nature, turns out to be constantly interfered with by her internalized patriarchal perspective, as has been mentioned in the case of GN^1, and more evidence can be found in her depiction of the New Women, male-female relations, and the balance between happiness and independence in marriage and career.

In addition to the views she shares with Mary Wollstonecraft, Lessing aligns herself with the feminist concepts held by Luce Irigary, Julia Kristeva, Virginia Woolf, and bell hooks. Being a marginalized female writer, Lessing regards writing as a weapon against dominant male discourse and believes in the revolutionary power of the feminist discourse, a stance echoing that of Luce Irigary and Julia Kristeva. Irigary puts forward the idea of "parler-femme" and argues that the presence of the female "has to be defined with a different discourse, a discourse of difference, since female is characterized by difference, diffusion, plurality, and multiplicity, logically and biologically" (Zhu Gang 231). Similarly, Julia Kristeva believes in a 'revolutionary' form of writing. For her, language is not only a "representation", but also "a material practice which can support political revolution": "There is a specific practice of writing that is itself 'revolutionary,' analogous to sexual and political transformation, and that by its very existence testifies to the possibility of transforming the symbolic order of orthodox society from the inside" (Zhu Gang 235). That is to say, the abandonment of the prevailing writing paradigm and the negation of rational discourse give rise to a sort of conversion from the inside. This stand coincides with that of Lessing, who holds that being marginalized means being able to

---

1 For detailed discussion on this point, see the third part of Chapter One entitled "Mixed perspectives in *The Diaries of Jane Somers*, *The Grass Is Singing* and *The Golden Notebook*".

obtain the space of resistance, being endowed with a view of both the inside and outside, and hence capable of subversion from within.

For Lessing, telling about female experience which is an indispensible part of the human experience goes beyond the limit of feminist issues, a stand shared by Virginia Woolf. Like Lessing, Woolf who chooses to write about female experience doubts the power of the feminist movement in the process of social transformation. She believes that "it is fatal for anyone who writes to think of their sex. It is fatal to be a man or woman pure and simple; one must be woman-manly or man-womanly... Some collaboration has to take place in the mind between the woman and man before the act of creation can be accomplished" (Woolf 2208–2209). Woolf's androgynous perspective of writing to a large extent coincides with the major concern of Lessing.

Lessing is also regarded as an African writer due to the attention she has paid to African issues. Her depictions of black women and her views in this regard correspond with bell hooks who is extremely concerned about the articulation of black women and its constructive power in their fight against various kinds of oppression. Like Wollstonecraft, bell hooks believes in the importance of articulation for women, especially that of black women. Believing in the constructive power of women's voices, hooks argues: "Radical/ revolutionary feminist thought and practice must emerge as a force in popular culture if we are to counter in a constructive way... This means that we must work harder to gain a hearing" (hooks *Outlaw Culture* 105). hooks seems to agree with Showalter on the point that female voice should "emerge as a force" so that it will become part of the dominating culture by taking the identity of a subculture, which is expected to become more initiative and active as it accumulated more energy. Being confident in the constructive power of female voice, hooks declares that feminism is "a movement to end sexism, sexist exploitation and oppression" (hooks *Outlaw Culture* viii). In contrast to hooks, Lessing holds that, compared with the objective of changing the world, "the aims of Women's Liberation will look very small and quaint" (*GN* 9). What's more, Lessing doubts the consistency of dogmatic beliefs, saying, "I am so sure that everything we now take for granted is going to be utterly swept away in the next decade" (*GN* 9). So is the mainstream feministic doctrine. Lessing, though eager to stand clear of feminism, corresponds with hooks on the point that it is the obligation of the female writers to let their own voice "gain a hearing" (hooks *Outlaw Culture* 105).

How unhappy she is about being labeled as a feminist writer, Lessing nevertheless is a steadfast supporter of women, "for the last thing I have wanted to do was to refuse to support women" (*GN* 8). For her, there is a difference between supporting women and supporting feminism. Taking *GN* for example, the book, Lessing admits in her preface, does tell about "many female emotions of aggression, hostility, resentment" (*GN* 6), but it has nothing to do with feminism, nor should it be viewed as a weapon in the sex war as acclaimed by both the friendly and hostile readings. *GN*, Lessing declares, is a window open to the female world perceived through a female perspective. There are girls in pursuit of freedom in the metropolis like Martha Quest, and middle-aged women struggling against the pressure from family like Kate Brown in *SBD* and sixty-five-year-old woman Sarah Durham in *LA*. In *DJS*, several aged women hold different attitude towards the outside world and the younger generation.

However, Lessing finds it hard to deliver the female voice as she has expected. Generally speaking, in the 1950s and 1960s, Lessing, sometimes unconsciously, regarded males as an inseparable part of, or even dominating force, in women's lives and women's happiness as lying in their successful relationships with men, such as in marriage. This understanding of women as dependent on men may easily turn women into victims of patriarchal society, according to bell hooks, not only because of male domination, but also because of women's own internalized sexism to evaluate themselves from the patriarchal perspective. Lessing seems to have been affected by this internalized patriarchal perspective, a weakness that has been discussed in Chapter One.

Lessing is blamed by some for her alienation "from the authentic female perspective" (qtd. in Showalter 311). But she has spared no efforts at presenting a female perspective. Later, in the 1980s, Lessing revised her view on male-female relations, a change in attitude for the idea that marriage is not inseparable from women's life if it only gives rise to male-domination. She takes the heroines in *Shikasta* (1979), the first volume of her *Canopus in Argos: Archives* series, as an example and argues that these women, though put in a subordinate position in society, "provide a quality without which the whole thing wouldn't exist" (Bikman & Lessing 58). She hopes to convince the reader of the fact that women are powerful even in a patriarchal society, for they try to redefine their relations with men and become immune to male's influence out of their own will.

To prove Lessing's unsteady perspective in handling female issues, a closer look at her female narratives is needed, among which the story of *LA* has a unique appeal, for it is about the love affairs of an old woman in her sixties. Through it, Lessing shows her concern for aged females, their love, their sex, and their relations with men. The heroine, Sarah, is working on a play based on the journals of Julie Vairon, a French beauty who has several unsuccessful love affairs and then commits suicide. During her preparation for the play, Sarah gets involved in several relationships with men of different ages: the twenty-eight-year-old actor Bill, the thirty-five-year-old American director Henry, an actor named Andrew, and the sponsor of her play, Stephen, a well-off middle-aged man. Sarah feels tortured by her love for and from these younger men for she believes that it is only in one's youth that one is "in a privileged class sexually" (Lessing *SBD* 141) while older people are deprived of the right of loving and being loved. Sarah's love story becomes Lessing's feminist narrative, one that helps her to probe into the world of the elderly, a marginalized group that deserves more attention in face of an aging society. Lessing's particular interest in this group of women and her keen observation of them, as depicted from the perspective of the "experiencing" and "retrospective" Lessing, add up to the inclusiveness of her writing in terms of perspective and subject matters, a contribution to her hybridity.

Lessing shows her concern for the middle-aged women in *SBD*, for instance the middle-aged crisis of Kate Brown. Having spent about twenty years bringing up her children and taking care of her husband, Kate, for the first time in her life, comes to realize that it has been "the characteristic of her life—passivity, adaptability to others" (Lessing *SBD* 22) and that she is no longer wanted as before. She is also tortured by the horror of getting old, so that one day, while walking in the street, she comes to an epiphany that in contrast to those "young, confident, courageous" (*SBD* 104) girls, a middle-aged woman can only be characterized by "caution" and "suspicion" instead of "confidence" (Lessing *SBD* 103–104).

In order to rid herself of this middle-age crisis, Kate decides to make some changes and accepts a temporary job as a simultaneous interpreter. To her surprise, she is appreciated and welcomed by her boss and new friends, which sets her free physically and spiritually as well as economically. Being successful in career, Kate becomes increasingly doubtful about her former choice of confining herself to family life. She wants to make breakthroughs, for instance, a change in her dress style, or a journey with one of her admirers. At the end of the story, the 45-year-old Kate, no longer needed as mother and wife, survives the crisis and finds a new life, just as she silently tells herself while watching a play, "One last effort and I shall be free. Freedom and peace, how I have longed for you both…" (Lessing *SBD* 176).

Kate, together with Anna and Molly, are middle-aged women who try to live independent lives after having fulfilled their responsibilities in family life. Apart from these women, who manage to survive their middle-age crisis, there is Martha Quest, a young girl who endeavors to pull through her own crisis. All of these female figures, coming from different age groups and with diverse identities, make Lessing's female stories a diversified narrative. What's more, the mixed feelings, especially that of the female, inform the reader of the social and life experience told by women themselves as supplementing or revising the existing presentation of the female.

As praised by Elaine Showalter, Lessing's dedication towards female issues with an intentional female-centered perspective contributes to subverting the conventional perception of women and female writers. Lessing, together with other writing women with the same spirit of resistance, works hard to do "the self-exploration, self-discovery and a search for a specifically female identity" (Showalter 369). By making their voice heard and by integrating into the mainstream culture the female text which turns out to be hybridized in terms of themes, styles, genres, images, and subject matters, female writers have won themselves a rising fame in a patriarchal culture. What's more important is that, as noticed by Showalter, Lessing and several of her contemporary female writers including Iris Murdoch, Muriel Spark, Margaret Drabble, A.S. Byattt and Beryl Bainbridge, not only inherit from the tradition of literary production, but also are innovative and conscientious in presenting female experience through new artistic visions. Therefore, they "have been able to incorporate many of the strengths of the past with a new range of language and experience" (Showalter 35). It is in this sense that Lessing's female narrative plays a part in her construction of a multi-voiced text, a text which protests against the male-dominated literary mainstream discourse.

Lessing is not sure about her own position in this fight against suppression. Even when she declares herself to be an anti-colonist, she can hardly stand with the colonized all the time. Similarly, no matter how conscientiously she strives to be an independent woman and acts as such a woman, she may not be innocent of any form of prejudice or she can speak out without being impeded by her own stand or judgment. Ambiguity and uncertainty may result in complexity and multiplicity, yet for Lessing this is a truer representation of life, especially women's life, including that of her won.

2.4 Difference and Sameness in a Simultaneity: Lessing, Forster, Woolf, Fanon, and Hooks

According to Bakhtin's dialogic principle, there will be "no mere diversity of voices but an exchange of utterances and a viewing of each of these utterances from the perspective of the others" (Zappen 41). In Lessing's case, either to assimilate or to revise, she keeps making adaptations to her own way of writing by making self-reflection as well as keeping a close eye on other people's writing and philosophy. There are exchanges of views or "utterances" among Lessing and other writers and theorists, and at the same time, exchanges between the retrospective Lessing and the experiencing Lessing. Her discourse therefore turns out to be a dynamic one full of retrospection and silent talks with others and with herself.

The interaction of individual writing experience helps to achieve the goal of representing the collective experience of humanity from a diversified perspective, a representation that is presumably more objective and all-embracing. Speaking each in a unique voice, Lessing and her contemporary writers and theorists assert their subjectivities on the one hand, and on the other hand join hands in literary experimentation in the sense that they each set models for later writers ideologically, culturally or technically, for "individual voices can take shape and character in response to and in anticipation of other voices" (Atkins & Morrow 214). As for Lessing, her discourse, by responding to, echoing with or contesting against the discourses of other remarkable writers and theorists, manages to accomplish the task of writing with dialogic effect. To understand Lessing in terms of the above mentioned heteroglossia, the author of this book tries to conduct a comparative study between Lessing, E. M. Forster, Virginia Woolf, Frantz Fanon and bell hooks, the chosen writers Lessing claims to be her favorites or tries to identify with, and theorists whose thoughts she is unconsciously indebted to.

Lessing is a skillful experimentalist, capable of handling different modes of writing. Some critics regard her as a self-made writer, denying any outside influence on her and putting her into a different category from such writers as Virginia Woolf:

> Nothing was given, little inherited. An English novelist like Virginia Woolf, when she began writing, did so with an inevitable consciousness of those—George Eliot, the Brontes, Jane Austen—who had gone before and wrestled with the same language, the same society, the same landscapes. If Doris Lessing has no such bearings to steer by, nor was she overshadowed by her predecessors. It could be 'her' Africa (Thorpe 4).

This view, however, does not hold up. Although Lessing has little formal education and claims to be an outsider to the dominant culture, she benefits from reading great European, American, and Russian writers. In her autobiography *Under My Skin: Volume One of My Autobiography, to 1949*, she writes that, during her earliest years in Africa, she was deeply absorbed in reading the books her mother purchased from far-away London, and she enjoyed the whole house of classical writings. Reading is a habit she formed in childhood and keeps all her life. Her list of favorite writers consists of both the realists of the 19th century and the modernists of the 20th century. Lessing cultivates in herself an ability to learn from these writers and play with different narrative skills.

No matter how squarely Lessing and her critics align her with the marginalized writers and intellectuals, she in fact belongs to the mainstream intellectuals in the postcolonial context. The similarities and differences between Lessing and Forster, Woolf, Franz Fanon, and bell hooks indicate that though she takes a marginalized position and claims to observe from an outsider-insider perspective, Lessing is a highly qualified mainstream writer and intellectual of her time who has the expertise to write for the benefit of her readers.

E. M. Forster

Lessing shares some viewpoints with E. M. Forster; for example, both of them believe that the relationship between the author, the text, and the reader should be an interactive one. They also agree that it would not be a good thing if "the face of the author draws rather too near to that of the reader" (Forster 33–34). Both speak highly of the 19th century realists and criticize the so-called "provincialism" in British literature. Like Lessing, Forster criticizes the provincialism as demonstrated by the "fake" social scene and uses Meredith as one particular example to show that it is his "home counties posing as the universe" that makes him "now lie in the trough" (Forster 90). Forster argues that narrowness in scope is responsible for Meredith's comparatively low status in British literature, a weakness that Lessing always blames some of the British writers for.

Lessing elaborates on the above subjects in her first collection of literary criticism *A Small Personal Voice*, which was published 29 years after Forster's *Aspects of the Novel* (1927). It is hard to know for sure whether the parallels are coincidental or stem from conscious borrowing, for Lessing never overtly states her admiration for Forster. Since Lessing reads Forster's criticism in her youth, she may have been influenced by him.

As for the author-text-reader relationships, both Forster and Lessing regard it as necessary for an author to remain distant from the text and the reader, so that there will be more room left for the latter two to act on their initiatives. Forster holds that it is unwise for the author to always assume a transcending gesture or to present himself as an omniscient narrator who knows everything about the character or the story all the time. Instead, shifting the point of view once in a while is a more effective way for the text to speak for itself. Sometimes, the author may find it more advantageous to place himself in the position of one of the characters, so as to offer an apparently impartial observation, which may probably win more trust in the reader. Other times, he may choose to take the position of a pure observer who knows nothing about the inner activities of the character, so that the task of telling or showing is given to the character and the text. For Forster, being omniscient or manipulative is not the author's only choice: "Instead of standing above his work and controlling it, cannot the novelist throw himself into it and be carried along to some goal that he does not foresee?" (Forster 95) Forster believes that as long as the writing begins, it is better to let the story move on by itself while the author "should not try to subdue any longer, they should hope to be subdued, to be carried away... All that is prearranged is false" (Forster 98–99). Forster, on the one hand, suggests that the author should be wise enough to know how to make his presence felt in the story, to make his authorial intrusion in various disguises; on the other hand, he has more confidence in the self-expressiveness of the text and the active role of the reader. Likewise, Lessing holds that whenever the writing begins, all the characters will grow up in their own way. Sometimes the development of the story and the characters may turn out to be out of the writer's control or expectation, which consequently calls for the author to hide his presence, a strategy best achieved with the help of diversified narrators or shifted perspective.

Forster argues that the relation between the reader and author cannot be defined as simply guiding and accepting, for the reader has his own initiative and power, and most of the time he "must sit down alone and struggle with the writer" (Forster 31). Lessing holds a similar view. To "struggle with" the author means that the reader must meditate on, doubt, or even question whatever the author says to him, to find out the true meaning behind various disguises, or to interpret the text without being manipulated by the author. There is always a dynamic relationship between the author and reader, since both of them may take an active role in the text and become more mature in the process of writing, reading, or "re-writing" the text. The author would become more experienced or uncertain during the process of writing, which means his views and judgments may change. As it will be discussed in Chapter Three under the subtitle of "Fluidity in Writing Philosophy", Lessing herself constantly revises her views and draws lessons from her own experience. By keeping a close eye on the outside world, she ensures that her writing could be characterized as inconsistent, fluid, ambiguous, changeable, and so on. Similarly, the reader may also become more mature in interpreting the text, which would make him more reluctant to blindly believe in whatever the author says. He will find the reading a much more pleasant journey if he continues struggling with the author. Leaving more room for the reader instead of relying on authorial intrusion makes the reading process a dynamic interaction, a win-win strategy for both.

Lessing and Forster also hold similar views on some of the key elements of a novel, such as time, space, and character. Generally speaking, modernist and postmodernist writers prefer to follow psychological time rather than physical time, and space is frequently used as a metaphor. Forster, though a well-acknowledged realistic writer who believes in time sequence as key to a story, shows his admiration for the modernist way of handling time:

> I am only trying to explain that as I lecture now I hear that clock ticking or do not hear it ticking, I retain or lose the time sense; whereas in a novel

there is always a clock. The author may dislike his clock. Emily Bronte in *Wuthering Heights* tried to hide hers. Sterne, in *Tristram Shandy*, turned his upside down. Marcel Proust, still more ingenious, kept altering the hands, so that his hero was at the same period entertaining a mistress to supper and playing ball with his nurse in the park. All these devices are legitimate, but none of them contravene our thesis: the basis of a novel is a story, and a story is a narrative of events arranged in time sequence (Forster 43).

Forster is not self-contradictory in this aspect. He holds that the sequence of time plays a crucial role, for "there is always a clock" in a novel. On the other hand, however, he appreciates the modernistic strategy in dealing with time, a strategy that is favored by both the realistic and modernistic authors. No matter how flexibly the time is presented in the story, there is no denying that a story is fundamentally "a narrative of events arranged in time sequence". Pretending not to hear the ticking of the clock does not mean that the author ignores the sense of time; instead, the sense may become heightened, and the story may turn out to be more complicated. This partly explains the complicity in Lessing's writing, who, as a fan and master of psychological time, deals with the time issue in a pro modernist and postmodernist manner in the so-called realistic novel *GS*[1].

In addition to time, both Lessing and Forster pay special attention to space. Forster speaks highly of those writers who have a sense of space in their writing, such as Tolstoy: "Very few have the sense of space, and the possession of it ranks high in Tolstoy's divine equipment. Space is the lord of *War and Peace,* not time" (Forster 50). He emphasizes that it is the artistic handling of space that makes Tolstoy stand out among novelists. It could be imagined that if Forster were born decades later and had had the chance to read Lessing, he

---

1 Lessing's handling of time in a mixed way boasting both modernistic and realistic features in *GS* has been discussed in detail in the first part of Chapter Two, entitled "From realism to post-modernism: *The Grass Is Singing* and *The Summer Before the Dark*".

might have put Lessing into the category of writers with a sense of space, for Lessing is notable for her artistic handling of space in her writing.

Lessing shares many views with Forster, but she disagrees with him on one thing: the moral obligation in a novel. Lessing believes that a writer should be burdened with moral responsibility, either overtly or covertly, and consequently a good literary work could not be an amoral one. On the contrary, Forster argues that the story "is neither moral nor is it favourable to the understanding of the novel in its other aspects" (Forster 51). Perhaps what Forster cares about more is the novel itself, while Lessing prefers to use it as an intellectual instrument against domination and imprisonment.

Virginia Woolf

In recent Lessing study, more comparative research has been conducted on Lessing and other writers, with Virginia Woolf frequently mentioned as such a case. One of the reasons is that the two share many similarities, including motifs of nostalgia and the idealized mother[1], modernist techniques, the spirit of experimentation, and the stance of an outsider.

Lessing rarely admits that she directly learns from Woolf, she yet regards Woolf as one of the great modernists who have influenced her writing. She once praised Woolf for her avant-gardeness in literary practice, "… her writing life was a progression of daring experiments. And if we do not always think well of her progeny—some attempts to emulate her have been unfortunate— then without her, without James Joyce (and they have more in common than either would have cared to knowledge), our literature would have been poorer" (Lessing TB 24). For Lessing, Woolf—together with her contemporary James Joyce—has contributed to modern literature through bold experimentation with new ways of writing, a practice Lessing is never tired of. Her admiration for Woolf is such that, upon receiving her Nobel Prize, she complained about the

---

1 Both Lessing and Woolf have shown concern for the mother-daughter relationship as well as the image of an idealized mother as a result of their family background and female identity, so that there have been quite a few mother-characters in their writing.

Nobel academy's negligence of Woolf and felt sorry that Woolf, who should have been at the top of the list, was not among the awardees.

Researchers and critics have long noticed the similarities and differences between Lessing and Woolf. Of the commonalities between the two, their shared status as outside-insider is the most important. As has been mentioned before, Lessing regards herself as an outside-insider towards both white and black society. She enjoys the status of being both on the margin and in the center, a status that allows for a comparatively sober and objective observation. Likewise, Woolf also sees herself an outside-insider and is somewhat happy about this identity. In *A Sketch of the Past*, an autobiographical essay published in 1939, Woolf writes, "I felt as a gipsy or a child feels who stands at the flap of the tent and sees the circus going on inside" (Woolf "Sketch" 2224). In *A Room of One's Own,* an expanded treatment of issues concerning the feminist movement, she emphasizes again: "I thought how unpleasant it is to be locked out; and I thought how it is worse perhaps to be locked in" (Woolf "Room" 2210). In *Three Guineas,* Woolf points out the importance of women being "outsiders" of the male-dominated world which means that women should be "both different from and separate from men" (Marcus 229). Throughout her life, Woolf frequently makes explicit her hatred for the institutionalized, disciplined, and ritualized world and explains in various essays her understanding of the inequality between male and female, and her strong wish to break through boundaries and limitations. While taking the stance of a transgressor in her fictional works, essays, and diaries, Woolf prefers to be so in real life, a stance shown in her distrust of suffrage and feminist politics, in her struggle for being a woman with a room of her own, for a transcendence over Victorian society.

The sense of alienation which accompanies Woolf for all her life comes from her childhood experience. In her Victorian girlhood, Woolf was not given access to formal education like her brothers, but had to stay at home to devour her father's extensive library. Due to her extraordinary familial and cultural background, she was encouraged to be an artist and performer and later she educated herself to be an avant-garde woman who dared to step out of the household and take part in social life and artistic work, to become finally the opposite of the Victorian Angel in the House. So her early childhood and education gradually shapes her into a rebel against the institutions and mainstream discourses. It is her education that "[brought] out and fortif[ied] the differences rather than the similarities" (qtd. in Marcus 227) between herself and the outside world.

Although she reiterates her preference for an outsider status, Woolf is an active insider, which is both a result of and disguise for her insider-ness. For instance, while talking about Woolf's outward aloofness from feminist activities, Laura Marcus asked and answered the following questions:

> Does placing women in the position of Outsiders allow Woolf to exempt them from the urgent decisions of the period, and would her position in 1938 have put her very close to a 'politics of appeasement'? 'Thinking is my fighting', Woolf wrote, thus suggesting not a disengagement from the exigencies of her time, but an acute sense of the specific responses she could, and would, make to them (Marcus 225).

According to Marcus, Woolf, though superficially not a fervent supporter of the feminist movement, is in fact a fighter equipped with powers of thinking and writing. Responding to the exigencies of her time in her own way, she is indeed an insider who thinks and acts from the perspective of an outsider. Similarly, on the issue of Women's Liberation, Lessing is always unwilling to be grouped into the avant-gardes of the movement. But she does care a great deal about women's existence in modern society and constantly addresses issues concerning women from a female perspective. Like Woolf, she is more a practitioner than a spokeswoman.

No matter how hard Woolf tries to keep a distance, her leading position in the Bloomsbury Group and her deep concern for feminist issues in her writing are all evidence of her involvement in social life, the feminist movement, and the political activities of the day. Because of this involvement, Woolf suffers deeply, which is partly accountable for her mental breakdown and suicide. But just as Florence Nightingale, the well-known "the lady with the lamp", once wrote in *Cassandra*, suffering is important, "for out of nothing comes nothing. But out of suffering may come the cure. Better have pain than paralysis" (as cited in Showalter 27). Without these disruptions and trials, including sexual abuses in the childhood, the loss of her mother and elder sister in her adolescence, the death of her father in 1904, the First World War, the destruction of her London home during the Blitz, and other incidents, Woolf might not have been so productive in her literary career. Without experiencing the differences between male and female, she might not have been so concerned about the gender issue. In a sense, it is the experience of an insider that brings about a productive and avant-garde Woolf. So is Doris Lessing.

In addition to Forster and Woolf, Lessing can also be compared with two other significant post-colonial theorists, Frantz Fanon (1925–1961) and bell hooks (1952–)[1]. The comparison will further demonstrate how Lessing best exemplifies hybridity.

Frantz Fanon

Originally a term in anthropological and biological discourses, hybridity, in the postcolonial period, is reinterpreted as closely connected with oppositions in the form of binary concepts, including colonizer and colonized, white and black, East and West, superiority and inferiority, purity and impurity, and so on. Confrontation, resistance, and paradox are its inherent meanings. As critic May Joseph states in *Performing Hybridity*, "the modern move to deploy hybridity as a disruptive democratic discourse of cultural citizenship is distinctively anti-imperial and antiauthoritarian development" (Joseph & Fink 1). Since hybridity is refreshed with the connotation of "anti-imperialism" and

---

1   bell hooks is regarded as one of the most successful crossover academics of the late 20th century. Her concern for issues of race, gender, and cultural politics is fully demonstrated in her writings, including *Ain't I a Woman?: Black Women and Feminism* (1981), *Feminist Theory: From Margin to Center* (1984), *Outlaw Culture: Resisting Representations* (1994), and *Feminism Is for Everybody: Passionate Politics* (2000).

"antiauthoritarianism" in the post-colonial world, the discussion is surely to cover Frantz Fanon, the significant postcolonial theorist.

Frantz Fanon, with his book *Wretched of the Earth* (1961) and his advocacy for using violence in the anticolonial struggle, is a landmark figure in resistance against imperialism. His philosophy of resistance serves as "a revolutionary manifesto of decolonization and the founding analysis of the effects of colonialism upon colonized peoples and their cultures" (Young "Colonialism and Humanism" 243). He shares with Lessing the belief that it is important to strive for universality instead of locality. To paraphrase Lessing, the development of the individual serves as a premise for the growth and maturity of the community. Well-motivated to adopt a universalistic perspective, Fanon finds his battleground in colonialism, while Lessing rejects the "parochialism" (Lessing *GN* 14) she sees in literature and art. Fanon is confident that it is possible to "reach out for the universal" through "one human being" (Fanon 197). Likewise, Lessing holds that in "writing about oneself, one is writing about others" (*GN* 13), for the objective of writing about individual experience is to achieve universality. For both Fanon and Lessing, universalism is a strategy against the prejudice enforced by any one group or culture.

Fanon regards it extremely important for the black people to fight against racism in order to obtain equal rights with the whites and to share in a universal identity a stand that is clarified in his *Black Skin, White Masks* (1952):

As I begin to recognize that the Negro is the symbol of sin, I catch myself hating the Negro. But then I recognize that I am a Negro. There are two ways out of this conflict. Either I ask others to pay no attention to my skin, or else I want them to be aware of it. I try then to find value for what is bad—since I have unthinkingly conceded that the black man is the color of evil. In order to terminate this neurotic situation…I have only one solution: to rise above this absurd drama that others have staged round me, to reject the two terms that are equally unacceptable, and, through one human being, to reach out for the universal (Fanon 78).

Having realized that black is "the symbol of sin" and that the physical differences arising from skin color can hardly be denied, Fanon admits that he struggles to find the way out of the predicament that "others have staged around" him (Fanon 78). To arouse people's awareness in this regard, Fanon resorts to universality, arguing that both blacks and whites are, first of all human beings, born equal and should enjoy the same rights and opportunities.

Similarly, while telling the story of black people, Lessing believes that there is no need to focus on a particular anticolonial discourse, as she has explained in the case of Moses in GS^1. For Lessing, to treat blacks and whites as equals does not mean to deny the differences between them. What is more important for a writer is to bear in mind is the idea of color-blindness, or to treat everyone as an independent person regardless of skin color and race. This attitude can also be a strategy applicable to male-female relationships, as she once explained in an interview:

Of course, I am for women's equality; of course, I consider women inherently equal to men. However, I would never maintain that men and women are alike. They simply are not. Physically, psychologically, and intellectually, they are not—which is not to say that women must be more stupid than men. They have other gifts. No two people in the world are perfectly alike; how can men and women be alike? (*Schwarzkopf 103*).

Instead of making the distinction between the superior and the inferior or writing off disparities, it is wise to acknowledge the peculiarities of each group, since they differ from each other "physically, psychologically, and

---

1 Lessing reflects upon her depiction of Moses which is blamed for her white-focused perspective and defends herself by claiming that it is a well-chosen perspective so as to show the life as it is. For more details, see the third part of Chapter One subtitled as "Mixed perspectives in *The Diaries of Jane Somers*, *The Grass Is Singing* and *The Golden Notebook*".

intellectually". *GS* sets a good example in providing the reader with a white-focused perspective, accomplished by a polyphonic third-person narrator that turns out to be a flexible and all-engrossing narration. Therefore, the seemingly white-focused perspective is in fact a highly hybridized perspective, capable of observing from various points of view, which Lessing claims as the most appropriate narrative strategy in dealing with the issue of skin color in this story.

While Fanon calls for universalism in his activism by way of the anti-colonial struggle, Lessing makes it the objective of her literary production. She experiments with various modes of writing so as to remove the limitations of any specific literary tradition to achieve universality in writing, which makes it more likely to go beyond the immediate time and space, a strategy that she has explained in the preface to *GN:*

The way to deal with the problem of 'subjectivity', that shocking business of being preoccupied with the tiny individual who is at the same time caught up in such an explosion of terrible and marvelous possibilities, is to see him as a microcosm and in this way to break through the personal, the subjective, making the personal general, as indeed life always does, transforming a private experience—or so you think of it when still a child, '*I* am falling in love', '*I* am feeling this or that emotion, or thinking that or the other thought'—into something much larger: growing up is after all only the understanding that one's unique and incredible experience is what everyone shares" (*GN* 13–14, italics original).

Believing that each individual is a "microcosm" who mirrors the bigger world he lives in, Lessing argues that the private and unique experience of each individual is just "what everyone shares" and the individual can act as the spokesman for the general public. Besides, to grow up means to gain a better understanding of the group experience or the wider world on the basis of personal experience, which, in William Blake's words, is "to see a world in a grain of sand, and a heaven in a wild flower"[1]. To present the group experience by drawing evidence from the personal experience is what she bears in mind while writing, and it is one of the stimuli that has brought about the story and structure of *GN*.

Lessing's concern for the individual-collective issue partly comes from the influence of the 19th realism. According to Ian Watt, the emergence of realism as an aesthetic category brought about an enormous change in the 18th century literature[2] that was part of a larger cultural change to draw attention to the individuals and their particular experiences. As Watt explains, the 18th century realism begins to pay attention to particular individuals, times, and places. Through personal experiences, literary realists intend to express general feelings which, as Lessing once argued in an interview, is why the individual, trivial as it is, is widely read, "If these writers in Russia had not claimed their right to an individual conscience rather than a collective one, we would not now be remembering and reading Gogol, Tolstoy, Dostoyevsky, Chekhov, Turgenev, and all the rest of that dazzling galaxy" (Kurzweil 206). This focus on "individual conscience" in contrast to the "collective" impresses Lessing, and she holds that it is obligatory for a writer to respect the individual, as this individual is the premise behind the progress of the whole group or community. For Lessing, individuality should be given priority over universality.

---

1   The two lines are taken from William Blake's 132-line poem "Auguries of Innocence". The first four lines of the poem—To see a world in a grain of sand/ And a heaven in a wild flower / Hold infinity in the palm of your hand / And eternity in an hour—comes from a Buddhist concept which claims that the infinite universe can be perceived through the microcosm composed by each subtle and individual being. The analogy fits in well with the oriental context, as the poem is seldom mentioned compared with other poems of Black such as as *Songs of Innocence and of Experience*.

2   According to Ian Watt, the term "realism" originally was used to define the painting of Rembrandt as against the then dominant classical painting. It was formally used as a literary term in 1865 in France. French Realists "asserted that if their novels tended to differ from the more flattering pictures of humanity presented by many established ethical, social and literary codes, it was merely because they were the product of a more dispassionate and scientific scrutiny of life than had ever been attempted before" (Watt 11).

However, universality has its own role to play, for Lessing. She desires to seek out the common ground rather than disparities among different sexes, groups, religions, convictions, and so on. Her objective in presenting individual experiences is to achieve commonality or universalism, since "all people and all human societies share fundamental cognitive, emotive, ethical, and other properties and principles" (Hogan xv). Naturally, Lessing regards "see[ing] in fact what we have in common" a more crucial task than identifying differences, and she further claims that only with this realization can divisions be overcome in the construction of a solid community. This consciousness of unity is not inconsistent to seeking individual conscience, since an individual should first of all keep his own thinking in the context of institutionalization.

Although Lessing talks about the issue of universalism from the perspective of writing while Fanon discusses it in the context of anti-colonial struggle, both realize the significance of the concept as a strategy for fighting against confinement. Fanon puts it in his fight against racism while Lessing applies it to her narratives. Her multiplied and often conflicting perspectives of both white and black, male and female, child and adult provide the reader with more insight into the text; her diversified narrative styles can hardly be labeled as simply realism, modernism, or post-modernism; and her all-embracing subject matters not only make her narrative highly hybridized, but also help her move towards the objective of universalism. To seek the commonalities out of difference, as expected by Lessing, has been achieved with the help of her hybridized narration.

bell hooks

bell hooks bears a strong resemblance with Doris Lessing, not only their shared gender, but also their mental growth and concern for women's living conditions. Compared with some of the pioneering feminists, bell hooks appears to be a woman with more courage and vision for the radical position she adopts in a climate of heavy racism and of white supremacist capitalist patriarchy, both external and internal. What makes her admirable is that despite a well-established scholar, she speaks out for the oppressed minorities in a more and more conservative environment, even at the price of her safety and reputation[1].

bell hooks represents a change in the intellectual mindset during the last two decades of the 20th century, a change in habits of mind that plays a significant role in Lessing's narrative style and strategy. In addition, as left-wing intellectuals, both women not only call for but also get deeply involved in transforming the established systems. Their radicalism undergoes changes as they respond to different social context, but they never give up their belief in a better world. They have their own concerns, yet both take the African issues and feminism as their life long pursuit in writings. Lessing is well-accepted as an African writer, especially in her earlier period of writing; and women also figure prominently, with the New Women in *GN* as the most striking example.

Like Lessing, bell hooks, African-born writer and female conscious, talks a lot about her fellow African men and women, their culture, their lives, and their future. During the 1980s, hooks presents an image of a woman warrior who is filled with moral indignation: yelling, interrogating, and talking back[2]. In 1981, when she was 29 years old, she published her first book entitled *Ain't I a Woman?: Black Women and Feminism*. In 1989, she published another book *Talking Back: Thinking Feminist, Thinking Black*. During the 1990s, hooks became more temperate. There is less anger or fury in tone, and understanding, empathy, forgiveness, and support take the upper hand. This shift can be found in her *Outlaw Culture: Resisting Representations* (1994), where hooks advocates healing by the ethic of love. Love takes the place of injustice and evilness. Love is regarded as an effective means for African women to gain equality and independence in a white patriarchal culture. She discusses the "outlaw culture" to a great extent in this book, arguing that the outlaw culture, a culture of the marginalized, including black people, women—black women

---

1   bell hooks is regarded as one of the most dangerous academics in America in *Professors: The 101 Most Dangerous Academics in America* (2013), and the author of the book Horowitz warns the "hapless students" of the lecture given by hooks (Horowitz 278).

2   Such words and phrases are taken from the title of her books and are representative of her style, especially in her earlier writings which, compared with her later ones, are more radical and furious in subject matter.

in particular and some other minority groups, and the people it represents should let their own voices heard and get themselves expressed in an authentic way so that they can resist the misrepresentations which are manipulated by the mainstream culture.

Both Lessing and hooks protest and fight against the suppression of and hostility towards women in a patriarchal society. While Lessing is unhappy to be categorized as a feminist writer, hooks complains that "feminist theory lacks wholeness, lacks the broad analysis that could encompass a variety of human experiences" (hooks *Feminism* 11), for much of the feminist theory is formulated by "privileged women who live at the center" (hooks *Feminism* 11). Regarding themselves as marginalized females, both Lessing and hook keep a distance from the existing feminist movement. Lessing wants to steer clear of it while hooks calls for a turn to "a mass based political movement" (hooks *Feminism* 11) to keep it revolutionary and transformative enough.

In addition to the shared concerns for Africa and female issues, both Lessing and bell hooks regard themselves marginalized by the dominant white culture. For Lessing, her marginalization is caused by the outside world and by herself. She willingly takes herself to be an outcast of the Western world, of Africa, and of other women, either consciously or unconsciously. bell hooks similarly speaks for marginalized groups in whatever chances she has. It is interesting to note that both regard it an advantageous status to be able to perceive the world as they do:

Living as we did—on the edge—we developed a particular way of seeing reality. We looked both from the outside in and the inside out. We focused our attention on the center as well as on the margin. We understood both. This mode of seeing reminded us of the existence of a whole universe: a main body made up of both center and margin. Our survival depended on an ongoing public awareness of the separation between margin and center and an ongoing private acknowledgement that we were a necessary, vital part of that whole (hooks *Feminism* 11).

hooks claims that being marginalized, one is endowed with a unique perspective which enables one to observe the world from both within and outside, a stand that has been co-hailed by Lessing, for neither of them are disappointed with this "inferior" position and turn it to their virtues. Lessing believes it is an advantage to keep herself detached from the center for the sake of a sober and critical thinking, while hooks regards herself a justifiable spokeswoman for the prejudiced black female who have suffered not only from the tyranny of men but also from the oppression of privileged white women who adopt a "condescending attitude" (hooks *Feminism* 11) towards non-white or poor women. Staying on the margin allows for an objective observation while getting involved in the life at the center emphasizes first-hand experience. Hybridity, therefore, makes it possible for Lessing to maintain the membership of the mainstream society while at the same time acts as the instrument for speaking for the people on the margin. This self-assumed identity of insider and outsider may not be indisputable, but their resolve to take the perspective of the marginalized does win them a larger audience, especially those practitioners who have been encouraged by their works in the fight against inequality and inhibition.

Despite quite a few similarities, there is however one difference between them: their passion and love for Africa are slightly different. For Lessing, Africa is her second hometown and her feelings for Africa are complicated. She looks back to that land from time to time, sometimes with nostalgia, sometimes with regret. While Africa is her cradle and stands for the memorable past, London is her final home. In contrast, for bell hooks, Africa is in the blood, a homeland she has spent all her life fighting for and its people she is seeking a better future for. In addition, although African issues frequently appear in Lessing's writings, what she cares most, perhaps unconsciously, is the struggle and survival of the white colonizer trapped in the black culture, as it has been discussed in the case of *GS*. "Africa and its inhabitants in Lessing's works are merely backdrop or instrumental to her white settlers' self-discovery, maturation, or epiphany" (Chen Jingxia 52). In contrast, hooks has always spoken and written for her fellow Africans, especially her black sisters.

Because of this difference, Lessing is by and large part of the white culture that misrepresents black people, a misrepresentation which is strongly opposed by bell hooks so that she makes this the top issue in her *Outlaw Culture: Resisting Representations* and tries to provide the readers with strategies to redress it[1].

In this book, hooks points out that white media control the representations of the outlaw culture. The white gaze speaks for the interests of the privileged rather than that of the black people who are unable to escape from the psychological impact of racism and white supremacist beliefs. Being the victim of internalized racism, they cannot express themselves clearly and accurately. Women, especially black women, are constantly portrayed in a stereotypical way, as informed by the white supremacist patriarchy. hooks further complains that some of their own spokeswomen, especially those feminists with power, are not qualified enough to speak for other women and the feminist movement.

Therefore, bell hooks calls for her fellow black people to resist misrepresentation. She believes in Malcolm X's advocacy for self-expression: "Never accept images that have been created for you by someone else. It is always better to form the habit of learning how to see things for yourself: Then you are in a better position to judge for yourself" (hooks *Outlaw* 181). In other words, to get rid of misrepresentations by the oppressive culture, there is a need to resist and to find one's own voice.

The dialogue between hooks and Lessing, or between non-fiction and fiction, can be found elsewhere, for instance, between Michel Foucault and Lessing. Both of them refuse to be identified with any specific label, both challenge the authority of the so-called professor-critic or academic critics, and both make efforts to seek alternatives as a gesture against a unified dominance,

---

1 *Outlaw Culture: Resisting Representations*, a collection of 20 essays and interviews, covers various issues of the outlaw culture. Here, hooks examines pictures of the outlaw culture misrepresented and misinterpreted by the contemporary cultural norms which are racism, patriarchy and sexism. To her, both white and black people, both men and women, should be held accountable for this. Consequently, hooks suggests that the outlawed should first of all unlearn the first-world or patriarchal mind-set, to get a clearer understanding of themselves and to strive against the manipulation by the mainstream culture.

either intellectually or literarily. Foucault holds that knowledge plays different roles in the construction of power relations, a flowing process with power moving fluidly between parties. Similarly, with the hybridized narrative, Lessing puts this philosophy into practice, empowering her writing and drawing strength from a mixture of skills, techniques, or styles. The hybridized narrative is a strategic tool to inject vitality into her writing as well as to protest against labelling.

One of the words that best characterize both Lessing and Foucault is resistance: resistance against dominance and power of any form. While Lessing's resistance is fully demonstrated in her literary production, Foucault's rebelliousness can be seen in his rejection of any dominating belief. As a philosopher and historian, Foucault "rejects identification of enlightenment with a unified science whose universal conditions would reside in Man... In reversing, dispersing, and criticizing what was taken to be universal, Foucault attacks what, in the present, has come to be regarded as *the* Enlightenment" (Rajchman 59, italics original). The Foucauldian knowledge has a role in the reconfiguration of the power structure because "all forms of knowledge are historically relative and contingent, and cannot be dissociated from the workings of power" (Downing vii). Thanks to the changeability of knowledge, the power structure is forever in the process of being constructed and reconstructed which echoes with Lessing's claim that nothing is fixed. For Lessing, literature is a strategic configuration and reconfiguration of power, or to be more specific in her case, all forms of narrative make a contribution to the literary work for its effectiveness. The effort made by each and every participant of the polyphony adds vitality to the text, which turns the text into a weapon against confinement and domination.

The comparison between Lessing, Forster, Woolf, Fanon and hooks demonstrates that Lessing is a writer with a border-crossing mind, a mindset that characterizes the postcolonial concept of hybridity: "Hybridity is a terminology and sensibility of our time, in that boundary and border-crossing mark our times" (Pieterse 238). She shares with some of her contemporaries the ideas of creative writing, the spirit of resistance, the power of words, and the actions that best reflect the time and her own thoughts. In a sense, like the power relations configured and reconfigured by all forms of knowledge, Lessing and her contemporaries construct and reconstruct a heteroglossia that allows for an infusion as well as co-existence of various forces.

If the heteroglossia constructed by Lessing and others can be regarded as a dialogue outside the singular text, her attempt at styles, genres and subject matters is a dialogue both with herself and others. The diversification as manifested in her concretized strategies goes beyond simple repetition, rather, it creates a Third Space for a fair play of voices at various levels and is a manifestation of her inheritance, integration and innovation in writing. In other words, the hybridized styles, genres and subject matters are all important elements in Lessing's strategic deployment of hybridity. Take the genre as an example. In his exploration into the discourse in the novel, Bakhtin argues that the hybridized genre is "the most significant and fundamental means in constructing a heteroglossia within a novel" (Ji Weining & Xin Bin 16), for the novel is open to all kind of genres. The mixture of various genres then gives rise to the ambiguity of the text which may further mobilize the initiatives of the reader and enrich the meaning of the text.

Her favour for the genre of travel narrative comes from the fact that travel narrative can best address such issues as identity, resistance, and group experience. The same is true for her writings about female experience. Hybridity therefore, not only comes to her as a strategic rhetoric for literary production, but also as an effective means for a new space.

Chapter Three
A Hybrid Construction of Lessing's Hybridity

I think that literature—a novel, a story, even a line of poetry—has the power to destroy empires.

—Doris Lessing

Since the above two chapters have shown that hybridity is a major feature of Lessing's writing, the author believes it is necessary to follow the trajectory of Lessing's hybridity and identify the elements that have come to influence Lessing the writer. In other words, since for Lessing it is a long process for this concept to take shape, and various elements must have partaken in the evolution and formation of her hybridity as a distinctive strategy, the present study feels it justifiable to assume that Lessing's hybridity itself is a hybrid construction made possible by various elements which have contributed to the making of Lessing as a hybridized writer. It is therefore necessary to have a close look at her theoretical ideas, in conjunction with a discussion of her intellectual background, the artistic as well as political and religious atmosphere of her time, and her own experience as an intellectual, social activist and writer, all of which has prepared Lessing to become what she is. This chapter therefore tries to analyze these elements through an observation of the informing context of the author, the influence of post-colonialism on her spiritual and intellectual growth, and last but not least, an in-depth discussion on the development of her writing philosophy.

The hybrid Lessing is best seen in her role as the author, one who both tries to control the text and retreat from it. The realist Lessing needs the author who makes decision to ensure that her text is "real" for her reader. Yet the decisive author in the postmodern age needs to be dead, some argue, if the text and reader are to be alive. In his essay entitled "The Death of the Author" published in 1967, Roland Barthes declares the notion of the "death of the author":

> As soon as a fact is narrated no longer with a view to acting directly on reality but intransitively, that is to say, finally outside of any function other than that of the very practice of the symbol itself, this disconnection occurs, the voice loses its origin, the author enters into his own death, writing begins (Barthes 142).

Since "the birth of the reader must be at the cost of the death of the Author" (Barthes 148), more attention should be given to the reader instead of to the author. As the author releases his control and stops acting as the sole and final authority over the text, the reader takes over and provides the condition for the existence of the text. The death of the author, then, gives rise to the emergence of the reader and more possibilities for the interpretation of the text. As long as the "voice loses its origin", and the intentions and biographical context of the author are no longer crucial in textual interpretation, the reader comes to the fore. Barthes tries to eradicate the traces of the author from within the text, as he further explains in an essay entitled "Introduction to the Structural Analysis of Narratives"[1] that the "(material) author of a narrative is in no way to be confused with the narrator of that narrative" (Barthes 282), the latter traditionally believed to be the mouthpiece of the real author. However, it is hard to ignore the presence of the author in the text, for whatever narrator the author creates and whatever distance between the author and the text, there is no denying the presence of the real author: its identity, intention and designs are evidenced in the choice of narrator and in the telling of the story.

---

1   This essay, translated into English, is collected in *Image, Music, Text* (1977), essays selected and translated by Stephen Heath, which contains some of Barthe's most significant writings about film and photography, and on the phenomena of sound and image.

Furthermore, there is a hidden author within the story. Different from the real author, this hidden author is to a large extent the product of the real author's experience, his cultural and social background, and his viewpoints and perspectives. The hidden author is not a completely separate "other", but another "self" of the real author that allows the latter's voice heard through it. Shen Dan and Wang Liya argues in *Western Narratology: Classical and Post-classical* (2010)[1] that the author's personal background is a part of the context that deserves attention from the narratologists:

> We should pay close attention to the impact of one's life and the related social context in his writing... Classical narratologists care about nothing but the text itself. But it is evident in the following chapter that the post-classical narratologists have returned to the right path of combining the text with its social and historical context in their textual interpretation (Shen Dan 75).

Professor Shen holds that, in contrast to classical narratologists, post-classical narratologists reiterate the significance of "social and historical context" in the study of the text. Talking about the nature of the hidden author, Shen declares that it is misleading to evaluate the hidden author simply by the individual reader's response. She agrees with Susan Lanser and Booth that to find the manifold personality of the hidden author necessitates discovering the real author behind.

There can hardly be an author who does not change in his or her perspectives and attitudes. The complexities and obscurities that result from the manifold personality of the author give rise to fluidity and dynamics in the text, making the reader's task even more difficult as they explore the intention and image of the author. According to Eve Bertelsen (1985), an influential Lessing critic, it is not until Jenny Taylor's *Notebooks/Memoirs/Archives: Reading and*

1　*Western Narratology: Classical and Postclassical* (2010) is written in Chinese, co-authored by Shen Dan and Wang Liya. The quotation here is translated by the author of this book.

Rereading Doris Lessing published in 1982 that Lessing criticism began to cast its eyes on factors such as the connection between Lessing's context and her works. This turn in Lessing studies has been well-accepted and frequently discussed, resulting in a large number of critical essays or books focusing on the relations between the informing context of Lessing and her writing.

Apart from the necessity of taking the informing context into consideration, it is also advisable to explore from the perspective of the postcolonial theory of hybridity which is characterized as border-crossing. The postcolonial critique "makes sense of Lessing's frequent switching of modes and genres; and it explains her attraction to different forms of life writing" (Watkins and Chambers 4). In other words, Lessing's mastery of various styles and genres contributes to her hybridized narration and echoes the spirit of postcolonialism.

As a writer reaching maturity in a postcolonial world, Lessing carries the distinctive features of this period, with an objective to bring about change and overturn the authoritative power:

> Postcolonialism is about a changing world, a world that has been changed by struggle and which its practitioners intend to change further…It disturbs the order of the world. It threatens privilege and power. It refuses to acknowledge the superiority of western cultures. Its radical agenda is to demand equality and well-being for all human beings on this earth (Young *Postcolonialism* 7).

Young argues that as the result of the fight by the postcolonial practitioners against existing "privilege and power", the postcolonial world witnesses a reconstruction of the order system. In this sense, Lessing can be regarded as one of the postcolonialists who, by posing a challenge to "the superiority of Western cultures" and demanding "equality and well-being for all human beings on this earth" in writing, hopes to set up a new order benefiting all. To achieve this objective, Lessing makes the most of her hybridized narration, which turns out to be an effective postcolonial strategy in the struggle of resistance and subversion, a strategy that has been discussed in detail by Amar Acheraïou in *Hybridity, Postcolonialism and Globalization* (2011). Acheraïou points out that as the concept of hybridity has been broadened to "stand for inclusiveness, dialogism, subversion, and contestation of grand narrative" (Acheraïou 5), most postcolonial theorists and writers take hybridity as "a crucial emancipator tool releasing the representations of identity as well as culture from the assumptions of purity and supremacy that fuel colonialist, and essentialist discourses" (Acheraïou 5–6). Lessing falls into this category of postcolonial writers who use hybridity as an instrument against colonial authority and discourse. But Acheraïou also points out that hybridity may fall into the false hand of the dominating power:

> Particular attention is paid to the tensions and contradictions inherent in the handling of métissage in the ancient world; tensions between the perception of hybridity as, on the one hand, a means of cultural and epistemic enrichment and political empowerment, and on the other, a source of social disorder and racial degeneration (Acheraïou 2).

Acheraïou warns against the abuse of hybridity, which can either be viewed as "a source of social disorder and racial degeneration" or a tool for "political empowerment", with the former serving the resisting minority group while the latter the powered authority. Acheraïou's worry about the danger of hybridity is based on his view of the ways "in which hybridity was experienced, construed, constructed, and manipulated across history to serve various, often contradictory, cultural, political, ideological, and economic ends".

This worry however does not apply to Lessing. To understand Lessing's hybridity, it is necessary to have a look at the educational, intellectual, cultural, social, and ideological influences on her life and writing against the postcolonial background and her ever-changing writing philosophy. It is argued here that her hybridity grows from her protest against philistinism and the practice of labelling, from her rebelliousness that has been cultivated through a lifelong struggle and from her adaptability to a diversified writing strategy.

"A dialogic is formed by the different meanings within and between utterances" (Hohne & Wussow ix). In Lessing's case, her fictional writing as well as her literary criticism are voiced within one utterance, constantly talking to, disagreeing with or contradicting themselves. By explaining her writing motive, characterization and construction of the novel in interviews, essays or prefaces, Lessing foregrounds the voice of a real author which are productive or even self-contradictory in the story.

3.1 Protest against Philistinism and Labelling

Lessing believes that for most people, in particular the poor and elderly, "a roof over one's head" (Lessing *WS* 131) is the objective of a lifelong struggle for a sense of security, like the old women in *DJS*. But it is not a principle of survival for Lessing, who has moved many times to many places and therefore has led a life with a frequently changed "roof". Being mostly a "roofless" traveler, her writing turns out to be "roofless" and "rootless" in nature, attempting to break the bonds set by the era, tradition, or nationality of its author.

Lessing is a willing "roofless" or restless writer in part due to her dissatisfaction with British literature for its philistinism and labelling. She constantly complains about the philistinism that makes it too provincial to incorporate broader subject matters into itself. For fear of being put into this group of smallness and dullness as she points out in *ASPV*, she has made efforts to diversify her own writing, either in content or form:

> We are not living in an exciting literary period but in a dull one. We are not producing masterpieces, but large numbers of small, quite lively, intelligent novels. Above all, current British literature is provincial. This is spite of the emergence of the Angry Young Men... Yet they are extremely provincial and I do not mean by provincial that they come from or write about the provinces. I mean that their horizons are bounded by their immediate experience of British life and standard (*ASPV* 14).

Lessing blames British literature for its lack of exciting and fresh elements and regards it as "dull" and "provincial" since the content is mainly drawn from the limited experiences of native British writers. Due to this limitation in subject matters, criteria, and horizon, British literature is far less exciting, despite the fresh power from the Angry Young Men. This is not the first time that Lessing blames British literature for its narrowness. In a 1962 interview, she criticized Virginia Woolf for the narrow subject matter: "I feel that her experience must have been too limited, because there's always a point in her novels when I think, 'Fine, but look what you've left out'" (Joyner 204–205). Although a great admirer of Woolf, Lessing complains about the life confined in London and in particular in the Bloomsbury Group[1]. She points out that this is not an individual case, but typical of British literature as a whole. "Philistinism is endemic in Britain, and most particularly in London... What the British—no, the English—like best are small, circumscribed novels, preferably about the nuances of class or social behavior" (*WS* 113–114). Lessing defends for herself in this regard by quoting Maugham: "... Somerset Maugham felt that English writers were provincial, knew only England, and should travel" (Lessing *WS* 131). Like Maugham, Lessing regards travel as an effective measure against localization, since it enriches both local experiences and global awareness, in contrast to the "small, circumscribed" circumstances (Lessing *WS* 113–114). Lessing's own writing is "global" in style, genre and subject matter, all "roofless".

---

1   Woolf is one of most frequently chosen one to be compared with Lessing. Some critics believe that *GN* has a lot to do with Woolf which indirectly proves Woolf's influence on Lessing. Tonya Krouse believes that Anna Wulf, the middle-aged and successful female writer in *GN* is "a direct challenge to Woolf" (50) for "Lessing seems to take Woolf up as her own "angel in the house", whom she must kill in order to free her own writing" (Krouse 50). It proves Lessing complaints about Woolf's limitedness in terms of subject matters as well as life style. Confined to the Bloomsbury, a corner of London, most of Woolf's writings are centered on personal experience, about the upper-class female, or the privileged group, which is not to the taste of Lessing. Whether Lessing's complaints about the so-called narrowness in Woolf is justifiable or not, Lessing's writing is more diversified in terms of genres, styles and subject matters.

Besides "roof", Lessing frequently addresses issues such as "space", "territory", or "field", which are all heavily embedded with symbolic or metaphoric implications, like the following paragraph from *WS*:

> Along one street, turn a corner into another, then another, whose name I never looked at, for I did not care where I was, thought when I moved from one little knot of streets, or even one street, into another, it was moving from one territory to another, each with its own strong atmosphere and emanations, bestowed by me and by me need to understand this new place. Not to know its name, so that I could find it again, for I am sure I often walked along the same streets, past the same houses, but did not know it, for the capacities and understanding I brought with me were different on different nights. And besides, even in daytime a change of light or a shift of perspective will create a new view. You use a certain underground station often, you walk down the steps onto a platform you know as well as you do the street outside your house, but when you stop at the same station after your excursion, on your way home, you go up steps from a platform quite different from the one you set off from, ten paces away (*WS* 165).

Lessing finds it intolerable to stay in one place and prefers to move "from one territory to another" for experiences of different "atmosphere and emanations". Whether by nature or nurture, she is restless and keeps exploring new places and new things—in life, by strolling along the London streets at night and in writing by switching between different styles, genres, and subject matters. In addition to trying on new things or "stepping on" new territories, she is capable of gaining new insights from the old experiences. She claims that no matter how many times she has passed the same place, there is still something unknown to her, "for the capacities and understanding" she brings with her are "different on different nights". These familiar places and roads once again are strange to her, as a shift in point of view may lead to a different interpretation. This can be seen as an analogue to Lessing's hybridized application of narrator, voice, and perspective. By talking about "territory", "understanding", "shift of perspective", and "view", Lessing seems to clarify her own view on the effectiveness of her hybridized narration, which is achieved through a juxtaposition of narrator and perspectives, as well as a diversified genres and subject matters.

Because of this constantly refreshed perspective on the same territory—the place as well as its people—Lessing is able to identify the weakness in the British character, which partly accounts for the philistinism in British literature:

> Self-sufficing. Solitude-loving. And yet a group of these same people, in England, seems cosy, seems insular, and, confronted by an alien, they huddle together, presenting the faces of alarmed children…There is a dinkiness, a smallness, a tameness, a deep, instinctive, perennial refusal to admit danger, or even the unfamiliar: a reluctance to understand extreme experience. Somewhere—so the foreigner suspects, and for the purposes of comparison, while writing this I am one too—somewhere deep in the psyche of Britain is an Edwardian nursery, fenced all around with sharp repelling thorns, and deep inside it is a Sleeping Beauty with a notice pinned to her: Do Not Touch (*WS* 86–87).

Lessing aligns herself with the perspective of a foreigner and points out that British people, in her times, tend to indulge themselves in the sweet memory of their brilliant past instead of opening their eyes to a new world ahead, which may most probably turn out to be a world of uncertainty and danger, due to their inborn characteristics of self-satisfaction, timidity, and reluctance to change. Lessing blames the British people for their disillusioned sense of security and refusal to accept challenges, traits that she holds responsible for the narrowness of British mentality and literature. In contrast, she is willingly experimental in life as well as writing, moving forward with an adventuring spirit by keeping a keen eye on the outside world.

For fear that she might become one of those "provincial" writers, Lessing picks up such exotic subjects as African matters, which makes her a so-called

African writer on the one hand and distinguishes her from other British writers for this "otherness" on the other. Writing about African matters, in fact, is Lessing's strategy to cope with the provincialism in British literature, as well as her resistance against the literary mainstream by adding to it new subject matters.

But why African? Besides her own experience, Lessing declares that her interest in African issues is ignited by a former African writer Olive Schreiner, *author of The Story of African Farm*. Schreiner brings her to a new perspective into African issues in terms of consciousness. Believing that writing about the remote land of Africa might inject vitality and freshness into British literature, Lessing produces quite a few African stories. But, as mentioned in Chapter One, Lessing's so-called African stories are still stories about white exiles told from white-focused perspectives. Taking the view of the marginalized white, Lessing tells about the life, struggle, and destiny of the white colonials. But the stories of these exiles do provide the reader with a fresh experience into the life of both the colonizing white and colonized black, a hybridity that helps to reduce the provincialism of British literature.

Lessing cares a lot about the individualized voice, but at the same time, she "is a great recorder of our group life" (Byatt 15) as commented by A. S. Byatt, for she is involved in various activities in different periods of her life, from a fervent communist party member to a follower of Sufism. Lessing believes a writer should explore into the universal experience through the personal one. That's why the story of Martha Quest is in fact the story of a modern Every-woman, despite being "provincial". Growing out of the African countryside and tortured by an aspiration for city life, the young Martha Quest is a replica of Lessing and her contemporary white young girls. This universality growing out of the surface of "provincialism" is an example of Lessing's effort to go beyond the narrowness in British literature.

Lessing's disdain for the narrowness in British literature comes from her belief in the "largeness of attitude" (Thorpe 98) that characterizes many great literary works. When asked whether her achievements could be attributed to any specific writers, she says, "I think I was influenced much more by a kind of largeness of attitude, which is what you find in 'great literature', which was the opposite of anything around me" (Thorpe 98). For Lessing, to write with this largeness in attitude means to write about one's concern for all human beings—in particular the marginalized groups outside England—or to view the world with a perspective beyond local environment. Bearing this largeness in mind, Lessing experiments with various styles she has learned from those great writers. Her hybridized largeness alone has distinguished her from most of her contemporaries.

In addition to her complaints about British provincialism, Lessing constantly demonstrates her disgust at being categorized, an attitude that she reiterates in her writing. Per Wästberg (2007) once praised Lessing for her resistance to categorization, order, or any set rules and argued that due to the complexity and multiplicity in Lessing's writing, it was hard to give it a specific tag or make a classification among it. It is true that Lessing protests against putting things into simple categories, as she declares in an interview that "I don't like this business of saying something is only *that*" (Terkel & Lessing 26, italics original). For her, it seems that the world as well as writing could better be defined with "hybridity" than any other single word, if there should be such a single word.

As a writer who has been active for about 60 years and produced more than 50 books in almost every genre, Lessing constantly falls victim to labelling. Ever since her first book was published in 1950, Lessing has been given various labels. At first, she was regarded as an African or a Rhodesian writer, because of her concerns for colonial issues, in particular the life in Southern Rhodesia. In the late 1950s, she was called a Communist, for her passion for political issues. She was also called a feminist due to the popularity of *GN*, a label she is strongly opposed to. In her later period, due to her interest in Eastern religion and especially Sufism, she is put into the group of Sufi writers or writers of mysticism. Finally, her shift towards science fiction brings her the title of space-fiction novelist.

Lessing's resentment against labeling stems partly from her preference for universality. For Lessing, a major task of literature is to reveal the common experience of people, regardless of their location and individual experience. In a 1980 interview, Lessing expresses her resentment of being compartmentalized or to be defined as only "this" or "that":

> Critics tend to compartmentalize, to establish periods, to fragmentize, a tendency that university training reinforces and that seems very harmful to me. At first, they said that I wrote about the race problem, later about Communism, and then about women, the mystic experience, etc., etc., but in reality I am the same person who wrote about the same themes. This tendency to fragmentize, so typical of our society, drives people to crisis, to despair... (Torrents & Lessing 64)

It is a common practice for scholars to classify a writer into time periods. Lessing regards this practice as ridiculous, as classification or fragmentization will impede the reader from getting a sound understanding of the author and his work. A brief look at Lessing's personal experience will prove that freeing herself from rid imprisonment is her lifelong objective: She quit school against her mother's will at the age of 14; went to work in Salisbury as a secretary at the age of 16 to escape from her parents' control; she left behind her two marriages and two children and went to London; she quit her job as a secretary and tried to become an independent professional writer in London. Lessing keeps fleeing from various bondages and fights for freedom in life as well as in writing, an attitude that has been praised by her critics: "Mrs. Lessing's insistence upon her own artistic integrity and the freedom to write in diametrically opposed modes, as they suit her different interests as a writer" (Ingersoll xi).

Noticing that there is a "tendency of the human mind to see things in pairs—either/or, black/white, I/you, we/you, good/bad, the forces of good/the forces of evil" (Lessing *PWCLI* 15), Lessing argues that to apply any over-simplified standard to things in the world is a practice of categorization, which is incapable of making a faithful representation. To avoid categorizations, Lessing finds it necessary to change the habit of thinking based on binary opposition. For Lessing, writing is a simultaneous action dependent on both the will of the author and the broad social context in which it is completed. The writer may take whatever form he likes, for the novel is "whatever each author makes of it" (Montremy & Lessing 195) and therefore is self-contained. Lessing seems to have been deeply annoyed by the misreading of her work. In the preface to *GN,* she complains that their reviews "are humiliating, they are on such a low level, and it's all so spiteful and personal" (Newquist & Lessing 6). She believes that the writer is a storyteller who needs to be fully engaged in storytelling without interference from the outside. Yet critics as well as students are usually trained by the academy to read in a dogmatic way, which prevents them from listening to the real voice of the author. Having identified the weakness in British literature and found fault with literary critics and readers, Lessing casts her eyes outside England.

3.2 Rebelliousness Cultivated Through Lifelong Struggle

Resistance, struggle, and survival are among the words most frequent found in Lessing's writing. *GS* tells about a white female colonizer's struggle against the three-fold confinement from her husband, white society, and the black community, a struggle that ends in a tragic murder. *GN* tells about women's survival in a patriarchal society, their struggles for new relations between men and women, and their disillusionment with and protest against communism which they firmly believe in at the very beginning. *Children of Violence* series are concerned with the children of two world wars, especially Martha Quest who rebels against her colonial parents, the narrow community in Central Africa, and the sophisticated city of London and draws a vivid picture of the growth of the post-war generation. Generally speaking, most of Lessing's works are about escaping from imprisonments and struggling to survive. Consequently, an in-depth study of Lessing's hybridized narration should include a discussion of Lessing's rebelliousness, which grows out of her lifelong struggle against various hostile elements, including those she met in her childhood in southern Rhodesia, her self-made education, the two world wars, her participation in various social activities, her belief in and later disillusionment with Marxism, and philosophies such as Freudianism, Jungianism, and Sufism.

Her early life in the vast land of Africa was a period of exile away from the powerful metropolitan white culture and of freedom in the wilderness. This early life partly accounts for the rebelliousness which lasts through her life, "She had the freedom and space to live that largely solitary childhood (her brother being away at school much of the time), which makes for introspection, dreaming, a close fellowship with the natural surroundings, a freedom from early intellectual involvement" (Thorpe *Africa* 6). Brought up in such a wild environment, young Lessing grew to be a "wild" girl and aspired for freedom and mobility.

Lessing was living in the wild, yet she felt depressed and confined by the unhappy child-parent relation in the family, especially by the tight control of her mother. Looking back to this unhappy experience, Lessing later admitted in her autobiography that "I was dealing with my painful adolescence, my mother, all that anguish, the struggle for survival" (Lessing *WS* 32). In order to get rid of her parents' control, Lessing rushed into marriage but found that that was hardly a "proper marriage"[1]. After two divorces, which left her with three children, she moved to London in 1949, starting a totally new and independent life as a career woman.

Apart from the depression and chaos resulting from her personal experience, Lessing suffered from crises and threats in the 1920s in southern Rhodesia, a colonial society and a land of conflicts. The increasingly intense conflicts between the poor white colonizers and the colonized blacks, between the intruding white culture and the conservative local culture, made her more aware of the incompatibility between the two cultures and ideological systems. This was the society in which she grew from a five-year-old girl to a young woman in her twenties, and the society that forced her to escape. In a sense,

---

1 One of her novels is titled *A Proper Marriage* (1964), an entry in the five volume *The Children of Violence* series. This novel tells about Martha Quest's married life, which is involved with drinking and partying, heavily burdened by an immediate pregnancy, and shadowed by the threat of war.

her early experience in a "white-black" Rhodesia contributes to the formation of her critical spirit and perception of the world:

> There were various reasons why I had to develop an extremely clear and critical mind. It was simply survival... I was under terrible pressure as a child, which is true of every child, mind you, but I think it was slightly worse in my case. And then I was in this social set-up, which I disliked, this white-black thing. I can't remember a time when it didn't make me uneasy, even when I didn't know why I was (Bikman & Lessing 59–60).

Lessing realized that she had to "develop an extremely clear and critical mind" in order to survive. The African prairie not only provides her with a panorama of nature and the black-white context, but also cultivates in her a critical perception and a strong will to freedom. Having spent all her formative years in Southern Rhodesia, Lessing gradually realizes that she has to fight every inch of her way and "had to be critical about everything, all my life" (Dean & Lessing 87). Among the factors that make her a courageous and undaunted fighter, Africa should be on top of the list.

Besides the impact of life in Africa on the development of her spirit of resistance, violence, Lessing explains, has made her a doomed child who "was one of the generation brought up on World War I and then as much formed by World War II" (*WS* 15). The *Children of Violence* series, which Lessing acknowledges to be more or less autobiographical, begin when Martha Quest is about 14 years old. The stories tell that "Martha's soul, and that of entire generations, is in some way warped by the seed of violence within her, planted by a historical process which Martha can neither choose nor accept as her own" (ferro 18). Like Martha, Lessing spent her childhood under the gloomy aftermath of the First World War and grew into maturity with the miseries of the Second World War.

Being a child of violence, Lessing is particularly concerned about the issue of trauma. For her, only by seeing with their own eyes the disaster, wounds, and immorality brought on by wars, could people realize how important it is to say no to all these crimes of violence. The post Second World War period in England saw a slow recovery, diminishing national power and weakening world prestige, which resulted in uncertainties, doubts, and complaints about the status quo. The Cold War and the nuclear threat thereafter led to wide spread disillusionment and fury, with increasing calling for transformation and destruction of the old system. The New Left, a group of people who devoted themselves to reshaping British society culturally, socially, economically, and politically came to the scene at the end of the 1950s, with the first issue of the *New Left Review* published in 1960. A literary figure related to the left-wing intellectuals who made his debut at the time was the Angry Young Man, which got its name from John Osborne's play *Look Back in Anger* (1956). The hero of this play, Jimmy Porter, is a young "rebel without a cause, unable to find clear, widely shared directions for his disaffection" (Stevenson 20).

The strongest impact on the formation of Lessing's characters is therefore the social context and her involvement in the politics of the day. As a sensitive and adaptable mind, Lessing kept pace with the tumultuous political life. Her intellectual participation in the political controversy contributes to the formation of her radical ideas and rebellious attitudes. Being one of the new left intellectuals, Lessing was deeply concerned about transforming human consciousness and establishing a new habit of mind. For this reason, among others, Lessing is "among the most innovative of late 20th-century authors" (Stevenson 44) to bring about the intellectual transformation.

Lessing's political awareness was cultivated during her childhood, when almost everyone talked nothing but politics: "I can't remember a time when I haven't heard people discussing politics. This was probably my earliest education" (Dean & Lessing 87). Lessing is sensitive to political issues all her life: in the 1930s she became a fervent communist; in 1956, having disillusioned with the hypocrisy of some communist leaders and the practices in some of the socialist countries, she quit the communist party; while later she admitted that her former commitment to communism was an act of absurdity, she still actively involved herself in the political life wherever she moved. Political as she was, her understanding of politics changed, as her experience in the 1950s made her realize that should there be any universal ethic, it would never be an overtly political or religious one. This realization turns her from a political activist into a humanist. She frequently reflected upon her life during this period and put it into several of her most important works. *GN* and *MQ* are the two books offset in the 1950s, and her autobiography *WS* is mainly about her life in London. *GN,* in particular, integrates into the story her involvement in the communist party in her early years.

After her break from the communist party, Lessing became more introspective and critical. Arguing that a writer should care more about the well-being of all humanity and that writing should deal with universal instead of party interest, Lessing felt disappointed with political ideologies, which she believed to be "deceptive" (Schwarzkopf & Lessing 105) and benefit only a few. While reflecting upon her former political fervor about thirty years later, Lessing not only regarded it as lunatic, but also questioned the justifiability of any such "mindset" at any time:

> And yet it is hard from present perspectives to make sense of a way of thinking I now think was lunatic. Does it matter if one woman succumbed to lunacy? No. But I am talking of a generation, and we were part of some kind of social psychosis or mass self-hypnosis. I am not trying to justify it when I say that I now believe all mass movements—religious, political— are a kind of mass hysteria and, a generation or so later, people must say, But how *could* you believe... whatever it was? (*WS* 53, italics original)

Looking back at the 1950s London, Lessing realized that all mass movements or beliefs were a kind of "social psychosis or mass self-hypnosis". To her, beliefs and convictions were, most of the time, utilized by a small group for their own purposes. Partly due to her unhappy experience with party politics, Lessing advocated that a writer's duty is to warn the reader of the hypocrisy of ideological convictions and to help them break away from the bondage of such beliefs.

Having spent about 25 years in South Africa and most of the rest of her life in London, and as a child of violence and a fervent social activist, Lessing develops a keen insight into the issues of discrimination, tyranny, as well as resistance against any set rules. She constantly revises her view on the moral issue of the writer's function and of the author-text-reader relations. In a sense, this rebelliousness cultivated through her lifelong struggle, together with the cultural legacies from the life she has experienced, encourages Lessing to try every means to open up her writing to various voices. In this struggle against the mono-voice authority, hybridity turns out to be an effective strategy.

3.3 Fluidity in Writing Philosophy

Lessing spares no effort in expounding her views on writing, including her response to misreadings of her works, her motivations and objective in each book, and her evolution as an intellectual.

Believing that "any philosophy that lasts longer than fifty years must be a bad one, because everything changes so fast" (Lessing *WS* 195), Lessing constantly revises her beliefs and convictions in writing so as to keep up with the times. It is this adaptability cultivated in the context of her personal experiences and ways of thinking that contributes to her style of writing. Lessing's interpretation of key narrative issues and the evolvement of her writing philosophy can be found in her collections of interviews and literary criticism, in her fictional writings as well as her autobiographies[1]. Of the issues that have aroused Lessing's interest, the most frequently mentioned are the author's function, the author-text-reader relations, and moral issues within the text, all of which have affected her choice of narrator, voice and perspective.

The author's function

For Lessing, understanding the function of an author is a major concern in writing. Should the author address his reader in a direct and intimate manner, or try to distance himself from the reader and speak in a detached voice? Should

---

1 Most of Lessing's elaborations on her writing philosophy can be found in *Putting the Questions Differently, Interviews with Doris Lessing, 1964–1994, A Small Personal Voice, Time Bites*, and her two auto biographies.

the author speak in a condescending or intrusive tone to make the reader accept whatever he says? To better understand Lessing's attitudes on this matter, it is necessary to start with her arrival in London in 1949.

At the very beginning, Lessing had confidence in the transformative power of a writer and declared that: "I saw it as my duty to be politically active, to take to the field against injustice, and wherever I went, standing or sitting, to discuss political subjects" (Schwarzkopf & Lessing 109). She advocated that a writer's obligation was to teach and preach, to shoulder the responsibility of fighting against injustice, and in particular, to integrate political issues into writing. Due to her involvement in various social activities, Lessing regarded political issues as indispensable parts of writing and as effective means to raise awareness of transformation, which helped to advance society as a whole. Believing in the writer's role as a preacher and moral guide, Lessing, during her early writing, tended to use an intrusive authorial voice or transcending tone more frequently, therefore, more omniscient narrators and intrusive narrators in her writing.

Later, in a 1972 interview taken in her London home by Joyce Carol Oates, Lessing expressed her doubt about the mission of the writer as well as the function of literature: "I asked her if she was pleased, generally, with her writing and with its public response. Strangely, she replied that she sometimes had to force herself to write—that she often was overcome by the probable 'pointless-ness' of the whole thing" (Oates & Lessing 38). While admitting that some of her writings seemed to have failed to elicit public response or produce the subsequent social transformation she desired, Lessing nevertheless claimed that the writer should move on. She did not totally deny the premises of writing, though she was not so sure about its moral effect on society.

This seems contradictory, for on the one hand, Lessing advocated that a writer should keep going "whether literature accomplishes anything or not" (Oates & Lessing 47). But on the other, she grew pessimistic about the function of the novel: "I think people now go to sociological books more than novels for cues of how to live their life. I used to go particularly to novels to find out how I ought to live my life. But, to my loss, I see now I didn't find out"

(Hendin & Lessing 54). Compared with her trust in the writer's social obligation two decades earlier, Lessing became more hesitant and doubtful, a change she had not expected of herself. What's more, Lessing, the once fervent participant in political activities, declared that it is futile to bring political issues into literature:

> To express it poetically, politics is not as the beating of wings. And the writer is nothing but an isolated voice in the wilderness. Many hear it; most pass by. It has taken a long time for me to recognize that in their books writers should *distance* themselves from the political questions of the day. They only *waste* their energy senselessly and bar their vision from the universal themes of humanity which know neither time nor space (Schwarzkopf & Lessing 109).

Lessing admitted that political issues in a literary text in the 1980s were far from a driving power and that the writer's voice seemed to be "an isolated voice in the wilderness". The writer would find themselves heard, yet rejected by the reader. Therefore, it was better for the writer to "distance themselves from the political questions of the day", for this focus on political issues was too limited compared with "the universal themes of humanity". Having drawn lessons from her personal experiences and having turned from an enthusiastic political activist to a disillusioned writer, Lessing realized in the midst of her writing career that a writer could hardly be a savior of or preacher to the public. The writer should instead devote himself to the task of revealing universal truth. Declaring that "anyone who reads history at all knows that the passionate and powerful convictions of one century usually seem absurd, extraordinary, to the next" (*PWCL* 6), Lessing showed her doubt about the certainty or consistency of beliefs, value systems, or ideologies that must be confined to a certain context and therefore deserve little attention from the writer[1].

---

1   Due to this lack of belief in fixed ideas, convictions, values systems, or any set rules, Lessing turns to space fiction in her later writing, holding that space fictions can go beyond space and time, and therefore can be a more faithful representation of reality.

In addition to her abandonment of political issues in writing, Lessing's confidence in the writer's power also weakens. She declared that what a writer could do is "to write as truthfully as possible about himself or herself as an individual, because we are not unique and remarkable people" (Bigsby & Lessing 82). A writer was not an extraordinary person who could foresee, predict, and change the world; rather, he kept interrogating the world and tried to present the symptoms of the ailing society from his individual perspective, for "a writer's job is to provoke questions" (Frick & Lessing 164). Lessing emphasized writer's power of expression: "We can express things better. Our function as writers, I maintain, is to express what other people feel. If we're any good, it's because we're like other people and can express it" (Terkel & Lessing 28).

Entering the mid-1980s, Lessing revised her view of the mission and function of the author once again. In a 1985 interview, Lessing expressed deeper doubts in the transforming power of literature or of the writer. She admitted that while writing *GN,* she had firm belief in the transforming power of literature. But it turned out to be a delusion, for there was no such magic power in literature. She began to doubt "that state of mind, something I would never have dreamed of doing in my youth" (Rousseau & Lessing 156) and turned to the idea that what a writer could do is to arouse curiosity in the reader or offer insight into reality. Lessing declared that the writer should be an "igniter" rather than a manipulator of either the text or reader. Instead of giving a solution and direction to the reader, as Lessing formerly argued, the writer was to warn the reader of the possible problems of the present and future, since the writer was more sensitive to reality.

But that is not all. With her advancing age, Lessing became more pessimistic about the power of the writer and argued that the writer does not have the mystical power to predict the future, nor was he capable of igniting the curiosity in the reader: "I know the problems of the hour, which the whole world knows. The fact of having written novels doesn't give me any more clairvoyance than the average television viewer" (Montremy & Lessing 194). Here for Lessing the writer is no better than the common reader. After thirty years of writing, she took a drastic turn on the issue of the author's function[1].

With a revised view on the author's function, Lessing changed her narrative strategy in the later period of writing and tended to efface her presence from the text, to be replaced by more objective, cool-headed and detached narrators in her later works: "You have to write cold. You can't write hot; otherwise, it's no good" (Thomson & Lessing 191). She stressed the necessity of writing "cold", of remaining uninvolved and distanced so as to leave the text to the reader. The earlier Lessing disappears, one of a fervent social activist who believed in the transformative power of literary works.

However, Lessing never loses confidence in the writer's keen insight and expressive power. What a writer puts down on paper will inevitably show his moral attitude and therefore exert influence on the text and reader. The elements of a novel, such as subject matter, selection of characters, focus of narration, tone, voice, and style, prove that a writer tells and his presence can be felt in the text:

> In short, the author's judgment is always present, always evident to anyone who knows how to look for it. Whether its particular forms are harmful or serviceable is always a complex question, a question that cannot be settled by any easy reference to abstract rules. As we begin now to deal with this question, we must never forget that though the author can to some extent choose his disguises, he can never choose to disappear (Booth *Rhetoric* 20).

Booth argues that it is impossible for an author to completely "disappear" from the text, for there are always clues that give him away, and the reader may detect his presence. For Lessing, diversified narrators are such textual clues, including Lessing the writer as an omniscient narrator or implied author. Lessing the author can hardly silence herself in the text.

---

1   This change in attitude is not an isolate case, rather, it reflects the general mindset of the left-wing intellectual in the 1980s. Due to the changing historical and social context, left-wing intellectuals in the 19805 suffer from dissolution and failure.

The Moral Issue

Besides the dynamic role of the writer, Lessing's critical essays and interviews frequently touch upon moral issues. Lessing's attitude towards whether an artistic work should have a strong and clear moral foundation is never steadfast, for it is closely related to Lessing's view on the author's function. Lessing believes in the necessity of morality through preaching, persuasion, or suggestion[1]. But her belief in the moral sense of literary work has undergone a subtle change.

When Lessing was beginning to write in the 1940s, she firmly believed that a moral stance was an indispensable part of artistic work, and that the artist should be entrusted with the task of establishing a correct moral system for the public. Encouraged by the 19th-century realists and confident in the transforming power of the writer, Lessing claimed that it was the writer's obligation to introduce something positive into his writing, such as "the warmth, the compassion, the humanity, the love of people" (Lessing *ASPV* 6). A responsible writer "must become a humanist" (Lessing *ASPV* 6), with concerns for human welfare, values, morality, and dignity, and dealt with morality in his writing with an objective of bringing about changes first in his reader, and then in society as a whole.

In a 1980 interview, when asked if she still believed in the duty of the writer to describe the immorality of the system with her "small personal voice", Lessing's answer was "possibly". She was no longer sure about the author's influence on his reader, in particular on the issue of morality. Nevertheless, Lessing still had some belief in the moral responsibility of the author and tried to adjust her strategy of dealing with morality. For instance, in place of an omniscient preaching narrator, she sometimes chose the role of a sympathetic,

---

1   She even declares her dislike of some of her own works for their lack of moral orientation. For example, while talking about one of her well-accepted short stories "Hunger", which she regards as one of her failures, she admits: "What is wrong with that tale is sentimentality, which is often the sign of an impure origin: in this case, to write a tale with a moral" (Lessing *WS* 70). Lessing seems to regard it necessary to put the moral issue before sentimentality, at least in her early years.

forgiving, and tolerant observer.

Lessing's beliefs in the author's ability to persuade the reader echoes that of David Lodge, who regards fiction as a "rhetorical art" that should be utilized by the writer to persuade the reader "to share a certain view of the world" (Lodge X). Lessing's belief also corresponds with that of Tolstoy her predecessor, who was praised by Lessing for his strong sense of moral teaching: "He was known as much as a social critic and moralist as an author... He was described as the conscience of the world" (Lessing *TB* 27). This is one of the reasons Lessing put Tolstoy high on her list of the great 19th-century realists. She claimed that a writer should be socially self-conscious for the silent majority and refuse to succumb to injustice, discrimination, and tyranny.

Wayne Booth, in his essay "'Of the Standard of Moral Taste': Literary Criticism as Moral Inquiry", is another morality oriented critic as he discusses in detail the moral effects of art and criticism. He tries to answer each of the following questions:

Is genuine moral inquiry possible, or even pertinent, in appraising literary quality?... Is this work's moral quality an essential element in our judgment, not just of its moral value, but of its artistic worth?... How does one distinguish competent from incompetent judges, and how can even the most competent listener exercise inquiry about moral distinctions, not just between individual stories but among kinds of stories?... Are some kinds of story more likely to be harmful or beneficial to listeners? (Booth *Rhetoric* 242–254)

Booth first argues that there is no denying that "the moral powers of art" do exist in the text and that "those powers are real" (Booth *Rhetoric* 240). To preach morals effectively, authors must convey the idea through storytelling instead of playing the role of "mere exhorters" (Booth *Rhetoric* 240), for "stories are our major moral teachers" (Booth *Rhetoric* 241). The Bible and the stories it tells is a good example. Booth points out that there are three "epochs" in literary history in terms of attitudes towards the moral issue. During the first epoch, it was assumed that any work should have a moral value, a stand supported by classic scholars including Plato, Aristotle, and Horace. In the second epoch, however, more and more critics changed from "yes" to "no" on this issue: "Moral rightness or wrongness has little or nothing to do with literary or aesthetic worth, and debate about the moral worth of any artistic work consequently leads nowhere" (Booth *Rhetoric* 242–243). But there appeared a return to the "yes" again in the late 1960s, which he defines as the third epoch: "Not only in literary criticism but also in every artistic field, critics reopened questions about how stories change listeners and cultures. They thus began to reunite themselves—consciously or unconsciously—with the grand tradition of Plato and Sidney and Arnold" (Booth *Rhetoric* 244).

Based on David Hume's classic defense of literary judgment in "Of the Standard of Taste", Booth concludes: "In short, a justified ethical judgment depends, as Hume well knew, on a transaction between the ethical quality of the work and the ethical powers and attention of the listener" (Booth *Rhetoric* 246). That is to say, the ultimate justifiable interpretation of the moral judgment in an artistic work depends on two factors: one is the "ethical quality of the work", and the other is "the ethical powers and attention of the listener". All in all, criticism concerning the moral judgment of a work depends on the interaction between the author and the reader. It is, therefore, a question of the function, power, and relations of the author and the reader.

Like Wayne Booth, Lessing constantly meditates and elaborates on this topic. From *ASPV* to *TB*, from autobiographies to interviews, she never tires of discussing the moral value of a work, the mission of a writer, the response of the reader, and most important of all, the interaction between author and reader. Two of the most important questions she asks and answers are: Is moral value an indispensable element in both writing and judging what makes an artistic work good? Should the author be a moral teacher or guider? Lessing generally answers yes to both of these questions, for she has confidence in the moralizing and educating function of the writer.

This raises the questions of how, when, and where should the author exercises guidance on moral issues. To do so requires a tactical approach. Again according to Booth, the author should "place" and "judge", and a responsive reader will have his own judgment, which either agrees with the author or does not. A clever writer knows how to direct the reader in a appropriate way, so as to avoid undesired responses. For instance, the direct authorial intrusion may make the reader feel manipulated, so that he would rather go astray. Lazy readers may simply accept what the author says, rather than using their own critical judgment. The detached author may make the reader feel confused or lost.

Lessing has been so concerned about moral issues in writing that she not only constantly reflects upon her own handling of this issue, but also keeps a close eye on other writers' works. But her evaluation of other authors in terms of moral issue is unstable. Since she believes in the moral power of the literary work, especially in her early writing career, she admires those great 19th-century realists for their strong ethical power and social consciousness. But later, she realizes their weakness and believes that some of their works are provincial, being rooted in the local and trivial social situation. Even Tolstoy and Thomas Hardy fall into this group. Take Tolstoy's *Anna Karenina* as an example. Lessing believes that "the basic story is a story about nothing, about a local society, a very local, temporary set of social circumstances" (Bigsby & Lessing 72). Because of this narrowness, the moral effect and ethical judgments in these works are diminished. However, she does not think it good for a writer to be openly "moral". For instance, she puts George Eliot into the group of second-class writer, for "she was moral… I admire George Eliot enormously, I am not saying I don't. But there is something too cushioned in her judgments" (Bigsby & Lessing 71).

Just as her views on the writer's function keeps developing, Lessing's attitude towards moral values in literature keeps changing. Starting as a firm advocator for the necessity of moral value, Lessing later becomes doubtful about whether there should be any definite value system at a certain historical period, and whether people held certain beliefs. While still having faith in the moral effect in the novel, she yet has to admit that there is no fixed moral value. Despite these doubts or hesitations, Lessing remains a strong supporter of the writer's "small personal voice" (Lessing *ASPV* 21), a voice through which the artist can communicate with his reader directly and effectively, for "in an age of committee art, public art, people may begin to feel again a need for the small personal voice" (Lessing *ASPV* 21).

The Author-text-reader Relationship

Lessing's perception of the writer's function and ability to preach morality varies over time, and her interpretation of the author-text-reader relationship changes accordingly. With her increasing doubt in the power of the author, she puts more trust in the reader, claiming that "one can't choose one's readers; they choose us" (Torrents & Lessing 74). Having more confidence in the initiatives of the reader, she admits that readers are more difficult to identify, which consequently diminishes the power of the author.

In the 1950s, Lessing was quite optimistic about the moral power of the committed author and believed that the readers were willing to follow the guidance of this author as preacher. Therefore, the author was superior to the reader due to his power of interpretation and manipulation. But in the 1960s, in the preface to *GN*, after discussing the changing role of the author and reader, she concluded:

> And from this kind of thought has emerged a new conclusion: which is that it is not only childish of a writer to want readers to see what he sees, to understand the shape and aim of a novel as he sees it—his wanting this means that he has not understood a most fundamental point. Which is that the book is alive and potent and fructifying and able to promote thought and discussion *only* when its plan and shape and intention are not understood, because that moment of seeing the shape and plan and intention is also the moment when there isn't anything more to be got out of it (*GN* 22, italics original).

Here, Lessing seems to have confidence in her reader to understand her writing, though each reader may have his own interpretation. It is the interaction between the author, the text, and the reader that makes the novel a living being. This process of identifying the author's intention and carefully designed structure makes reading dynamic. She does not seem to worry about ambiguity in reader's interpretation, since ambiguity may create the possibility for the reader to read more closely and endow the novel with more freshness and liveliness. This belief of Lessing not only explains her textual arrangement, but also gives clues to the carefully designed hybridity in her works.

Having realized the benefits of a more active reader, Lessing gradually loosens her control on the reader and establishes a more flexible author-reader relationship in her writing. Sometimes she, as the author, is the superior; sometimes she tries to be a calm observer or outsider; sometimes she and her reader are coworkers or conspirators; sometimes she allows the reader the freedom to read independently; and sometimes she makes herself the reader's competitor. Even within one story, the author-reader relation may change, for the author's evaluation of and trust in his reader decides his way of handling this relationship.

In releasing her control of the reader, Lessing puts into practice the idea of "zero writing", a concept put forward first by Roland Barthes[1] and later echoed by T. S. Eliot. Lessing becomes more and more aware that it is necessary to distance herself from both text and reader, to be a more self-restrained author. When the reader takes the initiative, it becomes even harder to expect the reader's response, and the author may find it more difficult to manipulate him. For instance, Lessing once said that the readers' responses to *GN* were outside her expectations. On the one hand, it makes her anxious to realize "how far apart the intention of the author and the comprehension of the reader can be" (Schwarzkopf & Lessing 107). On the other hand, she feels relieved that "a book is a living thing which can bear many kinds of fruit" (Schwarzkopf & Lessing 107). She is happy to see the unexpected response from the reader and

---

1   As for the notion of "zero writing" put forward by Roland Barthes and flexibly applied by Lessing in her writing, see the detailed discussion in the opening part of Chapter Three.

the uncontrollable nature of the novel, for she regards it as the charm and force of the novel: "What's marvelous about novels is they can be anything you like. That is the strength of the novel. There are no rules" (Dean & Lessing 95).

Although Lessing grows to trust the reader, one of the reader's responses she dislikes is the attempt at finding the autographical parts of her writing. While most of her writings are drawn from her life experience and her observation of people around her, it is hard to find a real "Lessing" in her work. For example, the character Jane Somers, though seemingly just another version of Doris Lessing, actually comes from various people, including her friends and her mother. And in *The Four-Gated City*, Lessing's personality is "parceled out between the different characters" (Bertelsen "Acknowledging a New Frontier" 143). For Lessing, observation is fundamental in obtaining a comprehensive and objective view of life, hence, a faithful representation of reality rather than mere facts and details of the author.

Lessing further explains that even if there is something autobiographical, it "changes into something new as soon as the writing begins. During the process of writing, some unexpected transformation would surprise the author. A writer must depict the each character as specific circumstances demand. The characters may grow out of their own life, and sometimes even out of the expectations of the author. A writer should take special care when writing in first person to keep her own voice from taking the upper hand. Therefore, the writer has to let his character tell and see things in his own eyes.

While Lessing seems to give the reader more freedom in deciphering the texts, she knows it is impossible to erase the author from the texts. Believing that it is the author's duty to communicate with or to teach morals to the audience, she as an author keeps an eye on the reader, identifying their response to or reception of her novels and making adaptation accordingly. For Lessing, writing is a dynamic process which may bring about the growth of both the reader and the author, a fact that has been pointed out by one of the Lessing scholars Jenny Taylor:

Doris Lessing's fiction demonstrates particularly sharply the intricate ways in which a writer is *produced* and *reproduced* within a cultural formation, often by drawing on forms apparently outside it. It emphasizes not only the *complex* relation between author, text and reader, but also the different contexts and settings through which meaning is both *constructed* and made *active* by different readers' own subjectivity and social position. This process is *fluid*—there is no fixed author or reader. But neither is arbitrary or infinite (Taylor 9, emphasis added).

Taylor has noticed Lessing's changing position and concluded that it is this change that makes writing a "fluid" process. In this process of production and reproduction, Lessing has resorted to various modes and forms, as has been discussed in the first two chapters. "Fluid" is a right word to characterize Lessing. At times when she has belief in the writer, she is likely to make herself an interfering narrator in the story. When she begins to doubt the power of the writer, she chooses to step back so as to allow the reader to play a more active role. When she feels it unwise to lose control of the story, she interferes and cooperates with the reader. Then, if the reader's interpretation runs farfetched, she may compete with the reader for the meaning in the text. No matter what kind of author-text-reader relationship she chooses to build, the final goal is to endow the reading with dynamism and vitality.

In one of the essays entitled "Writing Biography", Lessing points out a significant difference between novel and autobiography, the personalities:

One of the ways one can use novels is to see the different personalities in novelists... Now here is the paradox. It is easier to see this map of a person in their novels than in the autobiography. That is because an autobiography is written in one voice, by one person, and this person smoothes out the roughness of the different personalities. This is an elderly, judicious, calm person, and this calmness of judgment imposes a unity. The novelist doesn't necessarily know about her own personalities (*TB* 99–100).

She explains that the novelist shows various personalities, quite unlike the "elderly, judicious, calm person" in an autobiography, and that the novelist usually does not have a single voice or tone. Therefore, there is no unity in the novel but fragmentation, splitting ideas, fluidity or confusion. At the end of the passage, Lessing goes back to Goethe again, quoting his view on reading to reach her conclusion:

> I think that he had learned a certain passivity in reading, taking what the author is offering, and not what the reader thinks he should be offering, not imposing himself (herself) between the author and what should be emanating from the author. That is to say, not reading the book through a screen of theories, ideas, political correctness, and so forth. This kind of reading is indeed difficult, but one can learn this sort of passive reading, and then the real essence and pith of the author is open to you. I am sure everyone has had the experience of reading a book and finding it vibrating with aliveness, with color and immediacy. And then, perhaps some weeks later, reading it again and finding it flat and empty. Well, the book hasn't changed: you have (*TB* 103).

Here, Lessing actually is talking about the author's function and the reader's response. She thinks that Goethe's view on reading is a passive one, yet this passive reading may bring forth something active, for "one can learn this sort of passive reading, and then the real essence and pith of the author is open to you". She believes in the dynamic relationship between the author and reader, because the reader's comprehension and interpretation of the novel is forever changing.

The dialogic relation here is not limited to author and reader, but is extended to the author's own voice and her text as a result of which an inter-textuality emerges.

Dialogism argues that all meaning is relative in the sense that it comes about only as a result of the relation between two bodies occupying simultaneous but different space, where bodies may be thought of as ranging from the immediacy of our physical bodies, to political bodies and to bodies of ideas in general (ideologies). In Bakhtin's thought experiments, as in Einstein's, the position of the observer is fundamental (Holquist 19).

This explains the fluid relationship between the author and reader as well as the endless production of meaning. Therefore, the "two bodies" involved in the same dialogue, one the speaker / the articulating author, the other the observer / the silent reader, perceive each other differently. With the change in the "position of the observer", the meaning brought forth by the dialogue varies. In this author-text-reader relationships, none of the three is fixed and therefore change is inevitable. As a result, the reader can take more initiatives in the production of the meaning together with the author long after the completion of the text.

The rhetorical strategic of hybridity enables Lessing to seek her individualized discourse under the system of a unitary discourse, to make her monologic utterance part of the heteroglossia. At the same time, her monologic utterance tends to be hybridized as the result of her intentional use of specific narrative elements. Perhaps no other writers have been so frequently challenged for the changeability in writing which tends to be ambiguous, disorderly, obscure, discursive, and dull. Her attempts at experimentation with styles and genres, though not always successful as in the case of space fiction, at least save her from the narrowness and provincialism of which she is so contemptuous.

Being a stead-fast left-wing intellectual and thrice-exiled writer, Lessing partakes of the social and historical heterogloassia and, at the same time, shows her determination to contribute her bit to the decentralizing practice characteristic of the time and in line with her own spirit and doctrine. When a narrative form with hybrid agencies becomes a marginalized construction, obtaining an "interstitial" position can be defined as "the outside of the inside: the part in the whole" (Bhabha "Culture's In-Between" 58), a position that makes it possible to observe with a detached yet vigilant and sober mind. While negotiating with the authoritative discourse, hybrid agencies assume no "supremacy or sovereignty" like those more advantaged discourses; instead, they offer representations from marginalized positions and speak for disadvantaged communities.

Conclusion

This study chooses to focus on Lessing and tries to argue that hybridity is a major rhetorical strategy used by Lessing to establish a dialogic mechanism in her writing, which is best demonstrated in the multi-voiced dialogue within the text, the interaction among the author, text and reader, Lessing's responses to or inheritance of other writers and theorists, as well as the adjustments she constantly makes in her writing philosophy. Lessing owes much of her position as a hybridized writer to two of the 20th century literary theorists, Mikhail Bahktin and Homi Bhabha, since the idea of polyphony and heteroglossia for one and the Third Space for the other best explain Lessing's strategy of hybridity.

Bahktin believes that the benefit of hybridity lies in its adaptability for both fusion and fission which gives rise to a multiple-voiced discourse against the single authoritative voice. While Bakhtin elaborates on the notion of hybridity from a discursive perspective, Bhabha turns it into a post-colonial strategy, declaring that the Third Space enunciations, made available by hybridity, entail a co-existence of the sameness and difference open to a multiplicity of voices in a multi-layered cultural context. Bhabha confirms the fluidity and changeability hidden within hybridity which is indispensable in the process of production and deconstruction of narration.

Bakhtin emphasizes the significance of establishing a dialogic mechanism inside and outside the text. He regards hybridity as an effective rhetorical strategy in the novel of Dostoevsky. Bhabha furthers the idea by turning it into a subversive strategy in the fight against colonial domination. He holds that in the Third Space—"the realm of the beyond" or "the one yet to be defined" (Sheng Ning 94), the cultural conflict calls for negotiation, redefinition or reinterpretation.

Thanks to the articulation and interpretation made by theorists such as Bakhtin and Bhabha, hybridity, a principally biological term, turns from a negative concept originally related to impurity, infertility and inferiority, to a much wider and more positive one denoting a source of vitality and constructiveness. As has been discussed in the introductory part, ever since the Victorian period, debates on hybridity has been focused on the question of fertility of mixed racial breeding. In the post-colonial context, the discussion takes on more analytical vigor and constructive power as a means of resistance against dominance.

According to Bakhtin, "the novel as a whole is a phenomenon multiform in style and variform in speech and voice" (Bakhtin 261). In Lessing's case, her writing turns out to be such a multi-formed text since it takes on a "variform" evidenced in her handling of narrating voices, narrators, perspectives, styles, genres and subject matters so that her text is characterized as inclusive, ambiguous, open and consequently highly constructive.

Her constructiveness, as has been extensively discussed in the above chapters, is itself highly diversified, taking different forms as they appear appropriate to her purposes. In *Love, again*, the narrating voice is a multiple one consisting of the omniscient third-person narration, the free-indirect speech and the interior monologue as accomplished by Sarah, Julie, and the diaries and journals. Hence, a polyphonic narrative which gives full play to both the external and internal voices of various characters while diminishing the authorial intrusion. Similarly, in *The Diaries of Jane Somers*, there is an interwoven of the first-person and third-person narration, a real author Janna within the story as well as the real author Lessing outside the story, together with the retrospective perspectives of Janna and Maudie, all of which combined makes the narration a complicated dialogue. While Janna's retrospective perspective depicts the mental growth of the young woman into her middle age, the retrospective perspective of Maudie shows the miseries of the old and the marginalized whose world can hardly be understood by the more advantaged or younger groups of people, for under most circumstances these so-called senior citizens are deprived of the chance of telling their own stories. Lessing's diversified perspectives can also be found in *The Grass Is Singing*, a story presented in a biased white perspective with or without

Lessing's own awareness, which is made blurred by a switch between the omniscient third-person narration and the limited third-person perspective of Mary. While the perspective in *The Grass Is Singing* switches between black and white, the perspective in *The Golden Notebook* can hardly be defined as either female or male, for the supposed-to-be female point of view is interfered with by Lessing's internalized patriarchal stance.

Apart from specific narrative techniques, Lessing's hybridity is further enriched by the diversified styles, cross-bordering genres and miscellany of subject matters. The latter, though not uncommon in other writers, work together with the former to create a new space for marginalized voices in the so-called heteroglossia which is the ultimate goal of hybridity. The two types of hybridity, either in form or in content, work together to construct a polyphonic narrative which gives full play to voices at various levels. In a polyphonic narrative, the dialogism growing organically out of a heteroglossia denies any ultimate meaning.

In addition, a brief comparative study between Lessing and several other theorists and writers including Forster, Woolf, Fanon and bell hooks further proves her construction of a hybridized discourse as a writing strategy in the macro-context of contemporary British literature. Besides, a diachronic study of Lessing's writing philosophy indicates that this philosophy has a direct bearing on her choice of voices, narrators and perspectives, which in turn proves that she is a writer against fixity in the habit of mind, singularity in modes of writing, and narrowness in both form and content.

By resorting to a hybridized narration, Lessing manages to go beyond the 19th century realism. Her postmodernist attempts at narrative theory and techniques entail a break with the traditional ways of storytelling or modes of narrative representation. Preferring to "play with, transgress, or otherwise meddle with these conventions" (Richardson 86), she tends to resort to different narrative techniques so as to motivate the progression of the narrative, a demonstration of innovation as well as a resistance against blind imitation. In fact, her experiments in this regard, in its extreme form, fall into the so called "de-narrative" group (Richardson 87) or meta-fiction which is an overt negation of conventional ways of story-telling. By emphasizing the artificial ways of story-telling, meta-fiction intends to remind the reader of the "unnatural" or constructiveness of the story, affirming that "there is no such thing as an objective, impartial narrative" (Richardson 87). Some of Lessing's works, if observed from this perspective, can be put into the category of meta-fiction due to her unique way of handling showing and telling.

As the result of the co-efforts made by both the (post)-modernist Lessing and realist Lessing, a dynamic author-text-reader relationship comes to the fore. It brings more freedom for the reader and the author, in the act of interpreting for the former and in the act of writing for the latter. Having achieved intellectual growth during the process of writing, Lessing the author tends to view the task of writing from an experiential perspective as the result of which a more flexible and diversified way of narrating is practiced. Whenever there is a looser control over the reader, the reading turns out to be more individualized, depending more heavily on the reader's personal experience and understanding, hence, a construction as well as reconstruction of the text. Meanwhile, the interaction among the three agents creates a dialogue which gives play to various tones and voices either inside or outside the text, a prerequisite for the emergence of a polyphony or heteroglossia which is characteristic of hybridity.

Lessing's mix of realistic and modernistic factors, according to Professor Yang Jincai (2009), is typical of contemporary British writers who are willing to travel back and forth between the real and the imaginary, a strategy capable of mimicrying and parodying the real. Since universality is based on individuality, it is worthwhile to have a close look at Lessing's writing experience so as to obtain a glimpse of the universal writing experience of her time. In addition, the multiplicity and complexity achieved by various strategies help Lessing to represent group experience through various individual experiences, as she holds it to be the ultimate goal of writing and the responsible of the writer to represent truthfully the experience of both the collective and the individual. Her writing, therefore, is not simply about Africa, London, young women, middle-aged married women, old women or people in any particular place and time, but rather, is about the common experience of humanity, about compassion and sympathy for the disadvantaged, about growth and maturity, about the humanity in the eye of the 19th century realists. What's more, Lessing also stands with the postmodernist writers for the doubt about watertight distinction between different genres or modes of writing, with a hybridized text which deny any simplistic categorization.

The advantages of hybridity lies in its capacity to break fixity, to dismantle authority, to redefine and reconstruct a world that is open to a multiplicity of voices, identities and cultures. The tone or voice issue, in Lessing's case, can also be interpreted from her "pursuit of English"[1], or her pursuit of a proper language and form to reflect the truth of life in literature, a self-defined literary voice. Feeling herself cornered with the dilemma caused by the limitations of traditional ways of writing as well as inspired by the emerging new ideas and new modes of writing, she tries hard to blaze a new trail, combining inheritance with innovation. This integration of both the old and the new, in fact, is dialogue or heteroglossia, a fusion of her introspective voice and experiencing voice both of which keep developing with the time on the one hand and constantly "talk" to each other on the other.

While the world has changed from one predominant with one voice to one multi-polarized by different voices, so is the world in Lessing's story. No single authoritative voice can speak for all, instead, the reader can hear voices of different groups of people in terms of races, ages, cultures, levels of education and so on, or they can view things in perspectives made possible by hybridized narrative strategies, as bell hooks once said: "To claim border crossing, the mixing of high and low, cultural hybridity, as the deepest expression of a desired cultural practice within multicultural democracy means that we must dare to envision ways such freedom of movement can be experienced by everyone" (hooks *Outlaw* 6). Lessing's hybridity, however, is more than cultural practice by left wing intellectuals in a post-colonial world,

---

1   It is taken from the title of one of her earliest semi-fictions *In Pursuit of the English* (1960) which tells about her first settlement in London and her efforts to make a living by herself, together with her two-year-old son.

it is also part of the narrative practice of a writer with critical imagination and innovative power. It is this practice that endows her with the freedom to speak out not only for herself but also for the silent majority and marginalized minority. It is her effort to construct a hybrid text that allows for more voices, "high and low", black or white, male or female, to get heard by more people. The underprivileged or once denied can have their voices heard thanks to the third space wrought by hybridity. In the case of Lessing, this hybridity results in a heteroglossia, to the effect of a blending of world views through literary production that creates a complex unity from diversified utterances. The various utterances delivered at the same time by the writer, the text and the reader, help to create a new space for a co-existence of powers capable of counter-balancing the dominating or mainstream discourse, literally, culturally as well as intellectually. For Lessing, hybridity is a strategy in her experimentation with various modes of writing, a disguise she uses to win the favor and trust of the reader, and last but not least, a weapon to fight against various form of imprisonment.

With the help of hybridity as the rhetorical strategy, Lessing establishes a dialogic mechanism which enables the dialogues to continue. The multi-levelled dialogic system in her writing consists of the following four types: 1) the one within the text, between the real author and the hidden author, between the author and his characters, 2) the one inside and outside the text, among the author, text and reader, 3) the one between the retrospective Lessing and experiencing Lessing, and 4) the one between Lessing and other writers and theorists.

Being one of the post-colonial writers, Lessing yet may not be the pioneer in this regard. For instance, Daniel Defoe in the 18th century tried to "define nationhood by insisting on difference and pluralism rather than common identity" (Guignery *et al.* 15). Joseph Conrad touched upon the issue of the hybrid in his colonial novel *The Heart of Darkness* (1902). Besides, since hybridity is often closely related to the issue of colonialism, it is no surprise that scholars use colonial fiction as textual support in their study of hybridity. Unlike those typical writers such as Conrad, Kipling and Toni Morrison,

Lessing is often excluded from the list of the post-colonial writing. Yet this study tries to show that she belongs to this category at least in terms of hybridity.

To approach Lessing's narration from the perspective of hybridity not only highlights her distinctive artistic feature, but also contributes to the study of post-colonialist and post-modernist writing in general. It should be pointed out that although Lessing critics have long noticed the hybridity in her, the study is limited both in breadth and depth. Similarly, Lessing herself seldom makes any clear or systematic articulation on the theory of hybridity. Lessing sometimes seems to resort to the strategy of hybridity without awareness, since neither her writing philosophy nor her narrative skill is consistent. While talking about hybridity as a distinctive feature of Lessing, this study, however, is careful not to use the term as a label for Lessing, since labelling is a practice which disgusts Lessing most.

While Darwin in his use of hybridity talks about the difference between the purebred and mixed species which has a bearing on fertility or productivity, Lessing applies the concept in her writing, consciously or unconsciously, to the effect of diversity in genres, styles and subject matters which makes her stand out among her contemporaries. Hybridity, therefore, is perhaps one of the best words to define her narrative skills and overall artistic feature. Her attempt in this regard, whether well acknowledged for its innovation or severely criticized for its immaturity, has injected vitality into contemporary British literature which partly accounts for her increasing influence worldwide.

Hvbridity resists simple replacement or dislocation of forms, styles, or identities and gives rise to more openness growing out of either integration or subversion or both. According to Robert Young, hybridity is like act of grafting, a process in which "any unlike living things" (Young *Colonial Desire* 24) can be forced together. No matter how incompatible it may seem, difference and sameness co-exist simultaneously. Likewise, the disparities in Lessing's handling of styles and genres can be defined as a sort of hybridity, for she feels free to bring something new out of the old or to turn the similar into the dissimilar.

Lessing disagrees with binary opposition, yet the binary opposition occurs not infrequently in her novel, a proof of "difference and sameness in an apparently impossible simultaneity" (Young *Colonial Desire* 24–25): the young vs. the old, female vs. male, children vs adults, black vs white, and so on. In a way, she tries to bridge the gap between the two by showing and presenting the differences and commonness at the same time. To erase the water-tight distinction between extremes, she first of all foregrounds their differences. The ambiguity arising from this mix-match makes the distinction less obvious and consequently a possibility for compromise or reconciliation is made available. The blurring of demarcations therefore is brought forth by the comparison and contrast. It is true that she is often blamed for this co-presentation of difference and sameness which seems to bring disorder to the text, as in the case of *The Golden Notebook* and some of her space fictions. Yet Lessing's writing is not a simplified fusion of elements. It may turn out to be an intentional act of hybrid which aims at decentralization and deconstruction for the purpose of contradiction and exposure from within. If hybridization occurs without her own awareness, or if a more natural hybrid construction calls for less doubt or challenge, it will make it easier for her individualized discourse to be incorporated into the heteroglossia. To integrate as well as to subvert, to project one's individuality while seeking common ground with others, this is the ultimate goal of hybridity and the essence of hybridization, at least so perceived by Lessing. And it is this kind of "a breaking and a joining at the same time" (Young *Colonial Desire* 24–25), usually a break from within and integration from outside, that distinguishes Lessing from others.

Lessing happens to be a privileged writer capable of speaking out both from the margin and from the center, an advantageous position or convenience brought forth by hybridity, as claimed by Robert Young. Young argues that to fight against domination, or to challenge the authority of the mainstream culture, one needs to take a stance of an outside-insider/ inside-outsider, like a ripple in the storm, being able to break from within while at the same time keeping in contact with the center, a goal best achievable in the context of hybridity. In Lessing's case, her popularity as a novelist, the wide audience, her frequent presence in public media, the award of Nobel Prize are all evidence of her influence on contemporary literature. In the meanwhile, her rich experience, in particular her early experience in colonial Africa and life-long enthusiasm for political agenda, plus her identity as a border crossing writer, have put her in a unique position for the marginalized experience. She consciously takes stand with the minority group while taking the advantage of a mainstream writer or intellectual. To highlight the hybridity in Lessing does not simply mean to emphasize the diversity of her work, but rather, to find out "how" and "why" she makes the best of this rhetorical strategy. Hybridity, though definitely not the only key to her success, does make her stand out among her contemporaries for the flexibility and innovation in textual construction, richness in textual interpretation and breadth in terms of motifs.

Although the author of this book makes efforts to conduct a systematic study on Lessing's narration from the perspective of hybridity, there are limitations. First, even if hybridity can be regarded as Lessing's writing strategy, more in-depth textual analysis needs to be made so as to prove that Lessing's is a steadfast practitioner of this strategy from the beginning to the end, with greater or lesser flexibility and creativity. Second, besides the observation made on Lessing's hybridity in terms of intertextuality, further study could be made on her indebtedness to the influence on her from Marxism, Freudianism, Jungianism and Sufism. Third, a closer look at the relation between Lessing, Bahktin and Bhabha is necessary to prove how effectively polyphony, heteroglossia as well as Third Space enunciations have worked into Lessing's hybridized narration. Hopefully, all this will be included in the future study.

Works Cited

Abbott, H. Porter. *The Cambridge Introduction to Narrative*. Cambridge: Cambridge University Press, 2002.

Abrams, M. H. Ed. *The Norton Anthology of English Literature*, 7th edition, Vol. 2. New York & London: W. W. Norton & Company, 2000.

——. *A Glossary of Literary Terms*. Beijing: Foreign Language Teaching and Research Press & Thomson Learning, 2004.

Achebe, Chinua. "An image of Africa: Racism in Conrad's *Heart of Darkness*". *Hopes and Impediments: Selected Essays*, 1965–1987. Oxford: Heinemann, 1988: 1–13.

Acheraïou, A. *Questioning Hybridity, Postcolonialism and Globalization*. London: Palgrave Macmillan, 2011.

Aldiss, Brian & Doris Lessing. "Living in Catastrophe, 1988". *Putting the Questions Differently, Interviews with Doris Lessing, 1964–1994*. Ed. Earl G. Ingersoll. London: Flamingo, 1996: 169–172.

Allardice, L. and Jones, S. "It's me? I've won after all these years? Doris Lessing: Interviews, audio, reviews and her own criticism." *The Guardian*. Oct. 12, 2007. Retrieved from http://www.theguardian.com/uk/2007/oct/12/topstories3.books.

Allen, Walter. *The Modern Novel in Britain and the United States*. New York: E. P. Dutton, 1965.

Anderst, Leah. "Feeling with Real Others: Narrative Empathy in the Autobiographies of Doris Lessing and Alison Bechdel". *Narrative* Vol. 23 (2015): 271–290.

Atkins, G. Douglas & Laura Morrow. Ed. *Contemporary literary* Theory. Amberst: The University of Massachusetts Press, 1989.

Bakhtin, M. M. *The Dialogic Imagination: Four Essays*. Trans. Caryl Emerson & Michael Holquist. Austin: University of Texas Press, 1981.

Barrish, Phillip J. *The Cambridge Introduction to American Literary Realism*.

Cambridge: Cambridge University Press, 2011.

Barthes, Roland. "Introduction to the Structural Analysis of Narratives". *Image, Music, Text*. Trans. Stephen Heath. New York: Hill and Wang, 1977.

Bertelsen, Eve. *Doris Lessing, Southern African Literature Series*. Johannesburg: McGraw-Hill Book Company, 1985.

Bertelsen, Eve & Doris Lessing. "Acknowledging a New Frontier, 1984". *Putting the Questions Differently, Interviews with Doris Lessing, 1964–1994*. Ed. Earl G. Ingersoll. London: Flamingo, 1996: 120–145.

Bhabha, Homi K. *The Location of Culture*. London & New York: Routledge, 1994.

——. "Culture's In-Between". *Questions of Cultural Identity*. Eds. Stuart Hall & Paul Du Gay. New York: Sage Publications, 1996: 53–60.

Bigsby, Christopher & Doris Lessing. "The Need to Tell Stories, 1980". *Putting the Questions Differently, Interviews with Doris Lessing, 1964–1994*. Ed. Earl G. Ingersoll. London: Flamingo, 1996: 70–85.

Bikman, Minda & Doris Lessing. "Creating Your Own Demand, 1980". *Putting the Questions Differently, Interviews with Doris Lessing, 1964–1994*. Ed. Earl G. Ingersoll. London: Flamingo, 1996: 57–63.

Bloom, Harold. Ed. *Bloom's Modern Critical Views, Doris Lessing, 1986*. Philadelphia: Chelsea House Publishers, 2003.

Booth, Wayne C. *The Rhetoric of Fiction*, 2nd ed. Chicago & London: The University of Chicago Press, 1983.

——. *The Essential Wayne Booth*. Ed. Walter Jost. Chicago & London: The University of Chicago Press. 2006.

Brewster, Dorothy. *Doris Lessing*. New York: Twayne Publishers, Inc., 1965.

Byatt, A. S. "Out of Africa: Review of *Under My Skin: Volume One of My Autobiography to 1949*". *The Threepenny Review*. Vol. 61 (1995): 15–16.

Carey, John L. "Art and Reality in *The Golden Notebook*". Ed. Annis Pratt. *Contemporary Literature*. Vol. 14-4 (1973): 437–456.

Clark, Emily. "Re-reading Horror Stories: Maternity, Disability and Narrative in Doris Lessing's *The Fifth Child*". *Feminist Thatcherism Review*. Vol. 98 (Islam in Europe) (2011): 173–189.

Cohn, Dorrit. *Transparent Minds: Narrative Modes for Presenting Consciousness in Fiction*. New Jersey: Princeton University Press, 1978.

Currie, Mark. *Postmodern Narrative Theory*. New York: ST. Martin's Press, Inc., 1998.

Dean, Michael & Doris Lessing. "Writing as Time Runs Out, 1980". *Putting the Questions Differently, Interviews with Doris Lessing, 1964–1994*. Ed. Earl G. Ingersoll. London: Flamingo, 1996: 86–95.

Dekoven, Marianne. "Modernism and Gender". *The Cambridge Companion to Modernism*. Ed. Michael Levenson. Shanghai Foreign Language Education Press, 2000: 174–193.

Downing, Lisa. *The Cambridge Introduction to Michel Foucault*. Cambridge: Cambridge University Press, 2008.

Draine, Betsy. "Doris Lessing and *Doris Lessing: The Poetics of Change* (review)". Ed. Patrick O'Donnell. *Modern Fiction Studies*. Vol. 42 (1996): 194–198.

Dunphy, Graeme & Rainer, Emig. Eds. *Hybrid Humour, Comedy in Transcultural Perspectives*. New York & Amsterdam: Rodopi Publishing, 2010.

Eagleton, Terry. *The Event of Literature*. New Haven & London: Yale University Press. 2012.

Ean, Tan Gim & Doris Lessing. "The Older I Get, the Less I Believe, 1991". *Putting the Questions Differently, Interviews with Doris Lessing, 1964–1994*. Ed. Earl G. Ingersoll. London: Flamingo, 1996: 200–203.

Eliot, T. S. *Notes Towards the Definition of Culture*. London: Faber and Faber Limited, 1948.

Edel, Leon. *Henry James*. Minneapolis: University of Ninnesota Press. 1963.

Fanon, Frantz. *Black Skin, White Masks*. 1952. Trans. Charles Lam Markmann. Northampton: Pluto Press, 2008.

Ferro, Nancy. "Doris Lessing: Children of Violence". *Off Our Backs*. Volume 2–3 (1971): 18.

Fishburn, Katherine. *The Unexpected Universe of Doris Lessing: A Study in Narrative Technique*. Connecticut: Greenwood Press, 1985.

Fludernik, Monika. *An Introduction to Narratology*. London & New York: Routledge, 2009.

Forster, E. M. *Aspects of the Novel*. Ed. Oliver Stallybrass. New york: Harcourt, Inc. 1927.

Frick, Thomas & Doris Lessing. "Caged by the Experts, 1987." *Putting the Questions Differently, Interviews with Doris Lessing, 1964–1994*. Ed. Earl G. Ingersoll. London: Flamingo, 1996: 156–168.

Genette, Gerard. *Narrative Discourse: An Essay in Method*. 1972. Trans. Lewin, Jane E. New York: Cornell University Press, 1983.

Gindin, James. *Postwar British Fiction*. Berkeley: University of California Press, 1962.

Gottlieb, Robert. "A Very Lush Garland of Writers". *The New York Review of Books*. Aug. 16, (2012): 818. Mar. 13, 2015. Retrieved from http://www.nybooks.com/articles/2012/08/16/very-lush-garland-writers/.

Gray, Stephen & Doris Lessing. "Breaking Down These Forms, 1983". *Putting the Questions Differently: Interviews with Doris Lessing, 1964–1994*. Ed. Earl G. Ingersoll. London: Flamingo, 1996: 109–119.

Guignery, V., C. Pesso-Miquel, & F. Specq. Eds. *Hybridity: Forms and Figures in Literature and the Visual Arts*. Newcastle upon Tyne: Cambridge Scholars Publishing, 2011.

Hagen, W. M. "Review of *Alfred and Emily*". *World Literature Today*. Vol. 83–84 (Jul. –Aug., 2009): 78.

Head, Dominic. *The Cambridge Introduction to Modern British Fiction, 1950–2000*. Cambridge: Cambridge University Press, 2002.

Heikinen, Denise. "Is Bakhtin a Feminist or Just Another Dead White Male? A Celebration of Feminist Possibilities in Manuel Puig's Kiss of the Spider Woman." Eds. Karen Hohne & Helen Wussow. *A Dialogue of Voices, Feminist Literary Theory and Bakhtin*. Minneapolis & London: University of Minnesota Press, 1994: 114–127.

Hendin, John & Doris Lessing. "The Capacity to Look at a Situation Coolly, 1972". *Putting the Questions Differently: Interviews with Doris Lessing, 1964–1994*. Ed. Earl G. Ingersoll. London: Flamingo, 1996: 41–56.

Herman, D., M. Jahn & M. L. Ryan. Eds. *Routledge Encyclopedia of Narrative Theory*. London & New York: Routledge, 2005.

Hogan, P. C. *Colonialism and Cultural Identity, Crisis of Tradition in the Anglophone Literatures of India, Africa, and the Caribbean*. Alberny: State University of New York Press, 2000.

Hohne, Karen & Helen Wussow. Eds. *A Dialogue of Voices: Feminist Literary Theory and Bakhtin*. Minneapolis & London: University of Minnesota Press, 1994.

Holquist, Michael. *Dialogism, Bakhtin and His World, 1990*. London & New York: Routledge, 2002.

hooks, bell. *Feminist Theory: From Margin to Center*. Cambridge: South End Press, 1984.

———. *Outlaw Culture: Resisting Representations*. New York & London: Routledge Classics, 1994.

———. *Feminism Is for Everybody: Passionate Politics*. Cambridge: South End Press, 2000.

Horowitz, David. *The Professors: The 101 Most Dangerous Academics in America*. Washington D. C.: Regnery Publishing, Inc., 2013.

Howe, Florence. "A Conversation with Doris Lessing, 1996". *Contemporary Literature*. Ed. Annis Pratt. Madison: The University of Wisconsin Press. Vol. 14-4 (1973): 418–436.

Howe, Irving. "Neither Compromise nor Happiness". *The New Republic*. Vol. Dec. (1962): 17.

Ingersoll, Earl G. "Introduction". *Putting the Questions Differently: Interviews with Doris Lessing, 1964–1994*. Ed. Earl G. Ingersoll. London: Flamingo, 1996: 2–9.

Ingersoll, Earl G. & Doris Lessing. "Describing This Beautiful and Nasty Planet, 1993". *Putting the Questions Differently: Interviews with Doris Lessing, 1964–1994*. Ed. Earl G. Ingersoll London, Flamingo, 1996: 228–240.

James, Henry. "The Art of Fiction". *The Norton Anthology of American Literature*. Ed. Nina Baym. New York: W. W. Norton & Co., 2007: 456–470.

Joyner, Nancy. "The Underside of a Butterfly: Lessing's Debt to Woolf". *Journal of Narrative Technique*. Vol. 3 (1974): 204–211.

Kapchan, D. A. & P. A. Strong. "Theorizing the Hybrid". *The Journal of American Folklore*. Vol. 112–445 (Summer, 1999): 239–253.

King, Holly Beth. "Criticism of Doris Lessing: A Selected Checklist". *Modern Fiction Studies*. Eds. Margaret Church & William T. Stafford. West Lafayette: Purdue University, Vol. 26-1 (1980): 167–175.

King, Jeannette. *Doris Lessing*. London: E. Arnold, 1989.

Kipling, Rudyard. *Kim*. New York: Doubleday & Company, Inc., 1901.

Knapp, Mona. *Doris Lessing*. New York: Frederick Ungar Publishing Company, 1984.

Kraidy, Marwan M. *Hybridity, or the Cultural Logic of Globalization*. Philadelphia: Temple University Press, 2005.

Krouse, Tonya. " 'Anon', 'Free Women' and the Pleasure of Impersonality". *Doris Lessing Interrogating the Times*. Eds. Debrah Raschke, *et al.* Columbus: The Ohio State University Press, 2010: 32–57.

——. "Review on *The Technology of the Novel: Writing and Narrative in British Fiction*". *Modern Fiction Studies*. Eds. John N. Duvall & Robert P. Marzec. West Lafayette: Johns Hopkins University Press. Vol. 56-2 (2010): 445–447.

——. "Freedom as Effacement in *The Golden Notebook*: Theorizing Pleasure, Subjectivity, and Authority". *Journal of Modern Literature*, Vol. 29-3 (Spring, 2006): 39–56.

Kuortti, Joel & Jopi Nyman. Eds. *Reconstructing Hybridity, Post-colonial Studies in Transition.* New York & Amsterdam: Rodopi Publishing, 2007.

Kurzweil, Edith & Doris Lessing. "Unexamined Mental Attitudes Left Behind by Communism, 1992". *Putting the Questions Differently: Interviews with Doris Lessing, 1964–1994*. Ed. Earl G. Ingersoll. London: Flamingo, 1996: 204–213.

Lessing, Doris. *The Golden Notebook.* 1962. London: Granada Publishing Limited, 1979.

——. *In Pursuit of the English.* 1960. New York: Simon and Schuster, 1961.

———. *Martha Quest.* 1952. New York: Simon & Schuster, 1970.

———. *The Summer Before the Dark.*1973. London: Jonathan Cape of Ltd., 1973.

———. *The Marriage Between Zone Three, Four and Five.* 1980. London: Flamingo, 1994.

———. *Under My Skin: Volume One of My Autobiography, to 1949.* London: Harper Collins Publishers, 1994.

———. *Walking in the Shade, Volume Two of My Autobiography, 1949–1962.* London: Harper Collins Publishers, 1997.

———. *Love, again.* 1996. New York: Harper Perennial, 1997.

———. *The Grass Is Singing.*1950. New York: Harper Perennial, 2000.

———. *Time Bites.* London, New York, Toronto & Sydney: Harper Perennial. 2004.

———. *The Diaries of Jane Somers.* 1983. Beijing: Foreign Language Teaching and Research Press, 2005.

———. *The Good Terrorist.* 1985. London, New York, Toronto & Sydney: Harper Perennial, 2007.

———. *Alfred and Emily.* London: Fourth Estate, 2008.

———. *A Small Personal Voice.* New York: Alfred A. Knopf, 1974.

———. *The Sun Between Their Feet: Collected African Stories, Vol. 2.* London: Flamingo. 1993.

———. *The Real Thing: Stories and Sketches.* New York, London, Toronto & Sydney: Harper Perennial, 1992.

———. *Prisons We Choose to Live Inside.* New York: Harper and Row. 1987.

Lewis, Simon Keith. "By Europe, out of Africa: White women writers on farms and their African invention". PhD. Diss. University of Florida, 1996.

Linfield, S. & Doris Lessing. "Against Utopia: an Interview with Doris Lessing". *Salmagundi*, Vol. 20 (2001): 59–74.

Lodge, David. *The Art of Fiction.* New York: Viking Penguin, 1992.

McGowan, Kate. *Key Issues in Critical and Cultural Theory.* Berkshire: Open University Press, 2007.

Marcus, Laura. "Woolf's Feminism and Feminism's Woolf". *The Cambridge*

Companion to Virginia Woolf. Eds. Sue Roe & Susan Sellers. Shanghai: Shanghai Foreign Language Education Press, 2001: 209–244.

Martin, Wallace. *Recent Theories of Narratives.* Beijing: Peking University Press, 2006.

Montremy, Jean-Maurice de. & Doris Lessing. "A Writer is not a Professor, 1990". *Putting the Questions Differently: Interviews with Doris Lessing, 1964-1994.* Ed. Earl G. Ingersoll. London: Flamingo, 1996: 193–199.

Morgan, Ellen. "Alienation of the Woman Writer in *The Golden Notebook*". *Contemporary Literature.* Ed. Annis Pratt. Vol. 14-4 (1974): 471–480.

Murfin, Ross. & M. R. Supryia. *The Bedford Glossary of Critical and Literary Terms.* 2nd edition. Boston: Bedford/St. Martins, 2003.

Newquist, Roy & Doris Lessing. "Talking as a Person, 1964". *Putting the Questions Differently: Interviews with Doris Lessing, 1964–1994.* Ed. Earl G. Ingersoll. London: Flamingo, 1996: 3–12.

Oates, Joyce Carol & Doris Lessing. "Joyce Carol Oates' Interview of Lessing, 1971." *Putting the Questions Differently: Interviews with Doris Lessing, 1964–1994.* Ed. Ingersoll, Earl G. London: Flamingo, 1996: 33–40.

Osler, Audrey. "Behind the Mask: Black Hybrid Identities (review)". *European Journals of Women's Studies.* Vol. 13 (2006): 293–295.

Palladino, Mariangela. "Migration Literature and Hybridity: The Different Speeds of Transcultural Change". *Journal of Postcolonial Writing.* Vol 48-2 (2012): 226–227.

Perchy, Graham. *Mikhail Bakhtin: The Word in the World.* London & New York: Routledge, 2007.

Perrakis, P. S. "Introduction". *Adventures of the Spirit: The Older Woman in the Works of Doris Lessing, Margaret Atwood, and Other Contemporary Women Writers.* Ed. Phyllis Sternberg Perrakis. Columbus: The Ohio State University Press, 2007: 1–24.

Pieterse, Nederveen. "Hybridity, So What? The Anti-hybridity Backlash and the Riddles of Recognition". *Theory, Culture & Society.* Vol. 18 (2001): 219–245.

Pratt, Annis. "Introduction". *Contemporary Literature.* Ed. Annis Pratt. Vol.

14-4 (1973): 413–417.

Prabhu, Anjali. *Hybridity: Limits, Transformations, Prospects.* Albany: State University of New York Press, 2007.

Puri, Shalini. "*Colonial Desire: Hybridity in Theory, Culture, and Race* by Robert J. C. Young; *Imperial Leather: Race, Gender, and Sexuality in the Colonial Contest* by Anne McClintock; *Postcolonial Representations: Women, Literature, Identity* by Françoise Lionnet, Review". *Signs.* Vol. 1 (1998): 532–535.

Rajchman, John. *Michel Foucault: The Freedom of Philosophy.* New York: Columbia University Press, 1985.

Raschke, D., P. S. Perrakis & S. Singer. "Introduction". *Doris Lessing Interrogating the Times.* Eds. Debrah Raschke *et al.* Columbus: The Ohio State University Press, 2010: 1–10.

Richardson, Brian. "Postmodern Narrative Theory". *Foreign Literature Study.* Vol. 4 (2010): 24–31.

Rousseau, Francois-Olivier & Doris Lessing. "The Habit of Observing, 1985". *Putting the Questions Differently: Interviews with Doris Lessing, 1964– 1994.* Ed. Earl G. Ingersoll. London: Flamingo, 1996: 146–156.

Rubenstein, Ruberta. "Notes for Proteus, Doris Lessing Reads the *Zeitgeist*". *Doris Lessing Interrogating the Times.* Eds. Debrah Raschke, *et al.* Columbus: The Ohio State University Press, 2010: 11–31.

——. *The Novelistic Vision of Doris Lessing, Breaking the Forms of Consciousness.* Champaign: University of Illinois Press, 1979.

——. *Home Matters: Longing and Belonging, Nostalgia and Mourning in Women's Fiction.* New York: Palgrave, 2001.

——. "Feminism, Eros, and the Coming of Age". *Frontiers: A Journal of Women Studies,* Vol. 22-2 (2001): 1–19.

Said, Edward W. *The Orientalism.* New York: Vintage Books, 1979.

——. *Culture and Imperialism.* New York: Vintage Books, 1994.

Sebestyen, Amanda. "Review of *The Good Terrorist*: Mixed Lessing". *The Women's Review of Books.* Vol. 3-5 (Feb., 1986): 14–15.

Seidman, Gay W. "Nostalgia Trip, African Laughter: Four Visits to Zimbabwe by Doris Lessing". *The Women's Review of Books*, Vol. 10-4 (January, 1993): 9–10.

Schwarzkopf, Margarete & Doris Lessing. "Placing Their Fingers on the Wounds of Our Time, 1981". *Putting the Questions Differently: Interviews with Doris Lessing, 1964–1994*. Ed. Earl G. Ingersoll. London: Flamingo, 1996: 102–109.

Showalter, Elaine. *A Literature of Their Own, British Women Novelists from Brontë to Lessing*. Beijing: Foreign Language Teaching and Research Press, 1999.

Sizemore, Christine W. "In Pursuit of the English: Hybridity and the Local in Doris Lessing's First Urban Text". *Journal of Commonwealth Literature*, Volume 43-2 (2008): 133–144.

Sprague, Claire. *Rereading Doris Lessing, Narrative Patterns of Doubling and Repetition*. Chapel Hill & London: The University of North Carolina Press, 1987.

Stevenson, Randall. *The Oxford English Literary History, Vol. 12, 1960–2000, The Last of England?* Beijing: Foreign Language Teaching and Research Press, 2007.

Stross, Brian. "The Hybrid Metaphor: From Biology to Culture". *The Journal of American Folklore*. Vol. 112-445 (Summer, 1999): 254–267.

Tate, Shirley Anne. *Black Skins, Black Masks: Hybridity, Dialogism, Performativity*. Aldershot: Ashgate Pub lishing Ltd., 2005.

——. "Foucault, Bakhtin, Ethnomethodology: Accounting for Hybridity in Talk-in-Interaction". *Forum: Qualitative Social Research*. 2007 (8-2). Jan. 5, 2016. http://blog.sciencenet.cn/blog-331736-663738.html.

Taylor, Jenny. "Introduction: Situating reading". *Notebooks/Memoirs/Archives, Reading and Rereading Doris Lessing*. Ed. Jenny Taylor. Boston, London, Melbourne & Henley: Routledge & Kegan Paul, 1982: 1–42.

Terkel, Studs & Doris Lessing. "Learning to Put the Questions Differently, 1969". *Putting the Questions Differently: Interviews with Doris Lessing, 1964-1994*. Ed. Earl G. Ingersoll. London: Flamingo, 1996: 19-32.

Thomson, Sedge & Doris Lessing. "Drawn to a Type of Landscape, 1989".

Putting the Questions Differently: Interviews with Doris Lessing, 1964–1994. Ed. Earl G. Ingersoll. London: Flamingo, 1996: 178–192.

Thorpe, Michael. *Doris Lessing's Africa*. London: Evans Brothers Limited, 1978.

Thorpe, Michael & Doris Lessing. "Running Through Stories in my Mind, 1980". *Putting the Questions Differently: Interviews with Doris Lessing, 1964–1994*. Ed. Earl G. Ingersoll. London: Flamingo, 1996: 94–101.

Tomalin, Claire & Doris Lessing. "Watching the Angry and Destructive, Hordes Go Past, 1988". *Putting the Questions Differently: Interviews with Doris Lessing, 1964–1994*. Ed. Earl G. Ingersoll. London: Flamingo, 1996: 173–177.

Torrents, Nissa & Doris Lessing. "Testimony to Mysticism, 1980". *Putting the Questions Differently: Interviews with Doris Lessing, 1964–1994"*: Ed. Earl G. Ingersoll. London: Flamingo, 1996. 64–69.

Upchurch, Michael & Doris Lessing. "Voice of England, Voice of Africa, 1992". *Putting the Questions Differently: Interviews with Doris Lessing, 1964-1994*. Ed. Earl G. Ingersoll. London: Flamingo, 1996: 219–227.

Visel, Robin. "House/Mother, Lessing's Reproduction of Realism in *The Sweetest Dream*". *Doris Lessing Interrogating the Times*. Eds. Debrah Raschke, *et al.* Columbus: The Ohio State University Press, 2010: 58–76.

Wall, Barbara. *The Narrator's Voice: The Dilemma of Children's Fiction*. London: Macmillan Academic and Professional Ltd. Co. 1991.

Walters, Margaret. *Feminism: a Very Short Introduction*. Trans. Zhu Gang & Ma Xiaorong. Beijing: Foreign Language Teaching and Research Press, 2008.

Wang, Joy. "White Postcolonial Guilt in Doris Lessing's *The Grass Is Singing*". *Research in African Literatures*, Vol. 40-3 (Fall, 2009): 37–47.

Walsh, Lynda. "Accountability: Towards a Definition of Hybridity for Scholars of Transnational Rhetorics". *A Journal of the History of Rhetoric*, Vol. 30-4 (Fall, 2012): 392–431.

Watkins, S. & C. Chambers. Editorial. *Journal of Commonwealth Literature*. 2008 (43-1): 4–7.

Watt, Ian. *The Rise of the Novel: Studies in Defoe, Richardson and Fielding.* Berkley & Los Angeles: University of California Press, 1957.

Werbner, Pnina & Tarik Modood. Eds. *Debating Cultural Hybridity: Multi cultural Identities and the Politics of Anti-Racism.* London: Zed Books, 1997.

Woolf, Virginia. "A Sketch of the Past". *Norton Anthology of British Literature.* 7th edition, Vol. 2. Ed. M. H. Abrams. New York & London: W. W. Norton & Company, 2000: 2218-2226.

——."A Room of One's Own". *Norton Anthology of British Literature.* 7th edition, Vol. 2. Ed. M. H. Abrams. New York & London: W. W. Norton & Company, 2000: 2153–2213.

Young, Robert. *Colonial Desire: Hybridity in Theory, Culture, and Race.* London & New York: Routledge, 1995.

——. "Colonialism and Humanism". *Race, Culture and Difference.* Eds. James Donald & Ali Rattansi. London: Sage Publications in association with the Open University, 1992: 243–251.

——. *Postcolonialism: A Very Short Introduction.* Oxford: Oxford University Press, 2003.

Zappen, James P. *The Rebirth of Dialogue: Bakhtin, Socrates, and the Rhetorical Tradition.* Albany: State University of New York Press, 2004.

白春仁，边缘上的话语——巴赫金话语理论辨析．外语教学与研究，2000(3): 162–168.

陈璟霞：《多丽丝·莱辛的殖民模糊性：对莱辛作品中的殖民比喻研究》．北京：中国人民大学出版社，2007.

邓琳娜，"生命的体验，自我的超越——多丽丝·莱辛小说苏菲思想研究"．上海外国语大学博士论文，2012.

邓中良，多丽丝·莱辛在中国的译介评述．英美文学论丛，2008 (6): 270–280.

纪卫宁，辛斌，巴赫金的异质语理论与话语分析．外语研究，2012 (2): 15–18.

姜仁凤．"莱辛主要小说中的空间与自我"．上海外国语大学博士论文，

2013.

蒋花:《压抑的自我，异化的人生——多丽斯·莱辛非洲小说研究》，上海：上海外语教育出版社，2009 年 .

——. 多丽丝·莱辛研究在中国 . 中国比较文学，2008 (3): 57–65.

凌建侯，"复调"与"杂语"——巴赫金对话理论研究 . 欧美文学论丛，2004(0): 66–81.

卢婧，20 世纪 80 年代以来国内多丽丝·莱辛研究述评 . 当代外国文学评论，2008 (4): 75–81.

生安锋，罗伯特·杨，后殖民理论的反思与期待——罗伯特·杨教授访谈录 . 当代外语研究，2010 (5): 1–17.

盛宁，"后殖民主义"：一种立足于西方文化传统内部的理论反思 . 天津社会科学，1997 (1): 87–96.

王宁，多丽丝·莱辛的获奖及其启示 . 外国文学研究，2008(2): 148–156.

吴晓都，巴赫金与文学研究方法论 . 外国文学评论，1995(1): 37–45.

颜文洁.《金色笔记》的符号学解读.南京师范大学博士论文，2014.

杨金才，当代英国小说的核心主题与研究视角 . 外国文学，2009 (6): 55–61.

张和龙，多丽丝·莱辛的女性主义思想 . 安徽师范大学学报，2011(1): 86–90.

张琪，论多丽丝·莱辛太空小说中的文化身份探寻 . 湘潭大学博士论文，2014.

赵晶辉，文学中的城市空间寓意探析——莱辛的五部曲《暴力的孩子》释读 . 当代外国文学，2011 (3): 5–11.

周桂君，"现代性语境下跨文化作家的创伤书写"。东北师范大学博士论文，2010.

朱刚:《二十世纪西方文艺理论》，上海：上海外语教育出版社，2001.

朱振武，张秀丽，多丽丝·莱辛：在否定中前行 . 当代外国文学，2008 (2): 96–103.

Abbreviations

AE	*Alfred and Emily* (2008)
APM	*A Proper Marriage* (1954)
ASPV	*A Small Personal Voice* (1974)
BDH	*Briefing for a Descent into Hell* (1971)
C	*The Cleft* (2007)
CV	*Children of Violence* (1969)
DJS	*The Diaries of Jane Somers* (1983)
FGC	*The Four-Gated City* (1969)
GN	*The Golden Notebook* (1962)
GS	*The Grass Is Singing* (1950)
GT	*The Good Terrorist* (1985)
IPE	*In Pursuit of the English* (1960)
LA	*Love, again* (1996)
MBZTFF	*The Marriages Between Zones Three, Four, and Five* (1994)
MQ	*Martha Quest* (1952)
MS	*The Memoirs of a Survivor* (1974)
PWCL	*Prisons We Choose to Live in* (1987)
SBD	*The Summer Before the Dark* (1973)
SD	*The Sweetest Dream* (2001)
TB	*Time Bites* (2004)
WS	*Walking in the Shade* (1997)

Acknowledgements

First and foremost, I am grateful for the help, support and instruction given by my supervisor, Professor Zhu Gang. Thanks to his valuable suggestions, I have sharpened my thinking and obtained more insights into the writing of this book. What's more, his professionalism, critical reading, and enlightening lectures on critical theories all have inspired and encouraged me, setting a perfect example for me in work and in life as well. His warmth, patience, generosity and charisma have enlivened the spiritual adventures during my stay in Nanjing University and would continue to be a stimulus in my future life.

I also wish to express my heartfelt gratitude to the distinguished professors of School of Foreign Studies, Nanjing University, from whom I have benefited a lot: Professor Wang Shouren, Professor Liu Haiping, Professor Yang Jincai, and Professor Chen Aimin. Professor Wang Shouren impresses me deeply with his knowledge and scholarship. In particular, due to his rigorous training, I have improved my academic writing. Thanks to Professor Liu Haiping whose amiability and professionalism make his lectures sweet memories in my life. Thanks go to Professor Yang Jincai whose lectures have endowed me with inspiration in the study of British and American literature. I am also grateful for Professor Chen Aimin, from whose instructions I get to know more about Chinese-American literature, another interesting field of study in the doctoral courses.

Thanks should go especially to Professor Wu Fen. Her kindness, readiness to help and precious suggestions on the study of literature have enlightened me a lot. I could hardly express my gratefulness to Professor Zhang Shengshu and Professor Li Yaxiong, for their love, care and support. I have benefited a great deal from my discussion with Professor Li Yaxiong whose keen insight into and enthusiasm for literature encourages me.

This book could hardly be accomplished without the support of the leaders of my university and many of my colleagues. It is their care and help that encourage me to search with my will unbendingly in my professional research and writing. My thanks also extend to my classmates, Xiao Lamei, Yao Chenghe, Xin Huimin, Fan Hao, Jiang Xianping, Zhang Zuan, Wang Lin, Chen Xu, Yu Lei, Ding Xialin, Feng Dong and Gao Mingyu, whose advice and questions push me to think twice before writing. In addition, I want to thank my dear friend Gu Tingting whose advice and kindness of sharing with me her own writing experience encourage me greatly.

Special thanks go to my dear friends Won Kim, Jessie and Ji Jiao at the University of British Columbia. I have been greatly inspired by Won Kim's perseverance, professionalism and optimism in academic research. Thanks to Jessie and Ji Jiao, who made the last phase of my writing on UBC campus unexpectedly smooth and fruitful.

I want to express my sincere thanks to Mr. Zhou Jianjun and Ms. Li Jun, for their steadfast support and love. If without their family-like support, I could hardly concentrate on my doctorial research and writing of the dissertation which is the fundamental part of this book.

My heartfelt thanks also go to my family who always support me unconditionally. In particular, I am deeply grateful for my husband, Mr. Lu Jun, for his trust, understanding and love. Last but not the least, I want to thank my daughter Lu Jiayin for her accompany and sweetness during the whole process of my doctorial study and the writing of this book.

Huang Chunyan
Nov. 20th, 2016